Praise for **Joanne Pence**'s **Angie Amalfi** Mysteries

"A winner . . . Angie is a character unlike any other found in the genre."
Santa Rosa Press Democrat

"Deliciously wicked . . . Don't miss one tasty bite."
Jacqueline Girder

"High energy and a high fun factor . . . Joanne Pence has an amazing knack for building fascinating characters and compelling plotlines."
Romantic Times

"[Pence] titillates the sense, provides a satisfying read, and arouses a hunger for yet another book in this great series."
Crescent Blues Reviews

"If you love books by Diane Mott Davidson or Denise Dietz, you will love this series. It's as refreshing as lemon sherbet and just as delicious."
Under the Covers

"Pence's tongue-in-cheek humor keeps us grinning."
San Francisco Chronicle

JOANNE PENCE

If Cooks Could Kill

AN ANGIE AMALFI MYSTERY

AVON BOOKS
An Imprint of HarperCollinsPublishers

This is a work of fiction. Names, characters, places, and incidents are products of the author's imagination or are used fictitiously and are not to be construed as real. Any resemblance to actual events, locales, organizations, or persons, living or dead, is entirely coincidental.

AVON BOOKS
An Imprint of HarperCollins*Publishers*
10 East 53rd Street
New York, New York 10022-5299

First Avon Books paperback printing: January 2003

Avon Trademark Reg. U.S. Pat. Off. and in Other Countries, Marca Registrada, Hecho en U.S.A.
HarperCollins® is a registered trademark of HarperCollins Publishers Inc.

Printed in the U.S.A.

10 9 8 7 6 5 4 3 2 1

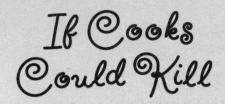

If Cooks Could Kill

Chapter 1

Connie Rogers glanced down at herself to make sure her brand new black lace Wonderbra was still doing its job and her boobs hadn't sagged as low as her spirits. She'd fixed herself up pretty hot for tonight's date in a leopard-print Lycra top with plunging V-neckline, short black polyester skirt, black diamond-patterned nylons, and sky-high patent leather heels, size 7 narrow. She normally wore a medium, but the narrow looked a lot better, and it fit. Almost. Not to mention that she'd risked razor burn by shaving her legs and underarms even though she'd last done them just three days earlier. Okay, so maybe that was overkill, but a girl could hope, couldn't she?

She sat alone at a window table in the Wings of an Angel restaurant. Her feet ached and her skirt seams screamed. She wriggled in the chair trying to stop the waistband from digging in quite so tight. She'd worn it to make sure her date liked what he saw. If he ever showed, that is.

If her willpower alone could have caused him to enter the restaurant, he'd have bounded in doing handsprings. She'd already smoothed the white linen

1

tablecloth, straightened the silverware, and twirled the single rose in the milk glass vase so many times half the petals had fallen off. The oversized gold-plated Anne Klein watch she'd splurged on at Costco showed 7:20 P.M. Not only was her date twenty minutes late, but since she'd arrived ten minutes early, if she were a thumb-twiddler, she'd have nothing left but stumps.

It wasn't as if she'd twisted his arm to go out with her. In fact, she'd never even talked to him, but she was a victim here. A victim of a blind date who'd stiffed her. What was with that?

Earl White, one of the three owners of the Wings of an Angel and the one who acted as both maître d' and all around waiter of the small restaurant, caught her eye. He was short and barrel-shaped, with hair resembling a shellacked brown helmet atop a face criss-crossed with wrinkles. He, too, glanced at his watch, then back at her with a shrug.

Being stood up was bad enough; the last thing she needed was an audience. She bet Earl had never been stood up. He was in his sixties, and not only single, but still bringing in a paycheck instead of living off Social Security, which made him one of the most sought after men at the North Beach Senior Center. She once heard there was a knock-down-drag-out over him between Gina DiGrazia and Beatrice Pikul-ski. Plus, he was straight, which in San Francisco, was not to be assumed.

Connie's best friend, Angie Amalfi, had helped Earl and his partners, Butch Pagozzi and Vinnie Freiman, build Wings of an Angel into a pleasant, albeit small, restaurant, and they'd grown close in the process. As a result, whenever Connie showed up, she, too, was treated like family. Maybe that was why Earl had taken such an interest in her plight a couple days ago.

She'd been talking with him about getting herself a dog. A little dog, nothing big or troublesome, but just something warm and alive to greet her when she went home after work. Something that needed her, that would love her unfailingly, through good times and bad.

Okay, so she had a goldfish. It was alive; it needed her, but it wasn't anything she could give a big hug to. Talking to it, watching its flat eyes and lack of reaction as it went around in circles no matter how heartfelt her story was, was an exercise in futility.

Earl had suddenly—rather rudely, truth be told—asked how her love life was going. She asked if zip, zero, nada was a clear enough answer. Before she knew it, he'd talked to his partner, Butch, who was also the restaurant's cook. Butch had called a nephew—apparently the only one in the family who'd made a name for himself—and arranged tonight's turkey of a blind date.

In truth, Earl, Butch, and Vinnie had all made names for themselves as well, only they called them "reps." Bad reps, unfortunately. The three had met doing time in San Quentin, and when they got out, they decided to go straight, so to speak. Vinnie was the brains behind the operation. He kept the books and kept Earl and Butch in line. Sort of.

Connie put an elbow on the table, chin in hand, and stared at the entrance to the restaurant.

She'd been so excited and nervous she'd skipped lunch today, and was living off a snack of large fries and a diet Coke from McDonald's. Okay, so maybe fries were a little fattening, but they were a vegetable, she'd been starving, and they had fewer calories than a Quarter Pounder . . . she hoped. Now, her empty stomach churned, adding injury to insult. The nephew had sounded too good to be true, and so far, it seemed he was neither. His name was Dennis Pagozzi, and he played defensive end for the San Francisco Forty-Niners. Connie might not be a sports fan, but she was quite willing to become one if it meant capturing the interest of a national conference player like Pagozzi, even if he was second string.

The way she understood it, he played only when someone else was hurt and pulled from the game. That meant his body shouldn't be as banged up as that of most football players. Generally, Connie preferred her men in one piece, although the way her love life was going lately, she'd settle for no-longer-on-life-support.

And he shouldn't be banged up at all now because it was spring, and there was no football. Not even practice.

She drummed her fingernails on the table, then, horrified, stopped, and made sure she hadn't chipped them. She'd spent a small fortune on fake nails that were painted at a diagonal—one half gold and the other red—Forty-Niner colors.

A manicurist had worked on the design while a beautician cut, styled, and lightened her hair. This was a special date, so she decided to splurge on a kind of Sharon Stone look—light ash blond, short, with a shaggy fringe that framed her face. Dramatic, sexy. Sure to make Dennis Pagozzi's toes curl, and another part of his anatomy straighten. He'd be impressed . . . if he ever got here.

She tugged at her skirt again. The seams were beyond screaming. They were howling now.

A couple came into the packed restaurant and picked up a take-out order. Connie took a sip of diet Coke and made sure none of it dripped from the glass onto her top. Many women having trouble with men could at least consider breast implants as a possible solution to their problems, but she was already a full C cup. If her experience was anything to go on, the size of one's bra wasn't the solution to anything beyond ogling.

Her best friend, Angie Amalfi, who was admittedly slim and petite, scarcely filled out an A, and she had a boyfriend. San Francisco Homicide Inspector Paavo Smith was not only crazy about her, but had proposed marriage. Actually, Angie's engagement to said cop had been the impetus that had caused Connie this predicament. It had made her realize that time was slipping by and she needed to work harder at finding the man of her dreams.

She thought she'd found him once, but ex-husband Kevin Trammel had turned out to be a nightmare. Some days it seemed the last time she'd had a good man to go out with, Calvin Coolidge was President. And she hadn't even been born yet.

All that was why she'd agreed to this blind date. If she were smart, she'd be home in her pjs, wrapped in a warm, comfortable robe and fuzzy slippers and curled up on the sofa with a bowl of popcorn and a good romance novel or a romantic movie on the VCR. Instead, she sat here uncomfortable, nervous, and hungry. What unlucky star hung over her?

"Here's some salad and bread, Miss Connie," Earl said. "I don't t'ink you need to starve just 'cause some jerk-off is late showin' up for your date."

"Thanks, Earl," she murmured. "But right now, I'm not even hungry." Okay, it was a lie, but she was too humiliated to eat.

"It's on da house." He left a green salad with Roquefort dressing, Connie's favorite, and walked away. The aroma of the French bread wafted up to her. She touched it. Warm. Firm crust. Soft center. Perfect for spreading butter which, unfortunately, was loaded with empty, straight-to-the-hips calories . . .

She checked her watch again. 7:30. Why bother with a guy who couldn't tell time? She kicked off her shoes and took a big bite of buttered, crusty bread. Heaven!

Just then, like magic, the restaurant's front door opened and a man alone entered. Connie's breath caught, causing her to nearly choke on the bread. She swallowed it in a scarcely chewed lump.

It quickly became obvious that the man who walked in was no football player. The only thing he resembled on a football field was a goalpost—tall and slim. He held an arm across his ribs as if in some pain, and stooped slightly because of it. He looked poor, as if he'd found his clothes in a Goodwill bag. Not that Connie was a clotheshorse like her friend Angie, but she knew cheap when she saw it.

Earl sped toward the bedraggled fellow, and unless he was another take-out-order customer, she expected Earl would throw him out. Earl confronted him just inside the door, near Connie's table.

"Excuse me," the newcomer said in a crisp voice. "I was told Dennis Pagozzi would be here tonight—"

"You got a reservation?" Earl asked.

"No. No, I'm not eating. I need to see Mr. Pagozzi—"

"Dat makes two a you," Earl murmured, "And he ain't here."

"Someone else is waiting for him?" The stranger's narrow face was pale, his hair dark blond and wavy. He looked like he'd lived a hard thirty-five or so years.

"Yeah, but we ain't got no room for squatters," Earl said haughtily, or as haughtily as he could manage with his diction and grammar. "Maybe you better get outta here, and when Dennis shows up, I'll tell him somebody's been lookin' for him. What's your name?"

"Who else wants to see him?" the man asked.

"Uh . . . nobody." Earl's eyes darted toward Connie just a second, but it was enough that the stranger turned her way and visibly started. Only after a moment of staring did his expression ease.

To Connie's astonishment, he headed toward her, his mouth a hard slash and his jaw firm. "You're Dennis Pagozzi's friend?" he asked. His eyes were dark, his gaze cold.

"Not exactly," she answered. Who was this filthy creep?

"But he's expected?"

"Yes—"

"Good." He grabbed the back of an empty chair at the table and pulled it out as if to sit.

"Hey!" Earl, his chest puffed out, also grabbed the chair and jerked it away. "I didn't hear da lady invite you, fella."

The stranger looked down at Earl as if he were a human mold spore, then yanked the chair his way again. "I'll leave as soon as I talk to Pagozzi."

Earl tugged it back. "Why don't you call him at home?"

The stranger's hand stilled on the chair. "I don't have his phone number with me—and it's kept private to protect him from football fans."

Connie could feel the other customers laughing at her. It was bad enough being alone at a table without having some bum play tug-of-war with a chair and announce to one and all he didn't want to be there. How mortifying was that?

"How do I know you ain't some poivoit fan your-self?" Earl demanded. "It's time for you to go, mister!"

"Poivoit?" the man asked.

"Pervert!" Connie said sharply, implying more than an explanation with the word.

He faced her. "It's cold outside. The fog is in." Now this jerk had the nerve to plead his case to her directly. "I've been trying to catch up to Pagozzi all evening."

She shook her head. "I don't—"

"A couple of minutes is all I need!" His voice was loud.

Connie's cheeks burned. He was a monomaniacal madman, but she didn't want more of a scene. "All right, already. Take a load off your feet. As if I should care."

"Miss Connie, you don't hafta do dis." Earl scowled pugnaciously.

"It's all right, Earl." Connie's teeth gritted. "I'm sure Dennis will be here soon."

A look of great relief flashed across the man's slender face as he settled into the chair. He didn't say a word, but she noticed the ravenous glance he gave the bread.

With a shake of the head, Earl turned to leave.

"Wait," she said, then to the stranger, "Since you're here, you may as well eat." Okay, she was being soft, and she knew it. What could she do? She was a nice person, even to a rude S.O.B.

His nostrils flared. "I'm fine."

Connie knew a hungry man when she saw one, pigheaded and vile or not. He looked exhausted, and judging from his stained and ragged clothes, probably hadn't eaten a decent meal for some time. Besides, much as she found him disagreeable, she could relate to anyone else stiffed by Dennis Pagozzi, the rat. "Why don't you bring him a salad, Earl? And more bread.

What would you like to drink? Coffee, maybe? A Coke?"

Her thanks was a fierce glare. "I said I'm fine."

Like hell you are, Connie thought. "It's no problem." She gave a firm nod to Earl. The waiter frowned, but went off to do as told.

"I'm Connie Rogers, by the way."

He glanced at her, bored, and then swiveled toward the door.

He was even ruder than she'd first thought. "And you are?" Didn't she at least deserve to know the name of this seething mass of insensitivity sharing her table?

"Max Squire," he mumbled.

Connie wondered if she should just go home. "Did Dennis tell you he'd be here tonight for sure?" Could she help it if a part of her still hoped the evening wouldn't be a complete failure?

He nodded, giving a heavy sigh as he sank against the chair, eyes half shut. "A guy at the 'Niners' gym told me," he said finally.

She noticed a tightening of his mouth, fine lines forming at the corners as if he might be in pain. "Are you feeling all right?"

He smirked, his voice weary. "Sure. I'm just great." She'd rarely heard such heavy sarcasm.

Earl brought him a glass of Perrier with a twist of lime. Squire drained it.

When he put the glass down, his gaze caught Connie's. "It's warm in here," he muttered.

Her discomfort with the uncommunicative man increased with each passing second. "You can take off your overcoat . . . if you'd like."

It was a gray, dusty, moth-eaten old thing. He removed it, trying to hold back a wince of pain, and let it drape over the back of his chair. Under the coat he wore jeans and a black turtleneck, faded and misshapen. His shoulders and chest were broader and more muscular than she'd expected. He simply needed some flesh on his bones.

Just then, Earl showed up with salad, another basket of French bread, and more Perrier. The stranger practically salivated. "Eat. It's for you," she urged.

He swallowed hard and shook his head.

"I insist."

He placed his hands flat on the table. "I can't pay for it. It's the reason I'm here to meet Dennis. I need money."

Despite his harsh tone and blunt words, the blow to his pride was evident. "Uh-oh. That means he won't be happy to see you," Connie said wryly, trying to lighten the mood. "So much for my great blind date."

He looked askance. "You have a blind date with Dennis? A woman like you?"

She couldn't tell if she'd been complimented or insulted. Maybe it was the new hairdo? Maybe it wasn't dramatic, and instead was butch? She surreptitiously patted it, then attempted to twist a fringe into a feminine curl near her ear. "What do you mean by that, Mr. Squire?"

Her question seemed to puzzle him. Instead of answering he faced the door again and simply said, "Nothing."

His irritating responses aggravated her. "Your words mean nothing, and you're flat broke. Big deal." She waited until she had his attention again. "Now that that's settled, will you please eat the damn salad?"

Surprise flashed across his solemn face, then, glowering, he considered the food. "What the hell," he murmured, and soon began to wolf down everything on his plate, plus the new basket of bread. As he ate, she ordered spaghetti and meatballs for both of them, asking Earl to bring it as quickly as possible.

"Want some wine wit' dat?" Earl asked.

She knew nothing about wine. House red? Did she want to spend the money? "I don't know . . ."

"A cabernet sauvignon would be good." Max's comments were off-handed, as if he was scarcely listening, but concentrating on eating.

"I'll try one—your choice," she said to Earl. "If it's not too expensive."

"It'll be okay, Miss Connie."

She glanced at Max. "Make that two."

He looked up, as if chagrined, and then huddled over the bread again.

As requested, Earl soon brought out the entrees. For a while, Connie ate in silence, studying Max's thin, aristocratic nose and high forehead. His eyes were intelligent, his mouth sensitive. When he noticed her staring, he made no comment. She turned her head, trying to figure him out. So far, she'd taken him for a bum, a jerk, and a creep. Yet something about him didn't mesh with his threadbare clothes or his clean but "unpolished" state.

"Are you new to the city, Max?" she asked.

He shook his head. "I used to live here."

"But not now?"

Reaching for more bread, he paused long enough to reply curtly, "No."

"Why not?" she asked, undaunted.

Dark eyes met hers, his lips curving thinly. "I go wherever the weather and my inclination lead me."

"Running away from something," Connie said.

His hand tightened on his fork. "Or trying to find it." The words were hushed.

The fierceness that radiated from deep inside him alarmed her, and she drew back, her mind searching for something more to say. "Are you hoping to live here again now?"

"You ask a lot of questions." His own breadbasket empty, Connie slid hers toward him. He took a piece to sop up the last bits of sauce from his plate.

Connie ate about half of her spaghetti. "How about some of this? I'm full, really." He needed it a lot more than she did. Especially in this skirt. Her stomach was going to have permanent grooves circling it from the waistband.

He glanced from her plate to his, seemingly bewildered by the now-empty plate in front of him. "Damn!"

"It's all right. I expect a man to have a good appetite."

He again made no reply, his jawbone working as if he were filled with anger, but at what?

Earl came over, still grimacing at the stranger.

"We'll have some coffee, Earl," Connie said. "And would you put the rest of my dinner in a doggie bag?"

"Anyt'ing you'd like, Miss Connie," Earl said, picking up her dish with a flourish, followed by a sneer as he took Max's empty plate.

"Where the hell is Pagozzi?" Max said, eying the clock on the back wall. "I didn't expect to be here this late."

"He seems to have stood me up, that's for sure." She was surprised that she could say it with a lilt to her voice, as opposed to the horrible way she felt a short while ago.

"He's usually not so unlucky," Max murmured, more to himself than to Connie. He stared at the clock once more, then shook his head and sighed. "That's my area of expertise."

Earl brought them both some coffee, and the doggie bag. She slid it toward Max, and he gave a slight nod in thanks, his cheeks flushed.

Connie spent most days in Everyone's Fancy, her modest gift shop in a lazy corner of San Francisco. She ran it alone, except for a college student who helped out a few hours each week. Her apartment building was just a couple of blocks away.

Sometimes, like tonight, she enjoyed getting away from her own neighborhood with hope of adventure, or at least avoiding the same old familiar routines. Unfortunately, this evening hadn't worked out the way she'd planned, although it hadn't been boring either.

Max folded his hands around the coffee cup as if enjoying its warmth, and she wondered at a man who appreciated something so ordinary.

"Have you known Mr. Pagozzi very long?" she asked.

"Yes."

"So, you must have known him when he was just starting out in football."

"Right." Max sipped the coffee and said no more.

"Did you work with the Forty-Niners?" she asked with enthusiasm.

He seemed to find her question funny. "Not at all."

"I see." She racked her brain for something more to say. "What about family? Are you married? Any kids?"

"No wife, no kids, no family who'll admit to it." His mood shifted, and he glared at her. "I suppose you come from a big, warm, loving brood?"

The derision in his voice stung. "Actually, I don't.

For years, it was just me and my sister, and we weren't close." Connie hesitated, but something about the way he dismissed her, as if he were the only person in the world who knew trouble, made her add, "A while back, she was murdered."

Shocked, his gaze met hers. Then the moment passed and he drained his coffee cup. "Shit happens."

His words stung. "That's one way to put it." The pain of Tiffany's murder had been overwhelming. The only good that had come of it—other than Paavo Smith finding the killer—was that she'd met Angie. Oddly, she and Angie were much closer than she'd ever been with her sister.

"I'm sorry," he said. "I didn't mean to—"

Earl cleared his throat as he stood stiffly beside the table. "Butch an' Vinnie say da dinner's on da house, seein' as how youse guys was here to see Butch's nephew an' he didn't show."

"You don't have to do that," Connie said. "No one's to blame."

"Please accept it wit' our apologies. An' Butch'll box Dennis's ears next time he sees him."

"He doesn't have to do that either," Connie said with a smile. Many years ago, Butch had been a prizefighter—bantamweight. He usually lost, and he was still a little scrambled-brained from a few too many head blows. She didn't know if it was the prizefighting that had led to his life of crime, or vice versa. "Thank you for the dinner, and be sure to tell Butch and Vinnie for me, too. I really appreciate it."

"Me, too," Max murmured, uncomfortable.

"Yeah, well, I guess you're bot' welcome. Have a good night, Miss Connie." Earl scowled yet again at Max, and left.

She glanced at Max. "I suppose it's time for me to get a move on."

"Pagozzi's not coming here any more tonight, that's for sure." He sounded disgusted.

She tried not to grimace as she wriggled her feet back into their stiletto torture racks, then took out her wallet, trying to figure out a tip.

"I looked at the menu in the window," he said. "Food's not too expensive here. That was about a thirty-dollar meal, so fifteen percent would be four-fifty. If you want to go twenty, that'd be six bucks."

"What are you, some kind of accountant?" Connie said with a laugh. She put a ten-dollar bill on the table.

He looked stricken by her words, then stood and put on his overcoat. The color that had returned to his complexion as he sat and ate disappeared once more.

"Max?" she said, worried.

"I'll be all right." He slowly straightened, an arm pressed again to his ribs. He helped her with her heavy wool coat, a shapeless navy blue one that reached to mid-calf, the kind her mother had taught her was "practical."

On Columbus Avenue, the foggy breeze blowing off the bay and slashing through the North Beach area was brutal. Connie's stylish hairdo was whipped back and swirled from side to side as if caught in an egg-beater. So much for trying to look gorgeous, not to mention all the gel and hairspray she'd used so that this wouldn't happen. She burrowed into her coat, and Max raised the collar of his thin overcoat. Between the cold and the pain he was obviously in, he looked ready to pass out. "I can drop you off somewhere," she said.

"No, thanks," he said, through unsteady breaths. "My hotel isn't far."

"It's no big deal. You look like you're hurting."

"Not . . . not really . . ." He was gasping more heavily. "Is your car near? I'll walk to you it."

She was relieved to hear that. She didn't relish walking the streets alone. "It's on the next corner. A little red Toyota Corolla—ten years old. I bought it a few months ago. So far, it's given me no trouble, and I can go all over the city on a gallon of gas."

"Sounds good," he murmured.

As they walked, he seemed a bit shaky—even wobblier than she was in her heels. Had she known him better she would have taken his arm to steady him. "The car's small enough that I squeezed it in between a Caddy and a fire hydrant. Parking lots cost a fortune in this area."

"Yes." He paused. "So I've heard."

He worried her. "Are you sure you won't need a ride?"

"No. Let's get you to . . . to your good-luck car."

As they hurried on without speaking, Connie felt she should do something, but he was a stranger to her.

"Here it is." The back seat of the Corolla was filled with boxes of supplies for her store that she hadn't carried inside yet, along with mountains of paperwork saved for federal and state tax purposes, while the front passenger seat had remnants of her last couple of McDonald's drive-throughs. She usually kept her car neater than this—a little—but she'd been busy.

The car was too old and cheap for alarms and remote-control buttons and had to be unlocked the old-fashioned way—with a key. "Thanks for walking with me, Max."

"Dennis was very much a loser tonight for not showing up. He is a nice guy, though. One of the best. Don't hold this against him." He stepped back, studying her. A lamppost was beside the car, and he reached for it, gripping it as if the pole alone was responsible for keeping him upright. "Take care of yourself, Connie."

His regard was unnerving. It'd been a long time since a man had looked at her in quite that way. "You, too," she murmured.

She didn't know what more to add, but leaving like this seemed somehow incomplete. He was a strange man, and an interesting one. She waited a moment for him to say something more, but he didn't. Standing there gawking at him was childish, so she smiled and said. "See you." When he still made no response, she bolted around the car to the driver's side.

He stood and watched, pale and wan under the streetlights, as she drove off.

What a weird character. She should just forget about him, think how lucky she was to be going home to her cozy little apartment. A half block later, she began to berate herself for having left him in such a sorry condition. He was hurting. What if he needed a doctor? She'd dumped him like rotten Limburger. How cold was that?

On the other hand, he was penniless and dressed like a bum. Was she crazy? What did she want with him? Nothing! By two blocks, though, guilt overcame her. She pulled over to the curb to build up the courage to face Max again and insist he let her drive him to his hotel or a doctor—his choice.

She angled the rearview mirror to check her make-up and make sure she didn't have a parsley flake stuck between her teeth.

Holy cripes! Her hair had frizzed from the heavy mist and stuck straight out from her head in weird, crinkly clumps. Any man who hadn't been appalled by such a sight was worth saving. Now, for sure, she had to make certain he was okay.

If he was walking along and looking fit, she'd just drive by and hope he wouldn't notice it was her. On the other hand, what did it matter if he did notice? She'd never see him again, anyway. Why should she care?

She made a U-turn in the middle of the block and headed back to the corner she'd left him on.

It was empty. She stopped the car and got out. He wasn't walking down the block they'd come up, and she didn't see him on any of the adjacent streets either. Apparently, he'd been able to move a lot faster than she thought he could.

You're such a jerk, Rogers! she thought. He'd probably been faking it all along. How much of what he'd said that evening was a lie? What was it about her that made men turn into a song parody—as in *don't believe their lying eyes*?

Feeling used and foolish—those words should be tattooed across her forehead—she flung herself back in the car and was speeding down the street when she passed a dark pile of rags against a building. She'd driven past them before they registered on her mind.

Stomping on the brakes, she backed up, threw on her hazard lights, and got out of the car.

She ran to his side, scared at what she'd find.

"Ronnie . . ."

What was he saying? "Yes, it's me, Max. Connie. I'm here."

"I'm late . . . too late . . . Ron . . ."

"Max!" she cried, kneeling at his side, shaking him.

He struggled to open his eyes, and when he saw her, his whisper was like a prayer. *"Help me."*

Chapter 2

The heavy metal doors opened and Veronica Maple walked out into the sunshine. She lifted her face and took a deep breath. Even early morning was hot in Chowchilla, a grim, dusty, ugly town in California's Central Valley. It was located about 40 miles from the "big city" in the area, Fresno, which even the inmates referred to as one of the world's armpits.

San Francisco was 150 miles away. It seemed more like a 150 light years.

None of that mattered to Veronica this morning. All she knew was that she was free. For the first time in three years, she was her own woman, and could walk the streets, go where she wished, see whomever she liked, and do whatever she wanted.

She turned one last time and stared at the sprawling, unadorned, concrete gray buildings that had been her home for the past three years. The Central California Women's Facility, 640 acres that made up the largest women's prison in the United States, and probably the world, had beds for 2,000 inmates, and housed around 3,500.

Once upon a time she'd thought a women's prison

would be a nicer place than one that housed men. Was she ever wrong. Deaths and mutilations, usually caused by other inmates, were rampant in the place. Getting out alive and unscarred meant she'd learned to kick ass with the best of them, and often better.

Hacking up a huge wad of saliva, she spit it hard at the gate. It hit. Yes! She wanted to dance, to laugh out loud. She'd have sung if she knew the words to any songs. The only words she knew went to children's songs. *Itsy, bitsy spider . . .* no, it didn't sounded right coming from an ex-con.

Ex-con.
Felon.
Thief.
Her good mood vanished.

She spun on her heel and sauntered to the bus stop, then squatted down on the arid, treeless road to wait. Brand new jeans, a blue-and-white striped blouse, cheap white running shoes, and a backpack to carry underwear and a few personal possessions had been given to her when she left.

Another "once upon a time" came to her—the time when she dressed so cool heads would turn, women's as well as men's. She reached up to touch her hair, pulled back in a barrette at the nape of her neck. It was so dingy it scarcely looked blond anymore. She used to spend a fortune on her hair. And on facials, manicures, even pedicures.

Her hands, dry, with sun-baked skin and short, broken nails, could have been a stranger's. She ran rough fingertips against her forehead. Relief that the three-year ordeal was over warred with bitterness. She'd been betrayed and arrested. No one did that to her and got away with it.

Normally, as a newly released prisoner, she should

have checked in at the office of her bald-headed probation officer. Not her, though. She made sure he wouldn't even know she was out until it was too late. Inside a cellblock, a few dollars could work wonders. Having been an exemplary prisoner made such schemes easy to pull off. Exemplary prisoner—that meant someone good at hiding all kinds of prison shit, playing the system, and having outside sources of supplies, from cigarettes to shivs, to trade for favors.

An ancient, once-beige, graffiti-marked bus rolled toward her, belching dust and black smoke as it came to a halt in front of the prison. The doors opened with a hydraulic *whish*. After waiting for the inmates' visitors to step off, she bounded up the stairs and gave a crumpled ten-spot to the driver. To her delight, he handed her change. Her smile spread as she swung herself into one of the black vinyl seats, its seams shredded from passengers past. To her, it was the most beautiful bus she'd ever seen.

She pressed her nose to the window and watched the scenery. Highway 99 had been pretty much forgotten when four-lane, divided Interstate 5 was completed as the fastest way through the sun-baked valley, and now, most of its vehicles were local passenger cars, old trucks filled to overflowing with lettuce and other green vegetables, and once in a blue moon, a bus. When the blinding, thick tule fog descended on the valley, they'd play bumper cars so often along a stretch of road near Fresno that it was called Dead Man's Alley.

Right now, though, it looked beautiful. She even liked the smell of the old bus's blue smoke diesel exhaust. Freedom was smelling whatever the breeze carried your way as you traveled wherever your heart and your money took you.

One quick detour, that was all she needed, then the world was hers. Kathmandu sounded pretty good at the moment.

The bus rolled into Fresno about 10:30 A.M. Veronica hurried from the bus station to the flat-roofed brick post office across the street.

A blast of air-conditioned air hit her. No one was in line, so she walked right up to the counter. "Do you have any letters for Veronica Maple at General Delivery?"

The clerk, a heavy, round-faced black woman with wide-spaced protruding teeth, frowned. Post office clerks tended not to like general delivery customers. While at times they were people vacationing in the area, they were more often drifters who looked bad and smelled worse. Veronica wondered how many showed up here still wearing their Chowchilla glad rags.

With a weighty sigh, the clerk stepped into the back room. Veronica held her breath. This was the first real test of how much she could trust him. Everything up to now had been promises, and she'd learned at about age twelve to put no faith in a man's promises.

Five minutes later, the clerk returned with a single envelope. "This is all of it," she said with disdain.

"Thanks." It was exactly what Veronica was expecting. She opened the letter and removed a pawn ticket.

A pawnshop, iron bars covering its windows, stood forlornly beside the Greyhound depot. She went in and handed the owner the ticket. From the back room, he carried a Japanese chest.

"I remember taking this in last week." When the elderly owner spoke, his missing lower front teeth made his words slosh. "A skinny Mexican-looking guy left it.

Had a little goatee. Ugly as sin, if you asked me. He talked good English, though. Better'n me, matter a fact. It's heavy, so be careful." Veronica didn't bother answering, the old fellow seemed to like having someone to talk to. "The guy said it had sentimental value for the family," he continued. "Looks kinda like an antique. Or maybe something brought over after the Second World War, you know. You got the key? I couldn't get it open."

"The family has the key," she said through gritted teeth. "How much do I owe you?"

"That'll be a hundred dollars."

As Veronica gave him the money, she noticed an old hammer among a pile of tools. "What do you want for that?"

"The hammer?" He stroked his chin, looking from the hammer to the way she was dressed. "Five bucks."

She gave him the money and took her possessions into the women's room in the bus depot. Her pulse raced as she used the claw side of the hammer to rip the box open.

The inside was stuffed tight with cloths. Frantically, she yanked them out until she felt the object she'd hoped for. Even through the cloth the shape was recognizable. She smiled at the familiarity, at the heaviness, at the sense that now, she was the one with the power and that no one could push her around anymore.

He'd come through for her; now, she had to do what she'd promised. She looked forward to it.

She hid the Smith and Wesson 9mm automatic at the bottom of her backpack and threw the chest and wrappings in the trash. Tossing her backpack over her shoulder, she sauntered up to the Greyhound station attendant and flashed him a big, sexy smile. Why not make his day? "I'd like a ticket for San Francisco," she cooed breathlessly. "One way, on the next bus out of here."

Angie Amalfi drove her immaculate new silver Mercedes-Benz CL600 coupe down West Portal Avenue looking for a parking place, otherwise known as a fool's mission in San Francisco. An unoccupied yellow loading zone beckoned, and she eased right into it, much to the irritation of the people behind her who were most likely also eying the illegal spot. She didn't care. Let them honk and glower and pound their steering wheels. Life was good; luck was with her; and the world was a panoply of baked Alaska straight from the oven, a pouffy dark chocolate soufflé, and flaming crêpes suzette.

She was engaged.

The to-be-married kind of engaged.

And she still couldn't believe it.

After an eternity of wishing, hoping, praying, hinting, and wondering if she'd have to resort to conjurers and mojo practitioners, one week earlier San Francisco Homicide Inspector Paavo Smith had proposed.

Before turning off the ignition, she glanced at her hand on the steering wheel. Her engagement ring, a unique half-carat Siberian blue diamond in an elegant marquise cut and a Tiffany setting of white gold, gave her goosebumps each time she looked at it, and then everything but Paavo and love flew right out of her head. Maybe she was being silly, but so what? This was a life-altering, karma-enhancing, family-churning event, and besides, she'd never been engaged before.

She kept pinching herself to make sure she wasn't dreaming. And looking at her ring. And hugging herself. And looking at her ring. She'd gotten two manicures in two days, trying to find the perfect accompaniment for Siberian blue. A natural French manicure was winning at the moment, since it didn't distract from the ring in the slightest. And her pale green Nina Ricci suit enhanced both.

God, but she loved being in love. She picked up her cell phone to call Paavo—just to say "hi" and to wish him a happy lunchtime, admiring the way her ring sparkled as she hit the phone's buttons.

The ring was especially precious because she knew he'd bought it with money he'd been saving for a new car. His Austin Healey was beyond ancient. If it was in good shape, it might be a collector's item. But the bailing wire and glue that held it together had destroyed any value beyond scrap metal.

Paavo wasn't at his desk, and Inspector Bo Benson answered the phone. Benson told her Paavo and his partner were called to a job in Japantown at Bush and Scott Streets, and it wasn't a homicide.

That gave her an idea. A brilliant idea, in fact. Gleefully, she made another phone call, and then, after rubbing a smudge off the dashboard, got out of the car. She was a little woman, with big brown eyes, and short brown hair with eye-catching red highlights, thanks to her favorite Fairmont Hotel beauty salon. Now, as she hurried up the quaint block lined with specialty shops and delis to Everyone's Fancy to hear all about Connie's blind date—holding her hand out in front of her to catch the sparkles of sunlight on it as she went—a quick halt stopped her from barreling smack into the closed front door. She tried the latch handle, but it was locked.

Why was the store shut down at this time of day?

She knocked and peered through the lace curtain behind the glass door. Nothing moved inside. Maybe

Connie was in the back room, sick or something. She'd talked to Connie yesterday, and she'd sounded upbeat and healthy. Why wasn't she at work?

Angie backed up and examined the store. Under a brick red awning, the window display hadn't been changed for at least three months. Boredom was hardly the way to entice neighbors into a shop they passed by every day. Connie needed to use a display with pizzazz, one that shrieked, "Buy me!" to window-shoppers. The linens, lace, doilies, and glass bottles gathering dust didn't even whimper.

Angie purposefully hadn't telephoned this morning, even though she was dying to find out all about the date, because they'd agreed to meet at one P.M. Had Connie forgotten and gone to lunch without her? Or . . .

What if something had happened to Connie on her date? What if she'd been in an accident?

It couldn't possibly be that she'd been so enthralled with that jock, that Dennis Pagozzi, or whatever his name was, that she'd gone home with him and decided not to come to work today, could it? A long night of wild, passionate, raw sex? No way.

That wasn't Connie's style. Or, to be more precise, it wasn't her kind of luck.

"Angie!" Helen Melinger, a broad-shouldered, well-muscled woman who owned the shoe repair shop next door, lumbered onto the sidewalk. "I saw you standing out here. Where the hell's Connie?"

"You don't know, either?" Angie asked. "Hasn't she been here at all today?"

"No." Helen folded her thick, muscular arms and scrunched her bulldog face. "I'm ready to piss my pants I'm so goddamned curious about that date she had last night. What the hell's wrong with her, doing this to me? Where could she be?"

"Good question," Angie said.

"Aagh, it's probably just that she's got a hangover. You know Connie around booze. She never could hold her liquor."

"True, but she doesn't drink much when she's nervous. She knows it goes straight to her head. I don't see that as being the problem." Angie was suddenly worried. "I think I'd better go over to her apartment."

"If you run into her, tell her I don't give a damn how sick she is, she'd better come to work tomorrow, or I'm coming to get her, understand?"

"I got it," Angie said, wanting to smile, but not quite sure if Helen was joking or not.

"And congratulations," Helen added gruffly. "Connie told me you were getting married."

"Yes. My cop friend finally proposed." She held out her hand to show off the engagement ring. Everyone she came in contact with had it stuck under his or her nose at some point before the conversation ended.

Helen took hold of Angie's finger, twisting it this way and that in the sunlight. "Look at that ice! Beautiful. Ring's got good fire and saturation. I like it." She dropped Angie's hand. "So, when's the big day?"

Angie was speechless for a moment, not expecting the gruff shoe repair woman to know the stone was a diamond, let alone its excellent qualities. "Well, I'm not sure yet," she murmured finally. "There's a lot of planning to do."

"Yeah. I guess so. Not that I've ever found out." She gave a raspy whiskey-and-smoke-laced laugh.

"Oh? You're single?" Angie eyed the woman. Forty-ish, self-employed, strong, motivated. In other words, exactly the kind of woman for her neighbor, Stanfield Bonnette. He could use some discipline, motivation, and hard work in his life. At thirty-something, he kept a job with a bank only because of his father's influence, not his dedication to the world of high finance. Helen and Stan. She liked it! Made for each other, and she could be the little Cupid who'd brought them together. Just as some good fortune had brought her Paavo. She smiled at Helen, starry-eyed. Ah, *amore!*

"Never found a man I could abide long enough to marry," Helen confessed. "Probably better off for it, too."

"You never know what might turn up when you least expect it," Angie said, her mind working. She was sure she could get Stan out to Helen's shoe repair shop on some pretext or other.

"Got to get back to work. Remember to tell Connie she'd better be here tomorrow or I'll kick her ass."

"Don't worry," Angie said. "There's no way I'd forget."

"I'm getting too old for this stuff, Paavo," Homicide Inspector Toshiro Yoshiwara groaned and huffed as he climbed down from the rafters in an abandoned garage.

"Come on, Yosh. It wasn't that high." Homicide Inspector Paavo Smith offered a hand as his partner leaped off a rickety wooden ladder, bypassing the last few worn-thin steps.

"I'm not complaining about the climb," Yosh said. "It was trying to speak Japanese after all these years. You'd think the police department would have someone else on the payroll to do it."

"They do—but not someone else who happened to be right around the corner when needed. You did a good job. The kid was scared, and now he's back with his mother." Paavo watched the young Japanese woman tearfully hugging her son, yet obviously torn between wanting to kiss him and wanting to tan his backside. Earlier, the five-year-old had gotten angry with her and run away from home. Around the corner from their apartment was a boarded up, dilapidated three-story building, the top two floors flats and a garage at ground level. In the back, a window leading into the garage had a loose board that could be pulled open wide enough for a child to squeeze through.

The police had been called to help find the missing boy. With the help of a bilingual neighbor, the mother explained what had happened. The police soon located the child, but he wouldn't obey the neighbor or his mother, and the cops didn't speak Japanese. He huddled on a flat piece of old, rotten wood that had been placed across some rafters at the top of the garage. It could hold a five-year-old's weight, but not an adult's.

Paavo and Yosh happened to be two blocks away investigating an apparent suicide when the call went out for Japanese-speaking assistance. As Yosh climbed up the ladder, he'd tried to remember the words and expressions he'd learned as a child. At nearly six feet tall, with powerful shoulders and legs, a thick neck, and stubbly hair, he looked like a cross between a sumo wrestler and the lead in a samurai movie.

When he reached the top of the ladder, the boy gawked at him and shrieked, and before Yosh had finished saying, *"Konnichi-wa. Omawari-san desu,"* or "Hello. I'm a cop," the child began to scramble toward his mother.

Now that the boy was safe, Paavo grew curious about the run-down building he found himself in. "Who owns this?" he asked one of the uniforms who had stood under the rafter, ready to catch the boy if he slipped or the board broke.

"The neighbors say its been abandoned for property taxes—a victim of rent control. The city owns it now but hasn't decided what to do with it," the young cop replied. "The upstairs flats are infested with rats, and people never see anyone go in or out."

Eight shoeboxes, arranged in a stack, were the only things in the garage that weren't coated with inches of dust and cobwebs. Paavo glanced at Yosh. "I wonder what's in them."

Yosh took out his pocketknife. "Let's find out."

Inside were baseballs. Yosh lifted one out and gawked at a valuable Roger Clemens autograph. "What the hell?"

Lifting out other balls, they found signatures from Barry Bonds, Pedro Martinez, Mark McGwire, and a number of lesser known players. Paavo and Yosh opened the other boxes and found the same thing. Several ballplayers had signed more than once.

"I wonder if this is someone's baseball collection," Yosh said. "Why here, though? Unless they're hot."

"Or fakes. Let's get them out of here. We can check them out—contact Robbery." He glanced at the neighbors gathered. "They won't last if we leave them."

After instructing a patrolman to send the boxes to storage, Paavo and Yosh left the garage and headed toward the city-issue Chevy. As Paavo took out his cell phone and called Robbery, a short, chubby man with a pencil-thin mustache and wearing a black suit with a red carnation in the lapel walked up to them. A fireplug with a flower.

"Inspector Paavo Smith?" he asked.

Paavo glanced at him, still on the phone. Yosh gave the strange guy an incredulous once-over before pointing to his partner.

Immediately, the little round fellow burst into a loud, operatic version of *"O Sole Mio."*

Paavo froze. *What the hell?* Then it struck him.

She wouldn't, he thought. As the octaves rose higher and the volume louder, he was forced to admit the awful truth: she would. He jabbed a finger in his ear, and spun 180 degrees, trying to finish his phone conversation. The singer followed, bellowing the tune with grandiose gestures, sobs, and catches in his throat at the heartfelt Italian lyrics, whatever they were. The fireplug had morphed into a singing windmill. A loud singing windmill.

People stuck their heads out of windows, cars stopped on the street, panhandlers forgot to ask for spare change, and a bus missed a turn and ended up on the sidewalk.

Paavo quickly ended the call and fled toward the Chevy. The tenor chased him down the block, still singing and gesticulating. Yosh was already in the driver's seat, his vision blurred by tears of laughter, while the other cops added a chorus of guffaws to the serenade.

With a diving leap into the passenger seat, Paavo glared at his partner. "Are you going to drive?"

As Yosh sped off, Paavo turned to see the tenor in the middle of the street, hands over his heart, mouth opened wide in song, eyes shut. A large truck was bearing down on him. Just then, Yosh turned the corner . . .

Chapter 3

Connie peeked into the living room around one o'clock. Max was still asleep. So much for going to work today. She might trust the stranger to sleep on her sofa, but no way would she leave him with all her possessions. They might not be much to others, but they were all she had, and she loved them. Besides, she'd let her renter's insurance lapse.

The last man to use her sofa that way had been her ex-husband whenever she'd thrown him out of the bedroom. Lots of big rumpled cushions made it comfortable, and the color was a practical brownish-gray. Years ago, a salesman, who could have taken lessons from her no-nonsense mother, had told her it would go with anything, and he was right—from the small house she'd rented with Kevin, to this little one-bedroom apartment in an older building filled with mostly long-term elderly neighbors.

Dark hardwood floors in need of refinishing ran through the hall, living room, and bedroom, and the walls in those rooms had floral wallpaper that had faded and yellowed with age. She knew better than to paint over it, and she didn't have the time or energy to remove it, so she lived with it, trying to brighten up the apartment with lacy white curtains over dark wood window frames, posters of plays and art exhibits, and of course, her one completely impractical pleasure—the one her mother had called "junk"—her stuffed animal and old-fashioned doll collections displayed on shelves, windowsills, and the backs of bureaus and tabletops throughout the apartment.

And now, as a finishing touch—a man in the living room.

Not that Max Squire was a particularly good-looking man, or anything like that. He was no Pierce Brosnan, that was for sure. Not even close to a Brad Pitt. His face was much too narrow, and the curls on his dark blond hair were too tight to look good in today's casual climate. His nose was too long, his nostrils too high, and his eyes too closely set. Even his mouth was perhaps a shade too well-defined for a man.

Her ex, frankly, was a whole lot handsomer. Both men were tall and blond, but Kevin had often worked construction jobs and had the bulk and strength of a man who did such work. Max, though broad shouldered, was lithe. Maybe she hadn't been so far off when she'd said he sounded like an accountant.

Last night, when he'd gotten into her car, he'd nearly passed out again, so she'd brought him to her home. Thank God she'd cleaned, vacuumed, and dusted the place the day before. Even changed the sheets—whether simply because they needed it or out of wishful thinking about her blind date, she wasn't sure. Well, actually, she was sure.

The sheets hadn't been that dirty.

Once they reached her apartment, Max told her he'd been mugged earlier that day. When he fell, he'd managed to protect his head, but the kids who'd robbed him—little Dennis Pagozzi wannabes in Forty-Niner jackets—had taken perverse pleasure in kicking him. He was sure he'd been badly bruised, but nothing more.

They took his money, and that was why he'd been looking for Dennis to borrow more. She decided not to question his story too closely. Since he didn't know how to reach Dennis by phone, and had to rely on hearsay from someone at the Forty-Niner gym to tell him how to locate the guy, Dennis hardly sounded like a close friend. Why turn to him when mugged unless Max had no other friends at all?

She'd run a warm bath for him and ordered him to take it after handing him a large terrycloth robe and the razor she used for her legs. She'd even put a fresh blade in it.

As he bathed, she'd covered the comfortable sofa with sheets, a blanket, and a pillow. Normally, she wouldn't have dreamed of allowing a strange man into her home, let alone to her bath and to sleep on her sofa, but he seemed in too much pain to be harmful.

Besides, something about him touched her. She had no idea why. How many women ended up dead because a pitiable stranger had appealed to their compassion? Was she crazy, or what?

When he'd come out of the bath, with his absurdly white legs protruding from the bottom of the robe and his feet bare, he'd looked so exhausted that she was sure she would be safe that night. Her life as well as her honor.

Damn.

She hadn't liked the way he'd grimaced as he'd lowered himself onto the sofa, so she'd suggested she take a look at his ribs.

He slumped wearily. "If they were broken, you couldn't do anything about it, so why bother?"

God, but he was negative. "I could wrap them for you," she said. "At least you wouldn't feel as much pain with each breath."

He kept the bottom of the robe clutched close about his waist as she slid the top off his shoulders. His arms and shoulders were milky white, while his chest, back, and rib cage were livid red and purple.

"You poor man!" Just looking at him made her wince. She found an old pillowcase and tore it up. As she wrapped it around his ribs, she said, "When you were passed out, you mentioned being late. Is there anything I can do to help you with that? Anyone you need to call?"

"I don't know what you're talking about," he said.

"You were muttering those words. You sounded agitated."

"You must be mistaken." His voice was firm, almost harsh, and his eyes bored into her.

Once she finished with the padding, she lifted the robe back onto his shoulders and gave him two Aleve.

While easing him down onto the pillow, she wrapped one of her arms around his shoulders in support. As she lowered him, bending with him, their eyes met. His were like pools of dark coffee, rich and penetrating. Heat swept over her.

As soon as he was firmly down, she pulled her arm away and stood, stepping back from him, her face nearly as red as his bruises.

She wasn't a horny teenager anymore, but a thirty-plus divorcee. Okay, so maybe it had been a long time since her last fling, but this guy was a stranger, a not-very-handsome, brusque, mysterious stranger.

So, maybe she was a horny divorcée? *Get over it, Rogers.*

He'd fallen asleep immediately, and this morning, he'd awakened while she was having her usual breakfast of a couple of slices of unbuttered toast and black coffee. Each day she started out as if she were on a diet; unfortunately, something usually got in the way of calorie counting long before the day was over. Sometimes, even before breakfast was over.

She gave him more pain pills along with a couple of poached eggs, toast, and coffee, shocked at herself for cooking an almost traditional breakfast. Angie would be proud.

Her mother had always given her poached eggs when she was sick, so it seemed like the right thing to feed him. Personally, she hadn't eaten a poached egg since she'd left home, and hadn't missed the watery concoction one little bit.

It'd also been years since either bacon or sausage had found their way to her refrigerator, not because she was a vegetarian or anything, but because they were too fattening. Also because toast or chocolate-flavored granola bars made for a quicker and easier breakfast. The fanciest she ever got was Egg-O waffles with diet margarine and lite syrup. She debated leaving Max alone while she ran over to Safeway to buy sausage, but decided she'd do it only if he seemed hungry. Since he hadn't finished his toast before falling back asleep, she guessed he needed sleep more than toast or sausage anyway.

Now, hours later, he began stirring and muttering.

The doorbell rang. The clock read 1:30, and she slapped her forehead.

She had to decide, quick. Did she dare tell Angie she'd taken some stranger into her home? It was bad enough she'd been stood up. Even to herself, she sounded really pathetic. How embarrassing was that?

Angie placed her hand on the door handle, ready to push as soon as Connie buzzed it open from her third-floor apartment.

Instead, after a long wait, Connie appeared in the doorway. "Hi, Angie," she said brightly as she stepped out onto the sidewalk.

Connie wore one of her more garish dresses—a day-glo pink with V-neckline and short skirt—plus she was all made up. This was not the appearance of a woman at death's door. Or of one who'd just crawled out of a bed of passion. More like looking to crawl into one.

"Were you just leaving?" Angie asked. "Heading for your store, maybe? Or . . . somewhere else?"

"No, not at all," Connie replied cheerfully.

"Why didn't you buzz me in?" Angie was confused. "What are you doing down here?"

"I figured it was you," Connie answered.

Angie wondered if her apartment needed cleaning, or something. "I went to the shop to meet you for lunch."

"Oh, shoot! That's right." Connie looked contrite. "With all the excitement of my date, I forgot to tell you I had a dentist appointment this morning."

"Oh, dear!" Angie hated going to the dentist. "Was it so painful you decided to stay home all day?"

"He had to use a lot of novocaine . . . and it took forever to wear off. My face puffed up like a chipmunk's. I couldn't go to work like that. Slurred speech, face swollen. What would people have thought?"

"Well, you look fine now," Angie said with a compassionate smile. "Shall we go? I can't wait to hear every little detail of your date last night."

"There's nothing to tell." Connie folded her arms. "Not enough for a five-minute break, let alone an entire lunch. He stood me up."

Angie didn't think she'd heard right. "Dennis Pagozzi?"

"Neither hide nor hair. Look, I've got to go."

Angie stared at her. "Wait! I can't believe it. He's Butch's nephew."

"Believe it, Angie." Connie's mood deteriorated with each word. "The guy must be flaky. It was embarrassing. But on the other hand, what else is new? It isn't the first time a blind date's ended up that way for me, and I'm sure it won't be the last. But I'm a big girl. I can handle it."

Angie's indignation over her best friend's treatment soared. "What a slime bucket!" she cried, throwing her arms outward. "I never thought Butch's nephew would be such a . . . a . . ."

"Dickhead?"

"Exactly!"

"Who cares?" Connie said.

"That's the attitude!" Angie's jaw was firm, her whole being determined to make things right. "I'll find the perfect man for you. The world needs more love it in."

"Sure it does." Connie said without conviction. "And while I'm holding my breath, I'm going back inside to nurse my sore mouth."

"Connie, wait!" Angie cried as Connie turned away. None of this made any sense. "What's going on?"

Connie stepped inside the foyer to the apartment building and left the door open a crack as she faced Angie again. "Nothing. I told you. I just want a break today. Don't worry about me. I'll be back at work tomorrow."

"But—"

Connie sighed. "You're so pushy, Angie."

"I'm pushy?" That took her aback. "Well, yes. Maybe sometimes. With good reason—"

"Good-bye!"

Angie quickly yelled as the door swung shut, "I don't suppose you have time to go to coffee and tell me again what it was like when Paavo proposed?" She heard the click of the latch. "No, I don't suppose you do."

She hated herself for having missed a good deal of her very own marriage proposal, having keeled over in a dead faint at Paavo's words. It wasn't shock, she was sure, but just an accumulation of everything else that had happened that particular evening.

Someday, she might even convince herself of that. On the other hand, she loved hearing about the proposal from Connie who, among others, had witnessed the whole thing.

Hands on hips, Angie stood facing the closed door. That dentist story didn't hold an iota of truth. Connie never dressed up for her dentist, and always said the last thing she wanted to do around one was to look like she could afford to pay for bridges, root canals, or anything cosmetic.

If Connie didn't live on the third floor, Angie would have tried to see just what was going on inside her apartment. Never before had things been so strained between them that they'd held a conversation out on the street or, come to think of it, had she been given such a brush-off.

She didn't even get to tell Connie about her brainstorm regarding her neighbor Stan and Helen the shoemaker.

As she walked back to her car, the sense that whatever was causing Connie to act so unusual had something to do with last night struck her. She checked her wristwatch—just for fun, waggling her ring finger to watch the diamond sparkle as she did so. There wasn't time now, but tonight would be soon enough, and if no one had been murdered today, Paavo could join her in sleuthing it out. Besides, he loved the food at the Wings of an Angel.

Chuck Lexington hit "Send" on one E-mail and another popped open. He didn't much like computers, didn't like all the technological changes that he'd had to learn since the old days when he was a law enforcement officer. He'd enjoyed that time, even though he'd put in so many hours his wife had walked out and his kids had grown up without him ever getting to know them. Now, he felt more like a clerk, sitting and staring at a screen for hours at a time. The phone rang while he was reading yet another E-mail. Without looking up, he answered.

"This is Joe Neeley at McDonald's down on Main Street," a male voice said. "I was told you're Veronica Maple's parole officer. She applied for a job here and was supposed to show up this morning, but she hasn't arrived. Do you know if she was released?"

Lexington wasn't sure what to make of the call. Maple wasn't one to consider serving Big Macs. "I don't know how you heard that. Her release isn't for a couple of days."

The question, though, made him uneasy. Nothing about Veronica Maple was ordinary, and especially not the woman herself. As they spoke, he pulled up her records on the computer.

"I was wrong." The information on the screen shocked him. "She was let go this morning."

"Thanks." The phone went dead.

Lexington stared at Maple's records with growing fury. How the hell had her release date changed without him being notified?

Something about the phone call bothered him as well. Lexington hit star-six-nine on his phone. Some aspects of high tech he liked. "The number of your last incoming call was four-one-five-three-nine-two . . ."

He scribbled down the number. Four-one-five was San Francisco's area code. He used the reverse phone directory on his computer for the full number. It belonged to a woman named Constance Rogers.

He jumped to his feet. What the hell was going on? And where was Veronica Maple?

Connie raced up two and a half flights of stairs to her third-floor apartment. On the last half-flight, she slowed down to catch her breath, smooth her dress, adjust her bra, and push at her rock-hard hair so that it'd pouf up a bit. One bad thing about this short hairdo was that gel tended to make it flatten against her head and look like a bathing cap.

Max just might be awake.

Something about him drew her to him. She liked the way he looked at her, like she was somehow special. That must have been it. Even—okay, it was colossal admission time—she liked having someone who needed her in her house, in her life. The words and tune of a schmaltzy Broadway musical tune popped into her head, *As long as he needs me . . .*

She waltzed up the rest of the stairs humming to herself, then quietly unlocked and opened her apartment door. No sound came from the living room. Tiptoeing to the doorway so as not to disturb him, she peeked at the sofa.

It was empty.

He must be in the bathroom. The door was open. Cautiously, she approached. It, too, was empty.

Was he in the kitchen? Hungry, perhaps? Some runny eggs and a piece of toast weren't enough for such a tall man's appetite. What had she been thinking? She should have used her Safeway Club Card and bought *both* sausage and bacon—and maybe splurged on a quart of chocolate Häagen-Dazs Vanilla Swiss Almond or maybe Ben and Jerry's New York Super Fudge Chunk.

The kitchen's appliances were last updated at least thirty years earlier. The miracle was that they still worked. The room had an almost art deco look to it with small white appliances atop sheets of ancient linoleum in a yellow, red, and black plaid. Red accessories made the room bright and cheerful, but nothing more.

At the far end of the kitchen the back door was ajar. Outside steps led down to a small yard where trashcans were kept until garbage day, when they were rolled along a small alleyway to the main street. She always kept that door locked.

Max's clothes, which had been folded and draped neatly over a kitchen chair, were gone, and in their place was the terrycloth robe she'd lent him.

He wouldn't have snuck out on her like that, would he? She wanted to believe he'd merely stepped outside for a moment, maybe to have a cigarette, and would be back soon. She wanted to believe anything except that she'd done it again—that she'd again opened her home and heart to a man whose own troubles left no room for her or her feelings or desires. The last thing she wanted was to get involved with that type again—her ex had been a complete course in needy personality.   •

Good thing she found all this out about him before she got any more involved! And even better that she hadn't mentioned him to Angie. This way, she could forget she'd ever met Max Squire, or that he even existed.

Too bad she'd kind of liked him.

As she stepped into her cozy living room, her mind froze. Her big, brown shoulder bag lay open on the oak coffee table. When she picked up her wallet, her heart sank.

All her cash—about a hundred eighty dollars' worth—was gone.

Chapter 4

"Isn't that sweet?" Angie thought. She'd returned home after her unhappy encounter with Connie and was on the sofa going through her mail when she came across a letter from *Bon Appetit* magazine. It was an offer for her to become their Bay Area correspondent, since the current one had resigned to become a full-time cookbook writer, and they were aware of her through the occasional but always wonderful restaurant reviews she wrote for the regional magazine, *Haute Cuisine*.

They enjoyed the whimsical style of her writing and thought she would add sparkle to the stories she wrote for them.

"Sparkle?" she murmured with a smile. She did have plenty to sparkle over these days, that was for sure. Diamonds, champagne, Paavo, love.

The offer from *Bon Appetit* dropped unnoticed to the floor as she stared dreamily out the window. The magazine had recently had a particularly nice spread on savory tea sandwiches . . .

Sidney Fernandez, known as "El Toro" by friends and enemies alike, stretched out on the back seat of his

black limousine and watched the bright neon glow of
the city at night. He loved his limousine. He loved the
plush red leather seats, the fully stocked bar with all
his favorite liquor, the television, the satellite phone
that worked even when he was in a valley or beside a
high-tech office building. He loved the way he never
had to worry about parking. He just had Raymondo
drive him around and around, picking up friends and
acquaintances, and once in a while pulling up to a gas
station so he could use the crapper. That was the only
thing still needed so he'd never have to leave his limo
at all—a toilet.

He didn't even care if he never took a bath or a
shower again. He washed up for other people, not
himself. He was getting so rich, so powerful, no one
would have the *cojones* to object to his stench anyway.
Come to think of it, they already didn't.

"What you laughing about, Toro?" a nasal voice
asked, snapping him out of his reverie.

"None of your business, Ju-li-us," Fernandez replied,
harshly eying the nervous, sharp-nosed goateed man.
"So keep your trap shut."

Julius Rodriguez sulked, as usual. Fernandez didn't
give a damn. He owned the guy. Rodriguez had been
one of Fernandez's men since they'd started out as
one of many street gangs in Los Angeles. Lots of guys
from the barrio wanted to call him "Hu-li-o" but since
Julius—like Sidney Fernandez himself—was third
generation and his knowledge of Spanish was limited
to swear words and common phrases, he preferred
the Anglo pronunciation. Anyway, Fernandez also
found "Julius" more in keeping with being a big
shot's main man.

"I was just wondering," Julius said. "Where we going?"

"No place. I'm thinking." Fernandez's three hundred pounds lumbered over onto his back, so his head lay on a stack of pillows covering the armrest, his feet braced against the one opposite.

Julius perched on the seat facing him. "No place. Great."

Fernandez glared at him. "Is she out yet?"

"She's trouble." Julius stared out the window. "You can't trust her."

"Who says I trust her? I want this job. That bitch owes me."

"And then?" Julius asked.

Fernandez smirked. "That's for me to know. So, she out?"

Julius sighed. "She got out today. I took care of everything for her. She's ours now."

Fernandez sat back and shut his eyes. *"Bueno."*

After a few more blocks of silence, Julius said, "Why don't we go find ourselves some chicks? I'm tired of just sitting."

Without moving, Fernandez ordered, "Get out."

Julius stared at his boss. "You joking?"

"You're tired of sitting, and I'm tired of listening to you complain." Fernandez struggled to sit up. "Raymondo! Stop here!" The car stopped in the center of Nineteenth Avenue, one of the major thoroughfares through the western side of the city. Brakes shrieked and horns blared outside.

"Come on, boss. I didn't mean nothing," Julius said.

"Me neither. No hard feelings."

"But—"

Fernandez pulled out a .357 Ruger. Julius leaped out the door and dashed down the sidewalk. Laughing, Fernandez gave Raymondo the signal to take off.

As the limo rolled through Golden Gate Park, Fernandez once again stretched his flabby bulk across the back seat. "Drive along the ocean. I got to relax. The sound of waves, they relax me."

"You got it, boss."

"This is gonna be big, Raymondo."

"I know, boss."

Fernandez rested his bulbous head and shut his eyes. He wanted to think of *her*, of the way it used to be between them, and could be again, without Julius's constant nagging and worry. He'd been the one to come through for her, to help when she needed it most, and she owed him big time. Also, she knew what he'd do if she tried to get away without paying. She'd help; no doubt about it.

"It's gonna be the biggest job of my life," Fernandez said to his driver. "After this, I may even think about retiring. What'll you do, then, without El Toro to drive around?"

"I'll be very sad, boss."

"I'm sure you will, Raymondo. I'm very sure you will be."

"So what that it's a corny old song?" Angie sat across the table from Paavo at Wings of an Angel and listened to him describe the tenor's serenade. "The sentiment is beautiful—that there's the sun in the sky, but my own sun, *sole mio*, is your face, *sta 'nfronte a te*. It moves me to tears just to think about it!" She sighed dreamily, her gaze slowly moving over Paavo's face. It was handsome, and to her eyes, the stuff of songs. Some people might think that it was too angular and hard, with his high cheekbones and intense blue eyes. Not her.

His hair was dark brown and wavy, and he wore it short and brushed conservatively back from his face. He was trim and fit, and about a foot taller than

Angie's five-foot-two, which meant she usually wore fun shoes with wondrously high heels around him.

"Well, maybe it's not such a bad song," he murmured, then cleared his throat, as if to hide the way her words had touched him. "Anyway, the cops with me sure enjoyed it."

She grinned at his discomfort. He hated showing any iota of sentimentality, yet hidden under a brusque exterior, he was one of the most loving people she'd ever met. "I'm sure they thought the singer was wonderful. They just didn't know how to tell you."

"Angie." He reached across the table and covered her hand with his. "It was thoughtful, unexpected, loving—but no more singers. Please."

She smiled ruefully. "All I wanted was for you to know how happy I am."

"I know, believe me. By now, the entire police force of the City and County knows as well."

"Good." She laughed. Even Paavo chuckled, proving he wasn't nearly as upset as he pretended to be.

Earl White scurried from one table to the next, serving desserts and coffee, collecting checks, and clearing dirty dishes, while continuing to provide for a steady stream of take-out customers. Angie hadn't realized Wings had started such a service. It appeared to be successful, amazingly so. Who would have thought so many people would have a yen for cash-and-carry spaghetti and meatballs?

Angie leaned toward Paavo, and in a lowered voice said, "As soon as Earl is free, I'll ask him what happened here last night between Connie and her date."

"So eating here wasn't due to a sudden lust for Butch's cooking," he said.

"If I was taking care of my lusts, we wouldn't be here now, believe me." She and Paavo had finished their green salad and small bowls of minestrone, and were working on the entrees—polenta and Italian sausage for Paavo, and Butch's spaghetti and meatball special for Angie—when she saw that Earl was free, and used her engagement-ring-laden hand to wave him over.

"How're you guys doin' now?" Earl asked as he bustled closer. "Wait! I almost forgot." He filled his lungs, spread his arms wide, and in an ear-splitting voice that grated like a flat bugle, erupted into "*'O so-o-o-le mi-i-o!*"

The other customers gawked in stunned silence, then burst into applause and laughter.

Paavo cringed as Angie beamed. "How did you know?" she asked.

"Da last take-out guy was a cop. Tol' us all about it. What a hoot! Miss Angie, you're too much."

Since Paavo looked ready to chew the table, Angie quickly changed the conversation to Connie's date. Earl told them all about the stranger Connie had dined with after Dennis had stood her up.

"Did they leave together?" she asked.

Paavo studied Angie's expression. "You don't think she'd take some stranger home with her, do you? She's smarter than that."

"Why, then, didn't she tell me about him?" Angie wondered aloud.

Earl had an answer. "Maybe 'cause dis stranger looked like a bum."

"Well, something kept her home from work, and me out of . . ."

The door opened and two men walked into the restaurant. The one in the lead dripped magnetism, money, and sexy good looks. Angie stopped talking and eyeballed him. Rarely did she see a man she'd call a hunk—other than Paavo—but this guy definitely fit the category.

He was at least six-three or -four, with shoulders that stretched from one wall to the other, and thick, jet black hair with an evocative lock carefully draped to touch his forehead lightly. His eyes were hazel, framed by long, black lashes, and his face chiseled. His clothes reminded Angie of a recent Saks Fifth Avenue ad, from his chestnut brown leather sport coat to the gold chains against a cream pullover, dark brown slacks, and Italian brown leather loafers. On his pinky rested an eye-popping diamond in a chunky twenty-four-carat gold setting.

She scarcely noticed the older, thinner, and smaller man in a dated off-the-rack pinstripe suit with wide lapels. He seemed to fade into the woodwork, while the first one lit up the room.

"Oh, my! Who's that?" Angie whispered to Earl as he rose from his seat.

"Not'in' like a day late an' a dollar short," he murmured. "It's Pagozzi."

It took all Angie's willpower not to swivel around and stare at the man and his cohort as Earl led them to a back table. Pagozzi looked like part of the high-rolling world of celebrity sports stars, the kind of man who'd have starlets and showgirls throwing themselves at him, while Connie—despite her love of loud, too-tight clothing—was really a down-home kind of girl.

On the other hand, Angie thought with a thrill, it might be time for Pagozzi to settle down with a real woman. Why should he bother with young, sexy playgirls when he could have Connie? A question better left unanswered.

Nevertheless, his own uncle Butch seemed to think

Connie was exactly what he needed, and Butch obviously had Dennis's best interests at heart. Connie's, too.

"Very interesting," Angie murmured, mental wheels churning and spinning.

Paavo cocked an eyebrow and glanced at the man who'd caused such a reaction in Angie. "He looks like a lot of jocks who've hit the big time," was his only comment, until, "Uh-oh."

Angie didn't like the way Paavo was frowning. "Why did you say—"

The question lodged in her throat as Dennis Pagozzi cast a huge shadow across the table. She had to lean way back to look him in the eye. "Hello."

He held out a large, strong hand. "I'm Dennis Pagozzi," his deep voice rumbled. "I understand you're Angie Amalfi, and you been a big help to my Uncle Butch and his friends getting this restaurant off the ground."

"Thank you," she said, her hand still swallowed up in his. "This is my fiancé, Paavo Smith. We've just become engaged." She freed her right hand and lifted her left toward him, ring finger extended.

"Very nice," Dennis said, then offered congratulations to Paavo as they shook hands. "Care if I join you?" he asked as he sat down in the chair Earl had occupied. "I feel terrible I missed meeting your friend last night. Man, my Uncle Butch is really piss—I mean, angry at me about it. See, what happened was, I nearly got knocked out during a pick-up game with some friends—we never get tired of playing, even during the off-season—and I spent my dinner in the infirmary. Do you think she hates me so much if I call her she'd hang up? I been told she's a great gal."

He looked so hangdog as he relayed his tale of woe

that Angie couldn't help but laugh. "If you tell her what happened, I'm sure she'll listen."

"Cool!" His face lit up with a big smile. "This restaurant's great, isn't it?" He looked around, eying everything much like a little boy in an ice cream parlor. "I been suggesting to Butch that they expand it so they can fit in lots more customers. I could help out, take part in it myself."

"Expand it?" Angie was shocked. "Don't you think that'd ruin the place? It's a small, romantic eight-table restaurant."

"Isn't that the problem?" He shrugged, then rose. "Well, I won't keep you. I wanted to say hello. What if sometime we get together and, you know, toss around ideas about how to make this place bigger and better? I been told you're real creative."

"Why . . . that would be most interesting," Angie said, pleased that someone, somewhere, appreciated her creativity. She tried to be creative, not that she often succeeded, but she always tried.

"Before I forget," Dennis said, "one more question. What was your friend's name again?"

A short while later, Angie was getting into the passenger seat of her car—Paavo preferred to drive—when she realized she'd never gotten an answer to her question. Had Connie left with the stranger last night or not?

Dennis Pagozzi was almost asleep when he heard the doorbell ring. He lived in a mansion in Sea Cliff, one of San Francisco's most exclusive neighborhoods. Most of his friends and teammates lived with family and kids south of the city in big suburban sprawlers with land and swimming pools. Dennis enjoyed city life, so the thirty-five hundred square feet of high-tech luxury he called home suited him just fine.

Few people knew this was his home, however. And those who did had better sense than to come to call at two A.M.

He went to the security video in one corner of his bedroom and looked to see who stood at the door.

He couldn't say his visitor was unexpected. He walked back to the bed, took out the Beretta he kept in his nightstand, and put on a black silk robe.

Holding the gun, he padded downstairs. The bell rang once more as he reached the door.

"Who is it?" he called. No sense letting on that he knew.

"Veronica."

Hearing her voice was like a knife through the belly. "Are you alone?"

"Of course!"

He opened the door a crack, giving her a quick once-over, then pulled it wider. Her gaze fell to the gun.

"Are you serious?" she said. "Is that any way to greet me?"

"Since when weren't you dangerous?" He slid the gun into the robe's pocket and held open the door as she entered. She looked good, damned good for a woman who'd done time, in a tight silver dress and gray stiletto heels. Her blond hair appeared freshly trimmed and feathered long and sexy. He remembered how silky it used to feel—how silky she used to feel—against his hands.

She perused the living room, slowly walking around over the white carpet, eying the two black sofas with a couple of black and gray checked throw pillows on one of them, the gray loveseat. She lightly fingered the big screen HDTV, the audio and video entertainment systems, and the entire wall filled with a variety of video game systems and monitors, the usual Nintendos and Playstations, plus more sophisticated arcade equipment. "Still into toys, I see," she said, her voice curling around him, as husky as he remembered it.

His chin tilted upward. He was glad she could see how far he'd come, but smarted at her criticism. "So? No harm done."

"You've done well," she said abruptly. "Extremely well. Almost . . . suspiciously well, I might add."

"Don't worry—it's all legit. From football. Not everyone's like you, Veronica."

"You had me worried there for a minute, but I should have known better." She laughed aloud as she sat down on the sofa and opened up the onyx cigarette box on the chrome and glass coffee table. "Cigarettes? That's all?" The mocking tone in her voice grated. Lifting out a Benson and Hedges, she held it between long red nails. "You aren't the man I used to know." She put the cigarette in her mouth and waited for him to pick up the lighter.

"I don't even use nicotine now. That's all I keep in the house, and they're for company." He held the flame steady as she drew on the cigarette, then sat down across from her. "I'm a respectable member of the community, in case you didn't know."

Her deep, throaty laughter rumbled inside him, made him want her in his bed. In the past, it had nearly cost him his career.

"Of course you are, lover." Her head dropped back and she slowly blew smoke high into the air. He eyed her long, smooth neck, the lightly throbbing pulse at the base of her throat.

"How did you find this house?" His words turned

clipped and dry. "I figured you'd phone when you got out."

"We have a few mutual friends," she said coyly, "whether you want to remember that little fact or not."

"I remember," he said with a frown. "So, when did you get out?"

"Today. Or, considering the hour, yesterday." She took a deep drag and let the smoke billow around her.

He inhaled it, remembering. "You didn't waste any time getting here."

"Why should I? I've waited for this a long time."

He smirked. "For me? I should have known."

Her red lips slanted into a look that was half-grin, half-derision. "You're such a sick bastard. You know what I'm here for. It's time to hand it over."

He raked his fingers through his hair and wished he were dreaming. She was more than he could bear. "It's not that easy, Veronica."

"What the hell are you talking about?"

"I got bills. Lots of them. My career . . . things . . . aren't quite as good as they were earlier."

"I sat in jail three years—"

"I know, but it's been tough. The economy is going south. My contract isn't getting renewed."

Her face hardened. "What are you saying?"

"I need the money a lot more than you do."

She jumped to her feet. "Max Squire put you up to this, didn't he? You two bastards think you're going to screw me again!"

"No! I haven't even seen him."

She pulled a gun from her handbag and pointed it at him. "Where's Max?"

Chapter 5

Connie woke up to a raging headache and black circles under her eyes.

Most of the night she'd lain awake berating herself for having been such a sucker. When she saw Squire lying on the street two nights ago, she should have called the cops and had him arrested for vagrancy! How far would he have gotten trying to steal out of their wallets, hmm?

When she finally fell asleep she dreamed she tracked him down. After devastating him with her charms into a mass of quivering unfulfilled desire, on his knees, pounding the floor with frustration, she picked his wallet from his back hip pocket, took out all his money, rolled it up, and slid it into her ample cleavage.

"Connie, forgive me!" he begged.

"Die, worm."

She sashayed away in a blaze of day-glo pink and matching four-inch spike heels. Comfortable ones. Definitely a dream.

She got up, showered, and used half a tube of Max Factor's Erase trying to hide her bags before putting on the rest of her makeup.

Yesterday, she'd searched her apartment for something, anything, Squire might have left behind to give her some clue of where he was living, but she'd found nothing. Big surprise. He didn't *own* anything to leave behind.

He'd told her he was staying near Wings of an Angel. She wondered if even that was true. Heck, maybe he didn't even know Dennis Pagozzi, and the whole thing was a scam to get a free dinner, a free night's lodging, and some ready cash.

What a stupid, schmaltzy, ignoramus sap she was! She was going to swear off men forever. She'd had it. End of story. Finito.

She was almost out the door to head for work when Angie phoned, singing the praises of Dennis Pagozzi.

"I'd like to know why you met him when he was supposed to have been my date," Connie snapped.

Angie's reply was measured. "He was sorry he missed you, and he's going to call."

Like this girl was born yesterday. "Well, let's forget about my job," Connie mewled. "I'll just sit here by the phone all day."

"He's handsome, and a sharp dresser. You'll be gaga over him, trust me in this," Angie urged.

"If gaga is close to nuts, I don't have far to go," Connie muttered.

Angie tried to change the subject. "Anyway, what's this I hear about you having dinner with some stranger? Earl told me about it. Some bum who was looking for Dennis as well? What was that about?"

"Damned if I know," Connie said brusquely. "Earl was right. He was a bum. I don't know, and don't care anything about him. Now, I'm going to work."

Connie hung up the phone, in no mood to hear any more about how great her missed blind date was, or how much Angie was in love, and definitely not how Angie thought everyone else in the world should be in love as well. Sometimes she could be really hard to take.

Before stepping out of her apartment, Connie looked at herself in a mirror to make sure no one had taped a sign to her back that said "Sucker." How did guys like Squire even find her?

Right then and there, she was determined to find *him*, and when she did, he'd be one sorry bastard. His ribs might not be broken now, but just wait.

Helen Melinger was sweeping the sidewalk when Connie approached. "Hey, there!" Helen barked in her usual gruff way. "So, you finally decided to get your butt back to work!"

"Buzz off!" Connie unlocked the door and slammed it behind her.

Helen leaned on the broom, gawking at her usually cheerful neighbor.

"Hello?" Angie said into the telephone as she shut off the Cuisinart. Ground pork, veal, and pork fat were swirling around with eggs, seasonings, and a heavy splash of cognac.

"Angelina Amalfi? This is Don Evans. I'm Director of Production at Sara Lee, Incorporated."

With the phone wedged between her ear and neck, she cut a whole goose liver into tiny one-quarter-inch squares. "As in Sara Lee cakes?"

"Exactly. We've heard wonderful things about your Comical Cakes, and—"

"I don't own that business anymore. I'm sorry." She would have hung up, but her hand was slimy and she reached for a napkin first.

"Wait!" the voice cried. "It's not the business, it's the

creativity we're interested in, and that's *you*. We'd like to start up our own line of festive and holiday cakes—some humorous, and all of them whimsical. The sort of thing you, we've been told, excel at."

She scooped up the foie gras and put it into a sauté pan with minced onions and butter. "What a nice compliment," she finally managed to say, as she wiped her hands and stirred the mixture.

"Miss Amalfi." He was sounding exasperated. "You don't understand. We were hoping you'd consider joining our team as a consultant as we start up this venture."

He was the one who didn't understand! If the liver cooked much more than a minute it would become rubbery, and her plans to surprise Paavo ruined. "Excuse me, but—"

"You've had experience in what the public is looking for along these lines—very successful experience," he continued. "Would you be willing to talk to us—"

"My liver is stiffening! I really must go." Her head cocked further and further as the phone began to slip. She placed it on the counter, then hurried to remove the liver from the heat and put it into a bowl.

"Your what? I'm not . . . anyway, Miss Amalfi, we'd love the opportunity to work with you, and we have an office right in San Francisco—"

A handful of pistachios went into the Cuisinart and she turned it on High. As she began to sauté the ground meat, the nuts clattered loudly and the blender whirred.

"Hello? Miss Amalfi? What's that strange noise? Hello? Hello?"

The Women's Facility was an oppressive cement monolith. Max almost felt a pang of pity for Veronica's having spent three years there. Almost. A sour-faced female guard led him through security to the visitor's area for the cellblock Ronnie had called home.

He sat on a stool facing a thick glass wall with phones on both sides. After some ten minutes, a jailer led a young black-haired woman to a chair opposite his.

"Who're you?" the woman asked. Her acne-scarred face was hard and the glare she cast made it even fiercer.

"I'm a friend of Veronica's," he said quietly. "I was supposed to meet her, but she isn't at the hotel."

The woman eyed him suspiciously. "You Dennis?" she asked.

Dennis? The past came at him in a rush. He wobbled dangerously on the stool, his head light and dizzy. After Veronica had been sent to prison, he'd gotten the impression that she'd once had an affair with Dennis, among others. He had no idea, though, that their relationship was at all serious, or that it had continued.

Dennis had been one of his few clients who'd been kind to him and offered help. He'd thought it was because Dennis had considered him a friend. Now, he wondered if it wasn't guilt.

"I'm surprised," he said finally. "I didn't think she'd tell anyone my name. She must trust you a lot."

The woman shrugged. "Guess so."

He tried to look worried. "I waited all day yesterday for her. She was released yesterday, wasn't she?"

"Yeah. Lucky bastard. Me, I got four more years here. She told me you're rich. Can you do something for me? Help me get out?"

"I'll see what I can do. But first, I've got to find Veronica."

"Why don't you ask her PO?" she said.

"I did. He didn't know where she was either."

"She said she was going to San Francisco, man. You should try her there. Isn't that where you live? Maybe she's at your place, waiting for you."

Maybe so, Max thought bitterly. He could imagine her there, with Pagozzi, laughing over what a lovesick fool he'd been. It shouldn't be too hard to find Pagozzi's home, to visit her there with the Saturday night special he'd picked up with Connie's money.

Damn them both!

He smiled warmly at the woman. "To think, I came all the way down here to meet her. Did she say she was going to San Francisco right away?"

"That's what I thought. Why the hell would she want to stay in this crappy town one minute longer than she had to?"

Connie's mood wasn't any better when she returned to her apartment that evening, especially after Mrs. Rosinsky, her landlady, confronted her on the stairs and demanded to know if she had a man living in her apartment. She should be so lucky.

Of course, she denied it vehemently, wondering if the landlady had seen Max leave. But that wasn't the case. Instead, apparently, some strange kind of police officer was looking for a man and thought he lived in Connie's apartment. He'd contacted her landlady, who had denied it, but now wanted to make sure she was right.

It was all too weird. On top of everything else, had she given sanctuary to a man wanted by the police? Even if he was, how would they know he'd spent one night there?

She kicked off her Hush Puppies as she flipped through the mail. Two bills, four advertisements. At least the numbers weren't reversed.

Tossing her jacket on a chair, she went to the refrigerator for a Lipton diet lemon tea and to ponder the food situation for tonight's dinner. It wasn't pretty.

The few customers who'd come into the shop that day were picky and didn't buy anything. Many more days like that, and she'd end up back at the Bank of America as a teller. Standing on her feet for eight hours giving money to other people was not her idea of a good time.

The hundred-eighty dollars Max had stolen from her was important. Most of it was grocery money. As she sprinkled some food into Goldie Hawn's bowl, she wondered if she might be reduced to eating fish food before her business turned around.

Goldie Hawn was lucky she was so small. Any larger, and she might end up battered and fried.

Connie cooked some instant rice, then sautéed onion and garlic in a frying pan and added about a quarter pound of hamburger, crumbled, a half can of peas, and a little powdered ginger. When it was cooked, she mixed it together with the cooked rice, sprinkled soy sauce over the concoction, and voilà, "Connie's Fried Rice." Okay, so it wasn't anything she'd serve company—and she wouldn't dare mention it to Angie—but it was easy, filling, and most important, cheap.

With each bite, irritation at Max Squire grew. How many times is one burnt so badly? She should track him down like a crazed bloodhound, then glom on like a rabid pitbull until he coughed up her money.

Dennis Pagozzi supposedly knew Max. Old friends, wasn't that what Max had said they were? Maybe

Dennis could tell her how to reach him. If she called Butch, he could give her Dennis's phone number.

God, but she hated the thought of phoning a man who'd stood her up! On the other hand, she was desperate, financially speaking.

She was steeling her nerve to punch in the Wings of an Angel number when the telephone rang. She was sure it was Angie again, wanting to get together "to talk." Why did people who had everything going well for them think that other people's problems could be solved by talking? God knows, if it was that easy, she'd talk so much she'd rival Oprah.

"Hello." She all but spat out the word.

"Is this, uh, Connie?" a man's deep voice asked.

"Yes," she said hesitantly.

"I'm Dennis Pagozzi. I called to apologize for missing you the other night. I was knocked out cold in a pick-up game. Spent the night in the infirmary."

Dennis Pagozzi! He'd actually called her. Was on her telephone. Right now.

She swallowed hard, thoughts of all the movies and books she'd enjoyed recently in which women had sexy Italian boyfriends swimming in her head. Maybe it was finally her turn.

It took a moment for her to find her voice. "How awful!" she croaked, then nervously cleared her throat. "Did you get a concussion?"

"It's no big deal. I'm okay. I was wondering if we could try again."

To hear him say those words was even more of a shock than the call, no matter how nice Angie had claimed he was. Cautiously, she said, "What did you have in mind?"

"How about dinner tomorrow night? I'll come by to pick you up. My uncle didn't like the way you ended up sitting there all alone with no one but a guy who knew me years ago to keep you company. It was pretty cold. I never treat my women that way—not any woman. I feel bad about it."

Something about his pat little speech grated. On the other hand, the way he said "my women" with that growling, masculine voice caused her heart to beat a little faster. God, what was with her? "Tell you what," she said, taking a couple of deep breaths. "I'll meet you there, but I'll get there on my own."

"Don't trust me?" he asked, sounding hurt.

"Why should I?" was her quick retort. Despite his sexy voice, he was a long way from being anyone she wanted to depend on for anything. Of course, she did want information on Max Squire's whereabouts, and perhaps he could give it to her.

"Hey, you're one tough woman." He chuckled. "I like that."

She smiled. "Maybe, if you're lucky, I'll feel the same about you someday."

"You will, Connie. You can bet on it."

After arranging a time, they said good-bye. Connie hung up the phone, but instead of feeling elation at the call, despite Angie's assurances, something made her uneasy.

Maybe she was gun shy because of her rotten experience with Max. Or maybe she just wasn't blind date material.

Chapter 6

When Paavo walked into Homicide, he was tired and cross from a grueling morning in court. The defendant's attorney was good, but with his client obviously guilty, his only chance was to make the police look like the bad guys in the case. It didn't help Paavo's mood any to know it was more a show for the jury than anything else.

The first thing he saw was an ornate silver coffee urn on a desktop near the entrance to the detail, and around it, yellow, green, and gold floral demitasse cups more than half filled with cold coffee. On platters were fancy little sandwiches, no crusts, cut into heart and flower shapes. A number of them, with one bite taken out, lay abandoned on plates besides the cold coffee.

He looked out over the large, oblong room that held the Homicide detail of the San Francisco Police Department. Homicide was a specialized department, part of the Bureau of Inspections, and housed centrally in the Hall of Justice rather than scattered over the neighborhood stations. Although Homicide was the top level for an officer not interested in supervision or administration to aspire to, right now, those few tough cops on the premises had their heads buried in their paperwork, refusing to meet his eye.

Elizabeth, Lieutenant Hollins's secretary, and de facto all-around helpmate for the homicide inspectors, a usually pleasant and chatty woman, in her fifties, with dyed red hair and glasses, stepped into the room, saw him, and froze.

"What's this?" he asked as she scurried by, almost as if she didn't want to be anywhere around him.

"Don't ask me." She picked up the outgoing mail, then hurried from the room.

Heads bent lower as he headed toward his desk in the back.

On the desk was an envelope with his name, written in Angie's neatly rounded script. Eyes peered at him as he opened it.

I hope you and your staff enjoy this treat—and it makes up for the singer.

Love, Angie

His own partner was one of the cowards. Paavo stared at him until he looked up. "What's wrong with it, Yosh?"

"Try it."

Paavo slowly walked to the coffee urn and poured himself a cup. From the smell alone, his stomach began to sink. He took a sip and nearly gagged. Rebecca Mayfield, the city's only woman homicide inspector, stood beside him. She was an attractive blonde, intelligent, tall, and with a figure sculpted to near perfection by workouts at a gym. Everyone knew, including Paavo, about her "secret" crush on him. They also thought she was a lot better suited to him than Angie.

"Strawberry?" he asked.

"Strawberry-and-vanilla-cream-flavored coffee . . . as far as we can tell," she said, her lips pursed.

"It's awful." Paavo's cup joined everyone else's on the table.

"Wait until you taste the sandwiches," Rebecca warned, unable to suppress a smile.

"What are they?"

"The watercress isn't bad, if you like veggie sandwiches, which these guys don't. But it was the pâté that really got to them."

"Christ," he muttered.

"You call it pâté. To me, it's chopped liver," Calderon's voice boomed across the room. Luis Calderon was Homicide's resident grouch. A Jack Nicholson wannabe, he could have easily played the guy in a Stephen King movie who scared little boys and girls. "Tried to wash it down with that strawberry crap. Thought my damn tongue would shrivel up."

Rebecca patted Paavo's arm. "I'm sure she meant well. It probably sounded very . . . romantic . . . to her. It's excellent pâté, if you like that kind of thing."

"I can't even think of where to send it," Yosh finally got the nerve to speak up from behind his desk. "If we offered it to the guys in City Jail, it'd probably cause a prison riot."

The entire detail laughed.

Angie walked two steps from her car and stopped, staring down at one of her black Ferragamo pumps with high platform soles. Stan Bonnette, a slim, preppy-looking man in tan Ralph Lauren slacks and a suede Brooks Brothers jacket, stood beside her. She'd convinced him to go to Connie's shop to buy his mother a birthday gift. "Before we go into Connie's, Stan, I've got to get the heel of this shoe fixed. It feels loose."

"How can you tell with those things? I think you need a blacksmith more than a shoe repair." He laughed at his joke. She didn't.

"A shoe repair is right next door to Connie's. Isn't that handy? Let's go inside."

Helen Melinger was concentrating on the sole of a man's shoe when the two entered. "Hi, Helen," Angie said. "How are you today?"

"Well, look who's here. What's up, Angie? I saw your pal drag herself next door this morning. I guess she's settling down a little, finally." Helen's greeting was good-natured as she swung the hammer down with a resounding *clang*.

"I hope. I'd like you to meet a dear friend of mine, Stan Bonnette. Stan, this is Helen Melinger."

The two shook hands. Angie waited for "Love in Bloom" to sound. "Stan is my neighbor," she chirped. "He's a good friend. Of Paavo's too." Heaven forbid Helen get the wrong impression about the two of them.

"Oh, nice." Helen scarcely looked up. Her muscled arm swung again. *Clang!*

"He works in a bank." Angie pretended not to see Stan scrunch his face up and cringe with each blow.

"Is that so?" Helen glanced up at the clock. Two P.M. "Banker's hours are getting shorter every day, aren't they?"

"It's my day off," Stan said petulantly. He was sensitive about his work habits, or lack thereof. "Why don't you show her your shoe, Angie?"

"Yes, my shoe. Helen is just a wonder at fixing things, Stan." She counted off on her fingers. "Shoes, purses, belts, um . . ."

"Motorcycles," Helen added with a wink and a smile. "I have a big Harley that sings like a bird."

"Isn't that exciting, Stan?" Angie asked, still not touching her shoe.

"Sure. Except that they're dangerous," Stan added.

"Not if you know how to ride them properly," Helen countered.

"It's not *how* to ride them, it's the way they're ridden," Stan proclaimed. "I hate how bikers head along the line that divides lanes, zipping between cars stuck in traffic. They should stay in one lane or the other, the way cars do. But instead, if you change lanes and you bag some guy on a motorcycle who's where he shouldn't be, usually right in your blind spot, it's the car driver's fault."

Helen put the hammer down and folded her arms. "You need to understand that motorcycles aren't like cars. They have only two wheels, in case you hadn't noticed. You've got to keep them moving so they don't fall over or stall."

Angie yanked her shoe off. "Here's—"

"If they can't handle traffic like everyone else," Stan pontificated, "they shouldn't be allowed in it. A no-motorcycle zone, that's what this world needs."

"My shoe?" Angie waved it around, hopping closer to Helen. Both Helen and Stan ignored her.

"What kind of a pig-headed attitude is that?" Helen growled. "If everyone rode motorcycles instead of big gas guzzlers, this country would be a lot better place. We could save the environment."

Stan threw back his head to bray a phony laugh. "A Sierra Club Harley rider. Now I've heard everything. A two-wheeling tree hugger."

Helen came around the counter toward him with deadly deliberation.

"The heel, right here!" Angie pointed vigorously, trying to get her attention.

"You haven't heard nothing if you bad mouth Harleys *or* the Sierra Club, buster."

Helen looked ready to deck him, and Angie had no doubt about the agonized outcome for Stan if it came to that. So much for matchmaking. "Uh, Stan, I think it's time for us to go."

He waved her off. "I can say whatever I want, lady—and I use that term only because I don't think it's polite to say everything one is thinking."

Angie couldn't believe her ears. Stan never stood his ground. Was he drunk? She shoved her shoe into Helen's clenched hand.

Scrunching the shoe as if it were tissue paper, Helen put both hands on her ample hips. "You can say what you want, you pencil-necked weenie, as long as you have the balls to back it up."

Angie wobbled dangerously on one shoed foot, tugging at Stan's arm.

He brushed her off. "Well, maybe mine aren't quite as big as you wish yours—"

"Why, you little—"

"Stan!!" Still hopping, Angie grabbed him around the waist and pulled. "Let's get out of here!"

"Hi!" Connie said from the doorway. "I thought I heard familiar voices. I was just heading home." She met Angie with a smile. "Got to get ready for my date with Dennis Pagozzi, thanks to you."

Angie gave a whoop of joy and quickly decided her matchmaking failure with Stan and Helen was only an aberration.

Connie gelled her hair into spiky strands that stood up on top and sprayed it into place. With this new hairstyle she should buy stock in Clairol. She added globs of black mascara to her lashes, gray eye shadow, and pink blush. After sheer black pantyhose, and strappy black sandals, she squeezed herself into a slinky Victoria's Secret black dress with a skirt so short and a neckline so plunging that if either was much shorter or lower, they'd have met.

Eat your heart out, Pagozzi.

She hadn't believed his concussion story one bit, but having him call made her feel a lot better about him. Angie's predictions about how much she'd like him, though, carried no weight after watching Angie try to matchmake Stan and Helen. Who was next? Charlton Heston and Rosie O'Donnell?

Covering up with her sensible, long, and bulky navy blue overcoat, she headed for Wings. When she walked in, she spotted Pagozzi immediately, and all thoughts about him feeling remorse for missing their date vanished. Who was she kidding? The guy was drop-dead, mouth-watering, giant-size Tom Cruise gorgeous. He stood up as she walked in, all six feet, four inches of him, in what looked like a deep red cashmere sweater and well-fitted black slacks. She stopped breathing. "Connie?" He smiled pleasantly.

"Hi, Dennis." She fought for composure. She was supposed to be cool here, not gape and drool like some brain-dead groupie. "How nice to finally meet you." They shook hands, he holding on a little longer than necessary.

"Same here," he answered, admiration in his eyes. "I'd like you to meet a good friend of mine, Wallace Jones. Everyone calls him Jonesy. Jonesy, meet Connie. She's the chi— er, gal, I was telling you about."

When she could finally tear her eyes from Dennis, she saw an older man also sat at the table. Skinny, wearing a pinstriped suit with wide lapels, he had a left eye that twitched as he looked at her.

He stood up and shook her hand. His hands felt dry and scaly, and his teeth looked the same.

Dennis held out a chair for her as she removed her coat. His pleasant expression expanded into a wide, happy grin, and he murmured, "Wow."

Ecstatic, she sat and then turned her attention to his friend. "What do you do, Mr. Jones?"

"It's Jonesy, ma'am. I'm a collector."

She raised her eyebrows in surprise. "How fascinating. What do you collect?"

"Sports stuff, I mean, mem-or-a-bi-li-a," he said slowly, as if he'd just learned the word and was testing it out.

"That's right," Dennis said enthusiastically. "And if we make this into a sports bar, like I'm thinking would be a real good idea, Jonesy will supply the stuff to sell, and we'd get a cut."

Facing him, she was struck anew at what a stunning man he was. "Why would you care about a sports bar when you play football?"

"A guy has to think about the future," he said. "Someday, when I retire, I'll need a backup plan. Of course, my contract will be renewed for next season. It's not like there's any problem."

"I see," she said, although she didn't, quite. Still, a man who thought about the future was fine in her book.

Dennis placed his hand on Jonesy's back. "No sense talking business tonight, friend. I'll call you." Jonesy took the hint and left.

The evening went by in a haze of glory. Dennis Pagozzi treated her like a princess, and he was large enough that she could feel almost petite around him. His hazel eyes had a way of gazing at her as if she were both interesting and intelligent.

She kept pinching herself to make sure this evening was real. That she was here, and so very happy.

Much too early, he escorted her to her Toyota. She'd hoped he'd ask her to go to a nightclub or out dancing. How many times could a girl say she loved to dance without appearing too obvious? But, no luck.

It was just a first date, though. He should call back. And maybe he really did have a concussion. At this point, she'd have believed him if he said he'd missed their blind date because he'd turned into Superman and saved Metropolis.

"I almost forgot," he said, as they neared the car. "You talked with Max Squire the other night."

Max who? was her first reaction, but she smiled and said she had.

"Did he say anything about how I could get hold of him?" Dennis asked. "I heard he was looking for me, but he didn't leave a phone number or anything."

That's the question she'd planned to ask *him*, back when she was able to hold a thought in her head. "He didn't say, specifically. Only that he lived near here—in easy walking distance. I suspect he might show up again."

"I see . . ." Dennis nodded, looking around. "Anyway, I got to go. See you around, Connie." With that, he hurried down the block to his Jaguar.

Connie hadn't even put the key into the ignition before she saw him drive off. What was he in such a hurry about?

Chapter 7

Veronica Maple sat in a coffee shop across the street from Wings of an Angel. When she'd first arrived in the city, she'd rented a Ford Escort—cheap, easy to park, and unmemorable—and she used it now to follow Dennis, to see if he'd go straight to Max Squire. Instead, he went first to a run-down apartment building in the rough China Basin area, where he picked up a sleazy-looking little guy with a pinstriped suit and an eye tic, and then to the restaurant.

Before long, the skinny guy left, but not Dennis. When he finally did, he walked out with some stacked blonde. They took separate cars, and judging from the directions the cars went off in, they weren't going to reconvene at some love nest.

From the outside, the restaurant looked like little more than a dump, although it did a decent business, especially in take-out. She'd peeked in the window and seen that it was clean and kind of cute, if you liked the cozy and intimate look. Definitely not what she'd consider a Dennis Pagozzi go-to place.

She had to find out what Dennis was up to. He wasn't nearly as malleable as when he was younger, and she didn't like his new assertiveness. He had the nerve to say "no" to her. Nobody said no to Veronica Maple. She thought he'd learned that years ago.

The three years she'd been in jail must have been long enough for him to forget. Or perhaps he thought her time there had softened her. If anything, it'd made her harder and tougher than the girl she once was.

They'd been clever. Neither one of them could simply take what they wanted—it was their way to keep things straight between them. No schemes, no double-crosses.

Now, though, it was working too well. Now that he was balking, she had to find a way to get him to go along, or find a way around him. Somehow, she would. No matter what it took.

Max Squire was the one she had to keep out of this, by one means or another. He knew too much, and he'd do anything he could to screw her over.

She'd prefer to get out of the city before he found her. Dennis swore he didn't know where Max was. For his sake, she hoped he was telling the truth.

The more she looked at the restaurant, the more she decided to check it out. What if Max was in there? What if the blonde was just a ruse?

She entered and stood at the door, looking around cautiously, peering at every corner, her right hand inside her large shoulder bag, her fingers wrapped around the handle of her Smith and Wesson. Inside, the restaurant was filled with the smells of Italy, cloth-covered tables with candles and single roses, wooden chairs, bottles of wine, and frilly white lace curtains adorning the tops and sides of the large window facing the street.

"You wanna table?" the waiter asked from his stand a little past the front door. Behind him were a couple of tables and swinging double doors to the kitchen. Most of the tables were to the right, as was the window.

She didn't see Max, or anyone else she knew. "I'm looking for Dennis Pagozzi. Do you know him?" she asked, stepping back from the disgusting little man.

"Sure. He's da cook's nephew. He just left, though. I don't t'ink he'll be back—"

"Butch is the cook here?"

"Yeah. You know him? He's—*hey!*"

She slipped past the waiter, toward the kitchen. He tried to step in front of her, but she ground the heel of her boot on his instep. As he hopped around in agony, she shoved the swinging double doors open and marched in.

She'd know him anywhere. Short, with wiry salt-and-pepper hair, a pugnacious grimace to his mouth, and an upturned nose, the only difference between the fleabag before her now, and the one she'd met years ago, was that his hair was no longer black.

Butch glanced up at her and stuck one hand behind his back. "What the hell are you doin' in town?"

"Isn't this interesting," she murmured, looking around the all-stainless-steel kitchen with its commercial-size ovens, sinks, and refrigerator, until her perusal hit the take-out boxes. She flipped open a Styrofoam lid and smirked.

"Hey!" the waiter yelled, and pulled the box away from her, too late.

"What're you doin' lettin' her in here, Earl?" Butch demanded.

Just then, another man bounded up the stairs from the basement at the noise.

"I didn' do not'in', Vinnie!" Earl cried. "She ran past me. I tried to stop her!"

Vinnie, wheezing from his dash up the stairs, was

short like Earl and Butch, but where Earl was stocky
and Butch was wiry, Vinnie sagged all over—cheeks,
jowls, chest, stomach, even his feet seemed to splay all
over the floor. If a pear could melt, it would end up
shaped like Vinnie.

His hair was straight, deeply receding at the forehead and with a bald spot at the pate. He looked at the
situation in the kitchen and ran his hand over his hair
as if to make sure the bald spot was covered. It wasn't.

"Who is she?" he asked the other two.

"If you're lookin' for my nephew," Butch growled at
her, "he ain't here. He ain't in town, even. An' he don't
wanna see you. You keep away from him!"

She laughed. "Do you really think your Dennis is so
clean?"

"What's goin' on?" Vinnie asked.

Butch ignored him. "His only mistake was gettin' involved with you!"

"Funny man."

She took a Benson and Hedges out of her purse and
grabbed a book of matches. "You always hated me,
didn't you? Maybe that's because you were jealous.
You wanted me for yourself, but I belonged to Dennis."

"You're sicker than I thought!"

She laughed, blowing smoke in the air. "You've got
a nice place here, Butch. With a couple of your friends,
I see. Friends from San Quentin, right?"

Vinnie's and Earl's heads swiveled from Butch to
the woman.

"What you gettin' at?" Butch asked.

"I think you know. Dennis's told me about you, Uncle Butch. You got caught twice, didn't you? First time
was just a little thing—auto theft, right? Still, it's a
felony. And then the second time. Burglary, wasn't it?
Another felony. That makes two strikes, Butch. You get

a third, and you know what that means in California—the jailer will throw away the key."

"Butch!" Vinnie yelled so loud his face turned beet red. "What the hell is this about?"

Butch glared at her. "She's an old girlfriend of Dennis's. She just got outta jail."

"An ex-con?" Earl muttered.

"I'd hate it if Dennis's uncle got into trouble." She smiled coyly at Earl and Vinnie while walking around the tabletop, her fingers lightly touching the take-out boxes, one by one. "It's too bad all of you left so much evidence laying around. It's my civic duty to tell the police, don't you think?"

"Get the hell out of my kitchen!" Butch rushed at her. Earl grabbed his arm, pulling him back. "The only thing I want to go to jail for is killin' you! It'll be worth every minute I'm there!"

"Easy, Butch," Vinnie said. "Nobody's gonna believe nothin' from her."

"You stay away from my nephew!" Butch bounded on his toes, like in his old prize-fighting days, unsuccessfully trying to yank his arm from Earl's grip. "So help me . . ."

"It's too late for that, sweetheart." Veronica smirked.

"Damn you!" Butch lunged again, but before he could break free, Vinnie hustled her out of the kitchen and out the door.

Instead of being angry at him, though, her reaction was even more chilling. She laughed.

The full moon cast a ribbon of white on the ocean just beyond the wide, gritty sand of Baker's Beach. Paavo and Angie took off their shoes and socks and walked barefoot. It was a rare night in San Francisco, no wind, no fog, only a peaceful stillness. To the north, the

Golden Gate Bridge spanned the narrow entrance to the bay, and to the south, high, steep rocks supported the posh neighborhood known as Sea Cliff. Waves from the Pacific lapped at their feet.

Angie was restless. Connie was going out with Dennis tonight, and she was wildly curious about it. She hoped Connie would have a good time. She deserved it. Life hadn't been easy for her.

Between anxiety and dreams of matchmaking, Angie was afraid that if she and Paavo had gone out to dinner, she couldn't have resisted staying away from Wings. Instead, she'd suggested they eat at his place and then bundle up and go for a walk on the beach. In early spring, San Francisco's beaches were usually cold and windy, if not foggy and rainy. Except for a few weeks each year, usually in September and October, only tourists went there without heavy jackets.

The cold water stung as it hit Angie's toes and she ran, lifting her feet high, to dry ground. Paavo chuckled at her. "Sissy," he said.

"You never told me if Homicide liked the pâté I made," she said suddenly, apropos of nothing. Paavo was used to that kind of thing.

"They thought it was . . . quite romantic of you."

She beamed at him. She couldn't help herself. Everywhere, all the time, with nearly every breath, she thought about him, and ideas would pop into her head, ideas that she absolutely knew would please him and let him know how much she loved him. Also, after the gut-rot motor oil the guys at the Hall of Justice drank, and the greasy doughnuts they ate, gourmet coffee and tea sandwiches had to have been a wonderful change.

"I'm so glad," she said, relieved. "Isn't it great to share the romance with your friends at work?"

Paavo looked a little stricken. "It's different," he admitted. He continued to walk through the cold waves while Angie darted back and forth out of their reach, but then, he was part Finnish. After learning that Finns enjoyed jumping out of a hot sauna to roll around in the snow, Angie knew she'd better be prepared for just about anything from Paavo. Her Italian blood couldn't begin to understand it, however. Just looking at his blue toes made her shiver.

"It's the happiest time of my life," she admitted, beaming at him.

He walked to her side on dry land and put his arms around her. "For me, too," he admitted, with a kiss that sent her head spinning. Then he tucked her close by his side as they continued their walk.

"I just wish I hadn't passed out when you proposed," she said.

He laughed aloud. "You didn't miss much."

"Hmm, I wonder . . ." An idea was beginning to form.

"You know, now that we've got this being engaged thing down, and we both like it," Paavo said, "have you ever thought about eloping?"

"Eloping?" She stopped dead, her jaw dropping. "Are you joking? I've dreamed all my life of a big, beautiful wedding. I just sent in subscriptions to *Bride*, *Modern Bride*, and *Bridal Guide*. I've bought an armful of books, including *Priceless Weddings*, *Planning a Wedding to Remember*, and *How to Set Your Wedding to Music*. I've already checked out four wedding boutiques and have seven more to go, from Carmel to Tiburon. I even tape the Lifetime channel twenty-four hours a day so I won't miss any of their wedding specials!"

After a long wait, he quietly said, "I always thought eloping would be romantic."

Hopefulness filled his voice, and she repressed a laugh. "It is, but not nearly so romantic as what I want. I can already see it in my head . . ."

"Oh?"

"You'll be standing at the altar, looking so handsome, and I'll be wearing the most beautiful gown in the world. At least a dozen bridesmaids will lead the way—"

"A dozen?"

"And my father will escort me to your side—"

"Scowling the whole way. The guy hates me, Angie."

"We'll have a Mass as part of the ceremony—"

"Not just quick 'I do's'?"

"With a children's chorus singing traditional hymns, several of them—"

"Angie, are you sure you don't just want to go to Reno? Or, maybe Las Vegas?" Paavo asked one more time.

His question pulled her out of her reverie. He just didn't get it. "Positive," she replied succinctly.

"That's what I was afraid of."

"This is a picture of the woman I'm looking for." Chuck Lexington handed Veronica Maple's mug shot to Luis Calderon. Calderon and his partner Bo Benson were the on-call inspectors at Homicide this week, which meant that any murders, suicides, or mysterious deaths that took place in the city and county from six A.M. Monday morning to six P.M. Friday night were theirs. A separate team took the weekends.

It was nearly midnight. Benson was home catching up on sleep, and Calderon was at the bureau, handling paperwork and writing reports until a call came in. And one would. In a city the size of San Francisco and with its crime stats, there was a homicide at least once a week, and a "suspicious" death about three times as often.

Calderon took the photo, then glanced at the probation officer hovering near his desk. "Sit down. Begin at the beginning."

Lexington gave him a brief summary of Maple's background and prison term.

"How do you know she's in the city?" Calderon asked when he was through.

"She bought a Greyhound ticket to here. I thought I had a lead on her whereabouts, but so far it hasn't panned out. That's all I can tell you. That, and the fact that she killed a pawnshop owner. I don't know what she got at the pawnshop. A ticket stub with her name on it was in the owner's pocket, and the item was gone. We suspect she picked up her item, killed him, then left town. I want her."

"So, you're here to find a skip?"

"She's more than a skip—she's a murderer. And I'm responsible for her leaving Fresno. There was a mix-up with the paperwork, and she was out of there before I knew it. An innocent man is dead as a result."

"If she's still in this city, we'll find her," Calderon said, steely-voiced. He didn't need any soft, overweight parole officer getting in his way. "You asking for an APB to go out on her? Where's the Fresno PD? We always work with them on cases like this."

"They're doing their own thing. I'm the one who tracked her to San Francisco." He tightened his lips. "They aren't listening much to me. But she was my case—and it's my job on the line now that she's vanished. I'm not about to sit around. She'll be long gone before they start checking in this area."

Calderon grunted, his most common form of communication. None of what the parole officer was saying surprised him. "We'll do what we can."

"When, or if, you find her, I want to know about it." Lexington leaned closer. "She's armed and dangerous, and has already killed once. I don't want to chance her doing it again!"

Calderon slid back in his chair, his mouth firm. "In this department, we know how to handle ourselves."

Chapter 8

Angie was in Stella's Bakery in North Beach carefully going over a recipe for a *Le Succès*, a meringue nut layer cake, with the head pastry chef. She wanted to be sure all four cakes she'd ordered were perfect. And heart-shaped.

The cake literally melted in the mouth, but it required more time and concentration than she wanted to give. For each cake, three heart-shaped layers of meringue, mixed with ground almonds, were baked separately. After baking, the layers were stacked, with caramelized almond butter cream spread over the bottom and middle layers and along the sides, and chocolate flavored butter cream on top. Slivered almonds were pressed against the sides of the cake and chocolate rosettes or other designs could be added on top for decoration. Angie was convinced the difficulty in making it was why French pâtissiers often wrote *"Le Succès"* on the cakes.

The chef was growing increasingly unhappy with each of Angie's comments. Meringues turned crisp and brittle after cooling, so the cake was a bit of a tour de force, and she imagined the possibility of being criticized over each flaw was not a happy prospect.

84

Nevertheless, she was working to convince him to give it a try, sure the boys in Homicide would be ecstatic over it, when who should walk in but her old friend and sometime foe Nona Farraday, restaurant reviewer on the staff of *Haute Cuisine*, a regional magazine for gourmands. Once, Angie would have crawled through ground glass to get that job.

On top of that, Nona was everything Angie would have liked to be. Tall, thinner than a breadstick, with high cheekbones, big, round, green eyes, and silky straight blond hair, she could wear clothes like a *Vogue* model. Her lips were a lot poutier than Angie remembered, and she wondered if a little collagen hadn't been added. Basically, she was someone Angie could easily hate, and often did.

"As I live and breathe," Nona cried. She threw her skinny arms around Angie, bent slightly, and they air kissed. "Whatever have you been doing with yourself? I heard your name come up in connection with something, but for the life of me, I can't remember what."

"My name?" Angie asked in surprise.

"I know. There's going to be an opening at *Haute Cuisine*." She smiled demurely. "I guess someone mentioned you. You might want to apply. You might have *some* chance. Perhaps."

"If I were interested, I'd take *Bon Appétit*'s offer."

Nona reached for the countertop to hold herself up, then laughed. "I couldn't have heard right. I thought you said—"

"I did," Angie stated. "My big news hasn't been announced in the papers yet, and I'm still trying to figure out a date for my engagement party, but look." She held out her hand.

Nona's mouth distinctly down-turned before she recovered with a big smile and a loud squeal. "Can it be?

You're engaged! How wonderful. Is it the cop?" Nona asked.

"None other."

"He's so sexy, I'll have to grant you that, Angie."

"Isn't he? I'm here ordering some special cakes for Homicide. That way, Paavo's friends can enjoy our happiness."

Nona's teeth clenched as she focused on the cakes behind the glass display. "I've got to get some cake for an open house one of my friends is holding at her art gallery. It would be much more fun, I'm sure, to be buying sweets for my fiancé's friends."

"It *is* fun."

Nona rested one hand on the counter, the other on her nearly nonexistent hip and angled toward Angie. "Maybe you've gone about this the right way," she said. "You've found a regular guy, maybe not real exciting, but *basic*, a guy who believes in things like marriage." Angie's eyes narrowed as Nona gave a toss of her head, making her hair whiplash away from her face. "Here, I've been going out with artists, chefs, restaurateurs, even a couple of film directors—poor ones, which is why they're here instead of Hollywood. What good has it done me?"

"I don't know how 'basic' Paavo is—"

"I'm not getting anywhere! These men are so busy trying to figure out themselves, they can't begin to take on the problems a woman might have, especially a strong businesswoman like *moi*." Nona ran a hand through her hair. She was a melodramatic nightmare.

Angie had had it. She turned back to the chef, whose eyes were starting to glaze over. If she wasn't putting out big bucks for the meringue, he'd have bounded back into his kitchen the minute Nona started talking. She addressed him. "It isn't as if my fiancé jumped onto the marriage bandwagon first chance he got, believe me, and—"

"You know what I mean, Angie," Nona interrupted. "At least there was *hope* for the two of you." She folded her arms. "All right. I'll admit it. Much as my life, my dates, my sex life have been wild and successful and exciting, I wish I knew someone like Paavo."

Angie did a double take. She tossed her recipe at the startled chef, giving him a quick thumbs up. He clutched the recipe to his chest and escaped.

Then she faced Nona, her mind quickly racing through the unmarried homicide inspectors she knew—and just as quickly came up with the perfect match. "No problem."

Dennis sat at a table at Fior d'Italia, a large restaurant near saints Peter and Paul's Church on Washington Square. He was early for their lunch meeting, but he was anxious to see Max Squire. He'd left word at the Forty-Niner office that if anyone should try to reach him, to give out his cell phone number. Sure enough, Max had called, and they'd arranged to meet.

The waiter, a young man with sandy-colored hair, one gold earring, and a well-scrubbed demeanor, brought him a Johnny Walker Red and water and put it on the table. "Say, you aren't Dennis Pagozzi, are you?" the man asked.

Pagozzi focused on the earring. "Yeah, I am."

"Wow! I watch the Forty-Niners all the time on TV. Can't buy a ticket"—he chuckled—"even if I could afford one! Man, seeing you here is great. Want to order? Wine? An appetizer? I'm Scott, by the way."

"Let's give my friend a few minutes to show up," Dennis said. "In fact . . . here he comes now."

Scott turned and tried not to look shocked as he

glanced from Max back to Dennis, as if to be sure he had the right man. "I'll show him to your seat," he said, baffled.

Dennis could understand why. Max's gaunt appearance stunned him, as well. He'd seen beggars better dressed.

He stood. "Good to see you, old buddy," he said, hand outstretched.

"Dennis!" Max shook his hand, his lips smiling, but his eyes hard. "Thanks for seeing me. I wouldn't have contacted you if it weren't important."

The waiter hovered near. "Can I get you something to drink, sir?"

Max glanced at Dennis's Scotch and began to shake his head when Dennis said, "Johnny Walker red—a double—for my friend."

"Thanks," Max murmured as Scott rushed off.

"So how you been?" Dennis asked.

"Well . . . not so hot, as you can see," Max said, gesturing at himself. "But that's not the reason I wanted to talk to you. You see—"

"Wait. After we order lunch. I didn't eat breakfast today." The waiter brought Max his drink, and Dennis ordered antipasto, soup, pasta, and prime rib for them both. "That okay with you, Max?" Dennis asked.

"Sounds great."

"And don't take too long," Dennis said to the waiter. "We're two hungry guys here." Scott dashed toward the kitchen, about ten feet off the ground.

"So, things haven't come together for you since that trouble a few years back?" Dennis asked.

As the table became loaded with bruschetta, baked brie, and roasted garlic, Max turned the conversation back to Dennis and his football career, as if he didn't want to talk about his own troubles. Not when he had a chance at a feast.

It wasn't until they were well into the prime rib that Max said, "Veronica Maple was released from prison three days ago."

Dennis tried to act surprised. "I heard she was expected to get out around this time. I didn't know exactly when. Why do you care?"

Slowly, Max lay down his fork and knife. "Don't play dumb. I know you kept in touch with her."

"But I didn't!" Dennis protested.

"She told people you did. People in the prison."

"Why would I? She meant nothing to me. Think, man! She ripped me off, too."

Max looked, at first, as if he didn't believe him. But then his eyes softened, questioning. Should he trust Veronica and her prison cronies over Dennis? Had he forgotten that Dennis had been the only one to help him in any way three years ago?

"I'm on your side in this," Dennis said. "I always have been."

Max ran his fingers through his greasy hair. "She's still got the money. Most of my clients were paid off like you were. The insurance company did right by you, didn't it?"

"Hey, Max. Calm down. They did okay."

"It's just me. I'm the one she ruined." His fists clenched. "I can't wait to get my hands on her!"

"You've got to forget about her. This isn't going to do you any good. Leave the city. Keep away from her."

"I won't do it. She's got what I want!"

"Max, let me give you some money." He pulled out a wad from his pocket. "How much do you need? Five hundred? A thousand?"

"It's not what I need now. It's the whole thing. She stole eight million dollars from my clients! Do you know what that did to me? To my reputation?"

"Here. Forget the eight million. It's a thousand. It's all I got with me—except to pay this restaurant—but you need more, you let me know. You were the greatest, Max. You helped me invest my money and make nearly twenty percent return on it. You stopped me from doing a lot of stupid stuff I wanted to do. If it weren't for you, I'd have nothing." Dennis placed it on the table by Max's plate.

Max stared at the money. "Tell me this. Did she contact you?"

Dennis waited a long time before he whispered, "No."

Max's eyes bored into him, colder than Dennis had ever seen them. "Tell me how to reach her."

Dennis slowly shook his head. "I don't know."

"Damn it, Dennis! If you're lying!"

Dennis noticed that the other customers looked up, concerned. "Forget her! She'll only cause you to do something that'll get you into more trouble."

"Like what? Kill her? Believe me, I'd love to. Once I get my money back."

"Max, listen to me." Dennis picked up his money and held it toward Max. "Take this money and leave town. Do it."

Max stood and knocked the money away, sending the bills flying across the restaurant. "I don't want your goddamned money! I want what's coming to me!"

Dennis stood as well, as Max stormed from the restaurant.

"I'm so sorry," Scott said, crawling around the floor picking up hundred-dollar bills. "Was he threatening you?"

"No. Not at all. He's just very upset." He left two hundred on the table to pay for lunch and a substantial tip. "When the pre-season games start, call the 'Niner office. There'll be couple of tickets waiting for you."

"Oh, wow. Oh, man!"

Dennis hurried from the restaurant and looked up and down the sidewalk for Max.

Connie's college helper was scheduled to work at Everyone's Fancy, so Connie took the opportunity to go to Angie's. She wanted to tell her about her date with Dennis.

Had Angie ever been right about the guy. All morning she'd been unable to keep still, leaping around the shop as if it were a step aerobics class, thinking about him. He was so cool.

Angie wasn't home. Didn't that just figure? The one time she had something exciting to tell her best friend about, said friend skipped out on her. What nerve!

Connie got in the car to go back home. The weather was clear, crisp, and warm, and going back to her solitary apartment wasn't her idea of a good time. She drove, enjoying the day, and soon found herself in North Beach, driving down the street where she'd found Max Squire passed out.

Whenever she thought about him, she still felt like a dork over the way he'd snookered her. Nothing like that had happened to her since high school, and then it had been over sex, not money.

Of course, her ex-husband had been the champion at really screwing her. Compared to him, Max was a piker.

Even in her family, B.M., or before men, it was her beautiful younger sister, Tiffany, who got all the attention and love from their parents. Tiffany had been no

more than a secretary, but a secretary in San Francisco's City Hall, where she hobnobbed with local
politicians. That made all the difference.

Such a job was far classier than working first as a
Bank of America teller or later as an insurance agent
for All Farm, like Connie had done. Tiffany talked to
their folks about political intrigue. Connie talked
about the need for liability insurance. Who was she
kidding? She was dull, even to herself.

During that time she met Kevin Trammel. Like her,
he had only a high school education, but he belonged
to a construction workers' union, made good money,
and was handsome as sin. Even Tiffany could scarcely
keep her eyes off him.

Connie knew he'd had problems with drugs earlier
in his life, but he told her he'd been clean for over six
months when they met. They dated another four
months, then went to Reno and got married.

Soon after, winter came, and construction slowed.
Kevin spent more and more time at home, while Connie went off to work. Money was tight. Two couldn't
live as cheaply as one, especially when Connie's pay
was low, and when he worked, Kevin's was compara-
tively high. He was used to buying what he wanted,
without a wife or anyone else to answer to.

She wasn't one to sit by with her mouth shut while
he blew their money. The resulting fights were scary.
Connie shuddered to remember how close to violence
each came. That should have been a sign of both their
immaturity and inability to cope with crises. And
more important, their incompatibility.

Before winter ended, he was back on drugs. He
stopped in spring when work started up again, but
then he pulled a back muscle and had to lie around the
house while it mended. Drugs helped ease the pain, he

said. Connie lived in dread of going home each day after work, wondering whether she'd find the loving man she'd married, or his evil twin, waiting for her.

Even worse was when he wasn't home when she got there, and she'd spend the evening worrying about the mood he'd be in when he returned. His good moods, eventually, simply weren't good enough, and the tension grew fiercer.

Ironically, she wanted to stay married to him through this time. She remembered the man who had charmed her, and she wanted him back. She tried to do whatever she could think of to get him back, including going to Alanon meetings.

For two years she tried, but the stress, financial strain, and unhappiness became too much. She contacted a divorce lawyer.

Kevin couldn't believe she'd abandon him that way. He needed her, while all she wanted was a husband she could depend on. Luxuries meant nothing to her, and she would have been perfectly happy with a couple of kids and a comfortable home. The kind of warm family life she'd never known. Was that too much to ask?

Was she bitter? Could she have gladly sent him through Angie's commercial-strength meat grinder? Never doubt it for a minute.

When All Farm Insurance downsized, she took her severance pay and used it to buy Everyone's Fancy. By that time, her parents were gone, and soon, her sister would be, too. Her little shop became everything to her.

The whole mess bummed her out until she met Angie and life began to pick up again. She'd lived like a loser because she'd let herself feel like one. Around Angie, she was different. Heck, Angie looked at her with respect—Connie ran a business, while Angie couldn't find the right job or business, no matter how hard she looked.

Respect didn't mean that Angie wasn't always after her to do something to add a little zing to the shop. Maybe she should think about ways to spruce it up, make it more inviting for return visits, and attract more drop-in traffic. Maybe Angie would be willing to help.

Connie would be sure to ask her.

Thoughts of past travails flew out of her mind as, with a jolt, the current one appeared in front of her.

Max was walking along the sidewalk, and running toward him was Dennis Pagozzi! The two were supposedly friends, so it shouldn't have been a shock to see them together, but it was.

They seemed to argue a moment, then quickly calm down.

It was all Connie could do not to drive onto the sidewalk—and into Max. Seeing Dennis with him made her wonder about him, as well, and if he got in the way of her fender, she couldn't say she'd be too broken up.

Instead, she drove as fast as she could to the corner and turned. Almost immediately, she realized she ought to take a look at what the two were up to, or at minimum, follow Max to demand her money back. By the time she drove around the block to where she'd spotted them, however, they were gone.

Chapter 9

Angie entered the offices of KYME , otherwise known as "Why Me?" radio, and approached the large reception area with a high, circular desk. Beyond reception were the executive offices and recording studio where Angie had once worked on a call-in talk show, *Lunch with Henri*, with chef Henri LaTour.

She was there now to pick up a list of top floral arrangers in the area. Last week, one of the station's talk-show hosts discussed big-events planning—weddings, bar mitzvahs, baby showers, graduations, and engagement parties. Angie telephoned and spoke with her on the air, and the host offered a list of decorators who specialized in floral arrangements, but it hadn't arrived. Most likely, it was stuck in clerical hell—the place requests wait for clerks to find the time to fill them.

There are some things a girl shouldn't have to wait for, and choosing the right help for her engagement party was one of them.

She explained why she'd come to the receptionist, who went off to search for Adrianne Marceau's list. As she waited at the desk, one of the station managers, a young curly-haired fellow with horn-rimmed glasses and a bowtie, walked in.

"Angie!" he cried. "Joel Witcomb. Remember me?"

"How can I forget?" she asked. Back when she worked there, she wasn't allowed to say a word on the show, just listen to Chef Henri mangle recipes. "I'm here to pick up floral recommendations because I'm—"

"You were such an angel to help us in the past here," Joel said. "I can't believe we let you go."

"Well, we all make mistakes!" She laughed, and he actually joined her. "Not that such things matter in the least anymore, because I'm—"

"I'd like to remedy that," he said with a toothy smile. "Pierre Takizawa, our current chef, will be leaving on Friday. His ratings just aren't what we'd hoped. We're going to be playing Country–Western music in that time slot until we get a replacement, which I pray will be soon, or we'll have no listeners left at all."

The other name for KYME popped into her head in neon colors: *cwime*. As in that station's broadcasts were a *cwime* to anyone with eardrums.

"As I said, I'm here for the floral arrangers, because—"

"I think you could do it," Joel enthused. "Instead of the Dixie Chicks, let's put on the Angie Amalfi Hour! You could talk about Bay Area restaurants, and also perhaps present a favorite recipe each day. What do you think?"

"As I started to say—"

"You can talk about how to prepare something exotic, and we could round out the hour with people calling in, asking you questions. How does that sound?"

Just then, the receptionist returned with Angie's list.

"Thank you," she said, then to Joel, "Good-bye." She turned and headed for the elevator.

"What's wrong?" He chased after her, flabbergasted. "Aren't you interested? Are you working on another radio show—"

"Goodness, no."

"TV?"

"Heavens!"

"Newspaper? Magazine?"

"No. Nothing like that."

The elevator doors opened and as she got on, she waggled her left hand in the air. "I'm engaged."

"It's too bad she won't elope," Yosh said to Paavo, then took a big bite from a slice of linguiça and artichoke heart frittata. "All this attention might be bad for you."

"Not for me, though!" Benson said, taking another slice. Dapper, African-American, and streetwise, he dressed like Joseph Abboud, and went through women like a rock star. "This is even better than yesterday's mixed hors d'oeuvres platter. They tasted good, but a couple of bites and they were gone."

"Don't even talk about her pâté," Calderon groused.

"Especially at breakfast," Bill Never-Take-a-Chance Sutter said between mouthfuls. In his late fifties, he kept threatening to retire from the force and get his pension, plus an easier, safer, and probably higher-paying job. Nothing like having someone around with his attitude to build up morale. "If Paavo's engagement goes on for long, I might postpone my retirement."

"I thought you already had," Rebecca Mayfield said sullenly to her nearly worthless, mind-on-fishing-holes-and-future-bridge-games partner. She cut herself a little more frittata—luckily, Angie had sent two of them—as if to drown her sorrows in food. "So, why not elope, Paavo?"

"She'd never go for it. Her mother's probably planning to rent out City Hall to fit all the people she wants to invite to the reception. Maybe Golden Gate Park. What else is big enough in this city?"

"The Cow Palace," Calderon called over. Not that he and everyone else in Homicide were eavesdropping. Not that they'd admit to it.

"That's scary," Yosh continued. "Can't you talk her out of doing something so huge?"

"Have you ever met Angie's mother?" Paavo asked.

"No."

"That's why you asked that question."

"I think I now know who Angie takes after."

Paavo visibly shuddered. "Don't remind me."

"Here's something to take your mind off your wedding," Calderon said, handing them a mug shot. "The name's Veronica Maple. She was released from Chowchilla Wednesday and apparently went down to Fresno, killed a pawnshop owner, and took off for the city. She has ties with a smalltime gang lord named Sid Fernandez, called 'El Toro.' He used to make his money on drugs, but bigger fish are moving in. He's having some trouble keeping his territory, I hear. Vice doesn't know where he might pop up next. Anyway, her parole officer, a guy named Lexington, was here trying to get help finding her."

"Why a PO?" Paavo asked.

"Sounds like he screwed up the case, job's on the line. He wants to bring her in himself. I told him we didn't go for cowboys here. Not our own, and for sure not outsiders from the valley. I don't know why, but something about the woman, the case, just smells like trouble."

Paavo nodded.

"Thanks for the info," Yosh said, studying the photo.

Just then a florist walked into Homicide wheeling a cart filled with flowers—a huge bouquet of red roses, and ten smaller ones with amaryllis, daffodils, and lilies. Out of Lt. Hollins's office came a loud *aaah-choo*.

"I had to see for myself if you were here, or if you were lyin', as usual," Butch said, when Veronica opened the door to Dennis's home.

"Now, you see." She was dressed in a high-necked, long sleeved black jumpsuit. "What do you want?"

He pushed past her and looked around. "I want to see Dennis. Where is he?" Butch said. He walked to the bar and poured himself a stiff shot of Chivas.

"You make yourself at home, don't you?" She gave the front door a shove and listened to the latch click.

"You have." Butch took a sip, and let the smooth warmth drift down to his stomach. "Why're you here? What the hell do you want from him?"

She stared at him. Her gray eyes seemed flat, almost soulless. "It's none of your business."

"I don't trust you, Veronica," Butch said. "And if Dennis does, he's a fool. Is he home?"

She smiled at him, a smile that never reached her eyes. "He's out buying some steaks for our dinner. Filet mignon. Just like an old married couple, wouldn't you say?"

Butch's body tensed. "Damn you, Veronica. You almost ruined his life once. Wasn't that enough?"

"Get out of here, old man."

He poured the rest of the Scotch down his throat and slammed the glass on the bar. "I'm going, and so will you."

"Don't count on it," she taunted.

He left the house before he could do anything he'd regret, but when he reached the sidewalk, he turned and looked back at it. He frowned, scratching his head. He had to admit he hadn't used his brain much over the years. Maybe that was because he knew it didn't work so good anymore.

Nevertheless, as he pictured Veronica with his nephew, his sister's pride and joy, he knew what he had to do. The question was, did he dare do it?

Chapter 10

"So, tell me about your date with Dennis!" Angie sat across from Connie at the Cliff House, a restaurant overlooking the ocean.

Connie opened her mouth when the waiter came by to take their order—golden red snapper in a coconut lime sauce for Connie, and fricassee of chicken with tomatoes, raisins, and olives for Angie.

"Say, aren't you Angelina Amalfi?" he asked.

"Why, yes, I am." Angie tried to remember if she'd met the young man before.

"I saw you on television sometime back, doing a video restaurant review. I'll have to get the owner. He'd love to meet you."

"Sure," she said, watching him dash off. She turned back to Connie. "Isn't that amazing? I thought no one watched my reviews, yet this fellow actually recognized me. But I interrupted you. You were saying about Dennis . . ."

"I met him at Wings, and—"

"Here she is!" The waiter beamed as he ushered in a distinguished man with a fringe of gray hair, a large jaw, and a picket fence of false teeth. "Miss Amalfi, I'd like you to meet the owner, Donald Kaufman."

"Miss Amalfi! What a pleasure to have you here," Kaufman blurted, his teeth clattering slightly.

"Thank you." She introduced Connie. "Your menu is a wonderful combination of Southwest plus San Francisco seafood."

"Do you think so? That's grand! Just learning you were here has given me an idea, if I might be so presumptuous." He pulled out a chair and sat. "I was wondering if you might be willing to work with me on this menu."

Angie stared. What was with him? "Work on it how?" she asked.

The waiter came by with a complimentary bottle of Charles Krug Cabernet Sauvignon Blanc, 1992, as the owner explained that he'd like to hire her as a consultant.

Connie caught her eye and nodded enthusiastically. What was with *her*? Angie wondered. "You don't need a consultant," she said firmly. "Now, my friend and I are here for some *girl* talk. We wouldn't want to bore you . . ." *(Hint, hint!)*

Kaufman's face fell. "Think about it, please. Give me a call when you're ready to talk." He handed her his card and left.

"Angie," Connie marveled. "What's wrong with you? He was offering the chance of a lifetime. The kind of job you've always wanted."

"No, no, no! I want to hear about *amore*. That's what life is really about!"

"Well, if you're sure . . ." Connie glanced back at the hopeful owner, letting her eyes wander through the fine restaurant with the gorgeous Pacific view.

An appetizer of seviche—raw halibut marinated until "poached" in lime juice, chili, onion, tomato, oregano, and olive oil—was placed on the table. "Compliments of Mr. Kaufman," the waiter said.

"Thank you," Angie said dismissively. Then, to Connie, "Tell me, did you like him?"

"Kaufman?" Connie's eyes widened.

"Dennis!"

"Of course. What's not to like?"

"Will you see him again soon?"

"I don't know. He didn't ask me. It's been three days. He hasn't called."

Angie's face fell.

"So, what did you think?" Kaufman materialized at the table. "Too much lime juice, perhaps? Seviche is temperamental."

Not nearly as temperamental as I'm going to be, Angie thought. She wanted to get back to Dennis's not calling Connie, but before she could say a word, a bevy of waiters paraded from the kitchen, each carrying a plate with a small portion of an entree.

"I've died and gone to heaven!" Connie cried. Kaufman hovered over them, grilling Angie with questions while Connie oohed and aahed with each dish. One of the waiters took over as sommelier, pouring wine to help Angie cleanse her palate from one dish to the other, while another stood off to the side and wrote down almost every word she said.

Finally, she could stand no more. She grabbed Kaufman's arm, dragged him to a far wall, and poked him in the chest. "Listen, I'm here to talk about love, damn it! I want to have a conversation with my girlfriend, but she's too busy stuffing her face to talk! Will you leave us alone?"

He twisted his tie. "But you know food, Miss Amalfi! Just to watch your expression as you take each bite is a full course in gastronomy. You're a dream come true to me."

"You are so dead!"

"All right, all right. Be that way." He stiffened his upper lip. "Go, now. I won't bother you any longer."

"Thank you!"

She marched back into the dining room, to find Connie in full swoon over a gigantic strawberry charlotte.

Paavo and Yosh came out of the Central Police Station, where they had gone to talk to a couple of uniformed cops about the stash of autographed sports paraphernalia they'd found in the abandoned garage. It was definitely counterfeit. No lead yet was available on who'd put it there.

As they hit the sidewalk, Yosh stopped, bent forward, and slowly peered first to the left and then to the right.

"What is it?" Paavo asked.

He held his finger against his lips a moment, then lowered it and whispered, "Just making sure there aren't any bakers, florists, or Italian tenors waiting to waylay us."

Paavo growled.

Yosh chuckled as they walked toward the car. "The good news is that Angie's so busy buying and making you stuff, she isn't snooping into your cases."

The two froze.

A man was getting out of a van with a huge stuffed bear.

In stark horror, San Francisco's finest fled to their car and sped off.

"We'll work together, like in the old days." Sid Fernandez placed his hand on Veronica's thigh and lightly stroked it.

"I think it'll be great fun," she murmured, and with

a toss of the head, looked over at Julius. "I love your plan." She flashed a smile meant for him alone.

She had walked two blocks from Dennis's house to the street corner where Fernandez's limo had been double-parked and waiting. Fernandez knew Dennis's home and was the one who'd told her where it was, but she wanted to make sure the two men didn't encounter each other unless it became necessary. She could control them better if they remained separated.

"You make our little 'strategy' perfect, Vero." Julius used what he thought was his very own pet name for her. *Vero*—truth. It made her want to puke, but that was all right. He was lots less revolting than the so-called El Toro, who didn't even have the good fortune to be bull-like where it mattered most.

"What's this Vero stuff?" Fernandez asked, squeezing Veronica's thigh. "We call her Ronnie, don't we?"

"Veronica is the name," she said.

He squeezed harder. "I thought you liked being called Ronnie."

"You can call me anything you like, Toro. You know that."

"*Bueno, puta.*" With that, he laughed hard. Julius joined him, as did Veronica. Fernandez was everything she despised in a man, but she needed him, and he didn't like his jokes dissed. He'd been the only one to help her when she was in prison, and he counted on her loyalty as a result. And had it. Up to a point.

"Now, we must get serious," Fernandez said. "In three days, Julius will have your identification. Everything is set. It should be perfect."

"It will be, boss," Julius said.

"That's it, then. It's up to you, Veronica, to get us in. Then the diamonds—all of them—will be ours."

"As long as I get my share," she said, "I can do it."

"You think I'd try to gyp my little *puta*?" Fernandez asked.

God, but she hated the fat bastard. "Only if you want to see your *puta* gut you," she replied.

He roared with laughter. "*Dios,* I love this woman!" He pulled her head toward him and nearly smothered her with a wet French kiss. She could feel Julius's eyes boring into her back, his jealousy a raw, livid, and very useful thing. She reached her hand out behind her, toward him, and he took hold of her fingers, their grasp hidden from El Toro's view.

Fernandez lifted his gaze while continuing the kiss. He'd missed her too damn much to be healthy, and he knew it, but she was the one soft spot remaining in his heart. Something about her had burrowed deep inside him years before, when they were little more than kids, first starting out.

Julius made it clear he didn't approve of the way Fernandez felt about her, but he didn't care. His kiss deepened, his hand cupping her breast. He'd searched a long time for a woman who thought like he did, and now that she was once again out of prison, she'd be with him, work with him, and—

The glass-covered bar area in the limo was polished until it shone like a mirror, and his eye caught a movement in it. He saw Veronica's back, her slim waist, her hips. For some reason, she had snaked one hand behind her, while the other pressed against the back of his neck, holding his mouth to hers.

Then, he saw Julius's hand reach for hers, their fingers entwined, like lovers . . .

Chapter 11

Paavo could smell pizza as he and Yosh walked down the hall on the fourth floor of the Hall of Justice the next afternoon. Normally, that would have made him feel good—a shared treat for one and all usually meant the successful conclusion of some particularly sticky or horrible case. He had his doubts, though, that business was the cause of today's celebration.

The first thing that struck him was the weird shape of the cardboard that had once held a pizza on it. As he neared, he felt the knot in his stomach grow. The pizza tray was heart-shaped.

Not again.

Even as he thought that, he knew he was wrong.

Again.

No pizza remained in the box, however.

"What's going on?" Yosh asked.

"Hey, Paav," Benson called. "That was great. Pepperoni, Italian sausage, three cheeses, loaded with mushroom and olives. Outstanding. The shape was a little weird, but no matter. We're getting used to heart-shaped food. In fact, heart-shaped steaks would be nice."

"Too bad pizza gives me heartburn," Calderon grumped.

"Heart-shaped barbecued ribs!" Sutter added, ignoring Calderon's remark.

"Heart-shaped ravioli, with a rich beef sauce." Rebecca was practically salivating.

"Heart-shaped biscuits and gravy"—Benson drooled—"with a slice of heart-shaped sweet potato pie on the side."

"Knock it off," Paavo said. "This isn't funny."

Yosh said nothing. He was too busy staring longingly at the empty cardboard. A glob of cheese and a piece of pepperoni had been left on the tray, and he scooped it up and ate it. The way he licked his fingers noisily confirmed Benson's raving about the pizza.

"It's all gone already?" Angie's voice bubbled over with good cheer as she walked into Homicide, her sometime friend Nona Farraday behind her. "Did you like it?" she asked Paavo as she gave him a quick peck. The Hall of Justice was not a place for displays of affection. Even Angie was quelled by the somber surroundings. But not Nona.

"Paavo, dearest!" she squealed. "Congratulations!" She threw her arms around him in a bear hug that, if it had gone on much longer, would have resulted in Angie grasping a fistful of blond hair.

Paavo backed up and thanked her, while Benson, Homicide's resident Romeo, moved in. "Hey, there." He acknowledged Nona, and without removing his eyes from her, said, "Angie, are you going to introduce me to your friend?"

"Sure. Nona, meet Inspector Bo Benson."

Bo was coolly extending his hand to grasp Nona's with some snappy comment when Angie hooked her arm in Nona's and spun her away. Paavo's eyebrows rose in wonder as Angie marched Nona up to Luis Calderon's desk.

Calderon slowly lifted his head from his reports, his eyes narrow, and focused hard on the two women before him. "Yes?"

"Inspector Calderon," Angie said, "I'd like you to meet my dear friend Nona Farraday."

Nona held out her hand. Calderon lifted himself to his feet, his knee cracking, and with a look of utter weariness, shook it.

Benson smoothed his jacket and took a step toward them, but Paavo put out his arm to stop him. Their gazes met, and Paavo shook his head. Benson's eyes widened, then his mouth spread into a grin, as the situation hit him.

"Who died?" Calderon asked gruffly.

"Died?" Angie asked. "You misunderstand—my friend is just here for a visit. She knew you were all having pizza for lunch, so she brought along a little dessert."

She glanced at Nona, who was gaping at Calderon as if her brainpower had bounded away like a slinky toy. Angie elbowed her. "*The dessert,*" she whispered.

"Oh! Of course! Here you are." Nona lifted a large cookie tin out of a shopping bag and put it on his desk, right on top of his papers. His scowl deepened. Then she opened the tin.

The smell of alcohol filled the room. Rum, to be precise.

"Holy Moses!" Bill Sutter cried, walking over to Calderon's desk. "Is it happy hour already?"

"What did you do?" Angie asked, puzzling over the soggy chocolate chip cookies in the tin. "The recipe called for only a tablespoon of rum."

Nona gave a come-hither look to Calderon. "I

wanted them to be *adult* cookies, so I tripled it." She lifted one out with her fingertips. "It's my recipe— Nona's Pecan Rum Chocolate Chip Cookies. Try it. You won't be disappointed."

Calderon noticed the other inspectors silently watching his every move. "Forget it. I don't eat pizza, and I don't eat sweets."

"You don't?" Nona dropped the cookie in the trash and stepped a little closer. "I don't either. It helps me keep my weight down." She held her arms out to the sides.

Calderon coughed lightly. "I see." He picked the cookie tin off his desk and handed it back to her. Without even looking at what they were, he grabbed a handful of papers and his suit jacket. "Got to go investigate a murder."

As Angie and Nona stared, he hurried out of the bureau.

"I'm sorry," Angie said.

"Don't be." Rubber-kneed, Nona sat on the edge of Calderon's desk and sighed longingly at the door he'd just exited. "He's so . . . masculine. I'm totally in love!"

"What a surprise to find you both here," Connie said, eying Angie and Dennis sitting together at Wings of an Angel.

Angie smiled innocently. "Butch made some lasagna, Dennis's favorite. He called Dennis, who was all alone when I arrived, so I invited him to join us for lunch."

"I'm glad to see you again, Connie." Dennis's cheeks dimpled when he smiled. Shades of Tom Selleck, Angie thought. He used to be her ideal man when she was a little girl. She wondered whatever became of him. Old age, she guessed. None of them was getting any younger, and looking at Connie and Dennis and hoping young love would blossom between them, while she was soon to become a wife, she felt more mature and sophisticated by the minute. Although it was too bad Paavo didn't have dimples.

"Dennis has an idea to expand the restaurant," Angie said, as enthusiastically as she could. Frankly, she hated the idea.

"So I've heard," Connie said.

"Say, Angie," Dennis turned to her, "wouldn't you say Connie is the perfect person to run some ideas past? She's got a good head on her shoulders. Practical. Sensible. I like that in a woman."

"You do?" Angie asked, delighted. "I'm so glad! Those are wonderful qualities, and Connie is one of the most practical, steady people I know. That's her— Constant Connie, in the flesh."

Her smile slipped a notch as Connie's foot met her shin under the table.

"Constant?" Dennis asked, confused.

"Dennis is also constant," Angie said. "He's loyal. Generous. Handsome." She was running out of adjectives.

"Well, he's more constant than some friends," Connie sniped.

Dennis looked lost, as if he couldn't hear his quarterback's audibles. "About the restaurant," he said, "I'm hoping to make this place hit the big time. Right up there where the Washbag used to be—you know, the Washington Bar and Grill."

Angie frowned. The place was at its height about the same time as Tom Selleck. What was Dennis thinking? She didn't want to call him on it in front of Connie. "See, he's full of ideas for business," she said brightly.

Just then, Butch bounded out of the kitchen holding

a bottle of wine and candles. Earl followed with a violin.

Angie's jaw dropped.

Connie glowered.

Dennis cleared the table of the menus so Butch could put the candlesticks down and open the burgundy. Last week's vintage. At least it didn't have a screw top.

Earl tucked the violin under his chin and began sawing away at something that vaguely resembled "You Are the Wind Beneath My Wings." Unfortunately, it sounded like a different kind of wind.

Other customers stopped eating, dumbfounded.

"If I'm part owner of a sports bar," Dennis shouted over the cacophony, "I could probably get some of the guys to drop in."

"They'd love this, all right!" Connie yelled back sarcastically.

"Absolutely!" Dennis's voice strained.

Angie made expressions at Connie to smile and be nice. It didn't work.

Butch poured the wine.

Connie snatched a breadstick and broke it in half. Instead of eating it, she reached for another and broke it as well. Angie didn't like the way Connie was eying her as she did so.

Butch had to strike a half dozen matches to light the candles.

Earl switched to "Feelings," a nails-on-the-chalkboard rendition that must have had the entire neighborhood of dogs, cats, and mice running for their lives.

As Dennis hoisted his wineglass, Connie reached for another breadstick, bumping it against Dennis's hand, which caromed against a candle that dived kamikaze-style onto a napkin. The wine sloshed from the glass, high into the air, to land with a splat on Angie.

The napkin burst into flames and ignited the table-cloth.

As her matchmaking plans went up in smoke, Angie doused the napkin flambé with water from her glass, while Butch smothered the tablecloth.

The violin's tune changed. Earl launched into a rousing rendition of Johnny Cash's "Ring of Fire."

Connie was glad to see Angie heading back from the ladies' room to clean up. Dennis had talked her ear off about his sports bar plans, as if she cared. She still smarted that he hadn't called her over the past week. To come in second fiddle to lasagna didn't make her feel warm and fuzzy toward him.

Angie returned wearing a big smile. What was with her now, Connie wondered.

"It's so nice that the two of you are discussing the place this way," Angie said. "I think it's important that two people, when they're seeing each other, are able to discuss all kinds of things, and work them out to-gether. Just like me and Paavo. We always discuss stuff. He tells me about his cases . . ."

Connie rolled her eyes. The only time Paavo told Angie about his cases was when he was telling her to keep her nose out of them.

". . . And we discuss what he should do next . . ."

Connie placed her hand to her mouth, needing to bite her tongue. Since when did Angie consider herself a homicide expert?

". . . And I always tell him about my business ideas and get his input . . ."

Paavo learned a long time ago it was easier to stop a train than to move Angie to a different track when she was in single-minded pursuit of a business idea.

". . . We're a team," Angie declared.

"Sure you are." Connie nodded. "Like Cagney and Lacey, or do I mean Lucy and Desi?"

"What?" Angie looked at her curiously. Recognizing sarcasm wasn't her long suit.

"Anyway," Dennis interrupted, "making this place bigger and better is a great idea, don't you think?"

Connie didn't know what to think. Dennis was excited over his ideas, but she understood Angie's reluctance. Wings was an inexpensive bistro with a pleasant atmosphere that caused it to have a number of loyal customers. She'd hate to see it lose them for something showy.

Showy, in her experience, didn't last long. Showy . . . like Dennis, who was now smiling at her and batting his long eyelashes. She smiled back—who wouldn't?—and could feel Angie scrutinizing them both.

"I'm so glad you two found each other," Angie gushed in a revolting display of sappiness. "As soon as I met Dennis, I knew you would get along. It was just like when I met Paavo. One look, and I knew he was for me."

Give me a break, Connie thought. She knew the true version of the story—one look, and Angie couldn't stand Paavo. The Great Stoneface, she'd called him.

"Now," Angie continued dreamily, "orange blossoms are in my future, and . . ."

All this mush just didn't do it for her, so Connie turned toward the door to contemplate escape. Immediately, though, Angie's voice, the restaurant, everything seemed to dissolve.

Max Squire walked in.

Connie began to get up from the chair, but then gripped the seat, trying hard to appear nonchalant. Max gazed at her for what seemed like an eternity.

As he approached the table, though, he ignored her. "Hello, Dennis."

Dennis stood, his expression serious. "Hey, Max. Good you could make it."

They shook hands and Dennis introduced him. "Ladies, this is an old friend, Max Squire. I just happened to run into him on the street yesterday. Max, this is Angie Amalfi, and . . . wait a minute, you two already met, didn't you?"

Max shook Angie's hand first, then turned to Connie. "Miss Rogers and I met briefly the other night."

Connie slowly lifted her hand to his. She wasn't sure who pulled his or her hand away faster.

"Is that so?" Angie's eyeballs had quite a workout as they bounced from one to the other.

Connie tried to regard Max as Angie might. His clothes were crumpled and worn. Jeans and a once-navy blue pullover were washed one time too many. His shoes were scuffed on top. She hated to think of what the soles must look like. His dark, mysterious eyes held hers, and when he looked away, her face burned. Why did she react that way? Damn him!

"Have a seat," Dennis said warmly, oblivious to the tension between his friend and Connie.

"Thanks, but," Max continued standing, "I didn't mean to interrupt anything. I can come back when you're free, Dennis."

"No, no," Dennis said. He grabbed a chair from a nearby table and slid it between Connie and Angie. "Sit. I asked you here for a reason. We're discussing expanding the place, and that's where you come in."

Max did as told. He looked everywhere but at Connie, yet she could feel his nearness. She tried to concentrate on Dennis's bright smile, his hazel eyes. *Looks, talent, money,* she told herself. *Looks, talent, money—*

"I do?" Max said, jarring her back to reality.

"Exactly." Dennis paused. "When the restaurant expands, we'll need more help."

Max folded his hands on the table and looked around. "It's a nice place."

"We'll have some work for you here. We'd hate it if someone as reliable as you went off and found work someplace else. We could use you, especially when the business starts to take off." Dennis was all sincerity and trust.

"Not me." Max shook his head.

"Definitely you, pal. Let me go get Butch." Dennis jumped up and headed for the kitchen.

Angie immediately faced Max. "So, you and Connie met when she was waiting for Dennis the other night?"

He gazed at Connie and didn't answer until she dropped her eyes to her lap. "That's right."

"You didn't tell me," Angie said to her friend.

Connie forced a laugh. "I don't tell you about everyone I meet in a day." She tried not to look back at Max, but failed miserably.

"Have you been in the city long, Max?" Angie asked.

"Not very," he said.

"Just passing through?"

"Not sure yet," he replied.

"I see. But you're here looking for work?" she prodded.

"Not really."

She sat back, arms folded in exasperation. Connie stifled a smile.

Just then, Dennis appeared, a big hand on Butch's elbow as he guided his little uncle into the dining area. Butch's bibbed apron hung below his knees, and the sleeves of his blue shirt had been rolled up to reveal forearms with an anchor and the logo of the U.S. Navy tattooed on one, flowers and "~~MOM~~" on the other. The word "Mom" was a little jagged, as if it might have been adapted from some other name sometime in Butch's history. Connie heard that back in the days when he was a prizefighter in the bantamweight division, before he lost many fights and began to grow jangle-headed, Butch used to have a lot of women after him. At least one probably caught him a few times. "Mom" might have been the last in a whole string of names.

"Uncle Butch, you remember my old friend Max Squire, don't you?" Dennis said.

Butch frowned. "Yeah, Squire." He stuck out his hand. "How's it goin'?"

Max stood and they shook hands. "Not bad."

"Max is looking for work," Dennis said.

Butch eyed Max, then his nephew. "Yeah? I don't know nobody hirin' right now. Times is tough."

Vinnie and Earl came puffing up behind the others.

"What's goin' on?" Vinnie asked.

"Dennis's friend needs work," Butch said.

Vinnie rose up, almost on tiptoe, and stood before Dennis's chair. "We don't need no more help."

"You guys are going to need someone to work here with you when the business takes off. Earl is slow now; he'll be completely over his head in the future."

"Whaddya mean, slow?" Earl put his hands in fists and approached Dennis.

"The restaurant needs improvement." Dennis glanced at Angie for confirmation. When she didn't move an eyelash, he turned back to Vinnie. "Me, Max and Angie are the ones to do it."

"Leave me out of this!" Angie muttered.

"Are you bailing on me?" Dennis was shocked.

"We don't want no more help," Vinnie said, his jaw stuck out. "We don't need it. Business is great as is." Just then two customers came in and Earl left to take care of them. They were there to pick up a take-out order. "See, what'd I tell ya?"

"It can't be great," Dennis countered. "The place is too small. I'm surprised you three have held on this long. Don't you understand—"

"I understand you're gonna get a flat nose if you don't stop badgerin' me." Vinnie waved a fist. "We like things the way they are. *Capisce?*"

"Forget it, Dennis," Max said. "I don't want the job anyway."

"Sure you do!" Dennis insisted, whirling toward Max now.

"I don't like it either," Butch said. "Too many from the past showin' up, first her, now him. What's going on, Dennis?"

Max paled, staring first at Dennis, then Connie. He turned on his heel and walked out.

Connie stood. "Max!" she called.

Dennis rushed out the door after him.

"What in the world is going on?" Angie also jumped to her feet and gripped Connie's wrist. "Do you understand any of it?"

"Not at all." They sat back down, but Connie's eyes never left the window as she watched Dennis and Max outside.

Soon they parted, Max heading south and Dennis north.

"Excuse me." Connie stood. "I've got to get back to work. My helper couldn't stay all afternoon."

"But—" was all she heard Angie say before she dashed outside.

Max was about a block ahead of Connie, heading south on Columbus Avenue. Staying within the shadows of the buildings, she followed him. He turned onto Mason, a street lined with three-story flats and a couple of small apartment buildings. As he walked up three steep blocks, she followed, gasping for breath by the time she reached the third. At a corner, he turned onto Vallejo and halfway down the block entered a yellow building with brown trim. Expecting it to be a roominghouse, she hurried after him, stopping when she read the sign beside the door. It was a homeless shelter.

She reread the sign a couple of times, then pushed open the door. Max stood at the registration desk.

"What are you doing here?" He sounded furious.

"You have to know. I want my money." She lifted her chin.

The clerk handed him a ticket with a cot number and a folded gray cotton-flannel blanket. He tucked the blanket under his arm and faced her. "It's gone."

"Gone?" If he lived like this, how could he have spent a hundred-eighty dollars already? "You spent it all? On what?"

"It doesn't matter. It was wasted." With a sneer, he walked away. His dismissal of her stung worse than his words.

"You wasted my money! You rat! You thief!" She dogged his heels. Visions filled her—of slapping him, kicking him, grabbing him by the throat and shaking sense into him, anything to get him to react to her and the awful way he made her feel. "How dare you do that to me when I was just trying to help you?"

He spun on her, his mouth twisted with bitterness. "You saw what just happened at that restaurant. Would I have put up with that . . . humiliation . . . if I had money?"

Shocked, she stared at him.

He walked into the men's room. So angry she didn't hesitate, she followed and slammed the bathroom door shut behind her. "I need it back! Why don't you get a loan from your rich friend Dennis? You two are so chummy! Why take from me? How am I supposed to live? I should move into a place like this right beside you, maybe? That money was important to me!"

He leaned toward her. "Of course it was. You're a woman, aren't you? Why isn't love enough for you?" His voice dropped, and his words were addressed more within himself than to Connie.

"What are you talking about? I invited you to my house—"

His head snapped toward her. "That was as stupid a move as I've ever seen."

Beyond fury, she yelled at him. "You were sick, damn you! That's what I get for caring!"

He bent over the sink and ran water onto his cupped hands. "You want money so much"—he splashed the water onto his face, then patted it dry with a paper towel—"put your money on Geostar Biotechnologies. It sells over-the-counter as GSBT. It'll make you back what I took and lots more."

"What kind of a smarmy line is that?" She yanked the paper towel from him, wadded it, and hurled it at the back of his head. "I'm supposed to take stock tips from a guy who lives like this? You're even crazier than I thought!"

An elderly man wearing a knit cap and layers of dirty, stained clothes, suddenly teetered around from the urinal, waved blithely at them, and stumbled out. He didn't seem to notice any necessity to zip up his sagging pants. She quickly lifted her eyes toward the ceiling. Max chuckled as he picked up the crumbled paper and put it into the trash receptacle.

His laughter was her undoing. "The hell with you, Max Squire!" she yelled, then turned and ran out of the dreadful place and into the street. There, she stopped, half expecting him to follow her out, apologize, anything. The paint-chipped brown door stayed shut.

"To hell with you!" she repeated, and stomped her way through the streets to her car.

Chapter 12

"You'll know where Max is, okay?" Dennis needed every ounce of willpower he possessed to keep from shouting at Veronica. "I convinced my uncle and Vinnie—Earl's opinion doesn't matter—to let him do their federal income taxes. They're due soon, which means he'll be in the restaurant trying to make sense out of the papers and receipts they've got stashed all over the place. I don't think they've ever filed before, and if the business is legit, they have to."

"So little Dennis wants to run a sports bar," Veronica sneered. "A legitimate, tax-paying sports bar. What a loser you are!"

They sat at a small table in the Porcupine, one of the best new restaurants in the city. She took a sip of Moët champagne and smiled as the bubbles tickled her nose. Champagne and oysters Rockefeller were her dream when she was in the slammer. Now, she had both.

"You just don't know how to think big, do you?" Dennis glowered at her.

"Right. A sports bar in a dump is big thinking. I'm so impressed." She leaned forward. "Listen, you pig, I'm sick of waiting for you. I don't give a goddamn about Max Squire as long as he stays the hell away from me. I want my cut now, and I want out. Do you understand?"

"The money I got isn't going to last forever, Veronica," Dennis said. "I got to think of the future—our future—and there's a lot a sweet little legitimate-looking operation like that can do."

"Don't give me that 'our future' crap. I gave up listening to you years ago."

"Hey, you and me. It's always been about us."

"No. It's always been about you and football. And now it's dumped you. Just like I'm going to. You've got two days, then life won't be so easy for you, Dennis."

"You can't threaten me."

"I think I just did."

He crushed the napkin, his teeth clenched. "Without me, you'd have nothing."

She smiled wickedly. "You forgot about Max. It was his system I tapped into. He'll know how to get into it, with or without you."

The words spat from his mouth. "You really think Max would do anything to you other than put a bullet through your cold little heart?"

"I know he would." She laughed in his face. "And now that I know how to locate him . . ."

"I could kill you myself. You bitch!" he shouted.

"That's what you've always loved about me, sugar, and don't forget it." With a dismissive sneer at his sputtering outrage, she smugly returned to her champagne and oysters.

Angie shivered as another blast of cold air hit her. The Porcupine was crowded, and she and Stan were stuck right near the front door, which meant every time someone came in or went out, she felt it. She hadn't wanted to stay home tonight. Paavo was working, and Connie was still fuming over their aborted lunch. Stan was her last resort, and anyway, she owed him for dragging him across town to meet Helen. He'd barely escaped that encounter with his life; Angie expected to see him turned into a human pretzel.

The seating arrangement didn't say much for a restaurant that had the best buzz, at the moment, in town. Just to bypass the reservations, she'd had to use her father's name with the maître d', something she didn't like to do routinely. Salvatore Amalfi had started as a shoe salesman and grown to become the owner of a chain of shoe stores and several buildings in San Francisco. He had more than a few friends in high places.

The restaurant wasn't at all what Angie had expected. One wall was brick, looking more like an outside wall than the inside of a top restaurant, and in keeping with the outside "theme," black rafters showed on the ceiling. Brown paper was placed on the tabletops instead of fine linen, and when the bread was delivered, the waiter just dropped a small, freshly made loaf on the table.

She guessed it was a rich man's rustic chic decor—alley dining at its finest.

A familiar-sounding voice cut through the noise of conversation and the clatter of the kitchen that stood open in one corner of the room, separated from the diners only by a high counter—she guessed so customers could be sure the cooks weren't spitting in the soup or anything.

Seated at a far table was Dennis Pagozzi, and with him, a woman. What was going on?

She hadn't noticed him when she and Stan had entered. She hadn't noticed much at all, since they'd been seated immediately by the door. Maybe her father's name didn't have quite the clout she thought it had.

Suddenly, Dennis and the woman stood to leave. What should she do? She didn't want Dennis to know he'd been seen with another woman, although she might not have been a date. They didn't seem like a loving couple.

What about Connie? Should she tell Connie she saw Dennis out with another woman? He wasn't exactly beating down Connie's door, but still, there was hope for the two of them, wasn't there? She also remembered the stark look on Connie's face when that other guy, that Max Squire, had entered Wings. Just what was going on there?

Suddenly, they turned toward the door. She bent down and stuck her head under the tablecloth.

"Angie, what are you doing?" Stan lifted his side of the supposedly chichi brown paper and peeked under the table at her.

"Shush!"

"Why?"

"I don't want some people to see me. They're leaving. Let me know when they're gone."

Stan straightened in his seat, munching on bread and salted olive oil, and Angie stayed under there, waiting and waiting . . . and waiting.

"Stan!" she whispered. "Stan!"

He stuck his head under the table again. "Yes?"

"Haven't they left yet?"

"Who?"

"The people I don't want to see me. A big guy with black hair and a blond woman."

"Oh, them. Yeah. They've gone. I didn't know who it was you were hiding from."

She sat back up and had to wait a minute before

telling him what a jerk he was because bent over that way, the blood rushed to her head and when she sat back up too quickly, she felt woozy. "You would have just left me sitting under the table, I suppose?"

"I didn't even know what you were talking about, so pardon me for living! I came here as a favor to you, remember."

A favor to his stomach was more like it. Stan loved to eat. Coming with her to this restaurant was no hardship.

"So, what shall we have?" Stan said, more to himself than Angie, as he drooled over the expensive menu. "Anytime you feel like doing more matchmaking, Angie, keep me in mind."

Chapter 13

"Angelina Amalfi?" asked a pleasant voice on the telephone.

"Yes." She found the web-page link she'd been searching for and clicked on it.

"I'm Kara Saunders, from KRAK-TV. We were recently talking about adding a cooking show to our Saturday morning line-up, and your name came up as a potential host for it. Someone remembered something you were involved in called . . . let me see . . . *Angelina in the Cucina.* Is that correct?"

Despite Angie's concentration on the Internet, she still cringed at the horrible name. The show never got off the ground. "That's right." Nope. That wasn't the information she wanted. She tried another link.

"We're going to hold some auditions, but I'll be honest, you're number one on our list. Do say you'll come and try out for us."

"What? TV? I don't do TV," Angie murmured. As the web page unfolded, she smiled. It was exactly what she was looking for, and right here in San Francisco, too.

The woman on the phone kept talking. "You aren't saying you're not interested, are you?" Kara asked, sounding crestfallen. "Don't you want to think about it? Hear the terms we're offering? The benefits? The publicity?"

A knock sounded. "Oh, my! Someone's at the door." She used the cursor to save the page to Favorites, smiling as she read about leprechauns and shamrocks. What fun! "I've got to run."

"But—"

"Good-bye!"

She put down the phone and stared at the web page a moment longer. Wasn't the Internet wonderful, and wouldn't Paavo be surprised? She could hardly wait to see his joyous expression, feel his gratitude, his love . . .

The knock sounded again, jerking her from her reverie. She dashed to open the door. It might be FedEx with the books she'd ordered about engagement parties. She'd hunted all over the city's bookstores, but couldn't find a thing that—

"Hi. Remember me?"

Angie stared in surprise at the man in her doorway—tall, blond, muscular, with a craggy face and twinkling blue eyes, and wearing a gray sweatshirt with cut-off sleeves and paint-and-grease-splattered jeans. A sort of Jeff Bridges or young Kris Kristofferson type. No way she could forget him.

"You're Connie's ex-husband," she said. "Kevin, right?" Of course, she knew his name was Kevin, but she didn't want to make him think she and Connie had spent much time discussing him, which, of course, they had. In fact, if she thought of all the things Connie had told her about Kevin, she'd blush.

"That's me." He put his hands on his hips and smiled.

She had no idea what he was doing there, but good manners won out. "Won't you come in?"

"Thanks. I wanted to talk to you about Connie." He slowly entered the apartment, taking in, first of all, the view of San Francisco Bay that stretched from the Golden Gate to the Bay Bridge, with Alcatraz centered like a picture postcard. "Kee-rist!" he muttered under his breath. His gaze then leaped to her antique furniture, entertainment system, and lingered a moment on the Cézanne lithograph. Was Kevin an art lover? If half of what Connie had said was true, she should tell him it was a reproduction.

None of her art or antique furniture were reproductions and she certainly didn't want him sitting on anything with a light fabric. "How about some coffee?" she asked. "I've got some cheesecake in the refrigerator as well. Why don't we sit at the table?"

She led him away from the living room to her dining area off the kitchen. The table and chairs were cherrywood. "Thanks," he said, plunking himself down with all the ease of a man making himself at home. Angie peered surreptitiously at his shoes. Old construction boots. At least he didn't leave a trail of mud. The building owner—her father—was really going to have to start paying a doorman once again. San Francisco wasn't the East Side of Manhattan. Doormen were unknown here except for a few exclusive condos.

"That sounds great," he said. "Connie always liked to eat those gooey chocolate desserts—women's desserts, I call them. Cheesecake is a man's food."

"Really? I'd never thought of it that way before."

"Yeah. Lots of my buddies feel like that."

"Interesting." She went into the kitchen and cut a slice of cake for Kevin. She'd made it that morning for

Paavo, who was coming over later. He liked cheese-cake a lot. Maybe Kevin was right? But Paavo also liked other cakes and pastries, more elaborate ones, like Italian Rum Cake . . .

After giving Kevin cake and coffee, and pouring herself a cup, she sat down. "So, what brings you here?" she asked.

"I'm worried about Connie." He stuffed a big piece of cake in his mouth, and made appreciative noises as he rolled it around on his tongue. *Obviously not too worried*, she thought.

She waited until he'd swallowed to be sure he wouldn't answer with a mouthful of mooshy dessert. "What are you worried about?"

"I heard she's been seeing some guy connected with football. The Forty-Niners. Big joke, huh?"

"What's wrong with that?"

He put the fork down, blue eyes widening. "So, it's true?"

"I'm not saying it isn't."

He looked stricken. "Those guys are out of her league. She's just a nice kid. Innocent, you know. I don't trust guys like that."

And Angie didn't trust *him.* "Connie can handle herself."

He finished the cake before asking, "Is he a nice guy, at least? Is he . . . white?"

She nearly spat out her coffee. "He's Italian, okay? Will that do?"

His eyebrows nearly touched his hairline. "Ohmy-god! Not . . . not *Joe Montana*?"

"Don't you think he's a little old for her? Not to mention that he's married?"

Kevin folded his tanned and tattooed arms. "I don't remember that that's stopped her before."

"If so, she didn't know it when she started dating such a guy!" Angie said indignantly, and suppressed the urge to stab him with his own fork. "Anyway, you just said she was an innocent."

He stood, sliding his fingertips into his back pockets, and strode to the window. "So, she *has* met someone who's a big deal." He stared at the bay a long moment. "I didn't think it'd happen."

Angie felt a twinge of pity for him. She made no reply. Was Kevin actually remorseful about the way he'd treated Connie? She knew Connie had been crazy about him, but when he'd been given the choice between his wife and heroin, the drug had won out. Angie wondered if he'd cleaned up sufficiently, and for long enough, that Connie would be interested in him again.

On the other hand, Connie had given him plenty of chances, and each time he'd failed her. Now she had a chance with Dennis Pagozzi, who was just about perfect in every way—except that he might be two-timing her. Or breaking up with that other woman so that he could be free to concentrate on Connie. Who knew?

"I guess you miss her," Angie said, not quite sure what to say or why she suddenly felt sympathy for him. Was she turning into a total marshmallow because of love?

His mouth tightened. "Could be." He did another once-over of her apartment. "I guess she'll be getting a place as nice as this, if she stays with this guy. Maybe even a house. She always used to say she wanted a house—just a little house to call her own, nothing more. Now, she'll be able to afford a mansion, if she can pull it off." He chuckled morosely.

"Pull what off?"

"Make the guy think she's in love with him. I know

how she feels about me . . . how we still feel about each other." He smirked, on sure footing once again.

What little sympathy she felt vanished. Angie didn't like the words or the attitude. "She doesn't have to pretend anything. I've seen the two of them together. This guy worships the ground she walks on. He treats her like a princess, and she adores him."

His smile disappeared. "The hell with her, then. Who cares, right? Well, I'm outta here. Thanks for nothing!"

Angie escorted him to the front door and opened it, glad to see the back of the loser. How had Connie stood him?

He stepped out into the hall, then faced her once again. "Say, when you talk to her, ask her if she can get a couple of Forty-Niner tickets for me, okay?"

"Dennis Pagozzi?"

Bleary-eyed, Pagozzi stood in his doorway in his robe and pajamas, trying to focus on the identification presented by the round, balding man. "Chowchilla Probation Department?"

Lexington stood tall. "That's right. I'm looking for Veronica Maple. Our records indicate that you are a longtime acquaintance of hers."

Pagozzi rubbed his face, wanting nothing more than a shower and a shave. "That was ages ago. I don't know anything about her."

"Mr. Pagozzi, we have reason to believe she's armed and dangerous. To you, and to others."

"What do you mean?"

"It appears that she killed a man in Fresno right after getting out of prison. She failed to report in to my office as required, which lends credence to her having perpetuated the crime. She was tracked to San Francisco, but we don't know where she's gone from here."

Pagozzi was suddenly wide awake. "Veronica? A killer? She was always just interested in money."

"People change in prison," Lexington explained. "They go in as white-collar criminals and come out hard, willing to do anything for a buck. She robbed the pawn shop along with killing the owner."

Pagozzi's nerves felt ready to snap. Veronica moved out last night after the blow-up at the restaurant, and he was glad. She'd changed, and hardened. He didn't think she could commit murder, but it wasn't the first time he'd been wrong about her. This time, he could be dead wrong.

His mind raced. "Thanks for letting me know. I'll contact you if I see her."

"Just what was your relationship with Miss Maple?" Lexington asked.

"Nothing. We hung out when we were young, that's all."

Lexington nodded, peering intently into Pagozzi's eyes. "For your sake, I hope it wasn't anything more than that. Here's my card. We have to get her before she kills again. Once a person like her starts, it can lead anywhere."

"That's exactly what I was thinking."

Connie glanced at the clock—5:55 P.M. Five minutes more and she could lock up shop, thank goodness. The day began much too early at six-thirty, in time for the New York Stock Exchange's opening bell. Stockbrokers were already at their desks in San Francisco—not a good way to live, in her opinion, but she was glad she could immediately get the answer to the question that had plagued her all night.

"I'm interested in buying a stock," she said to the

Merrill Lynch broker who answered her call, "but I want to know the price first."

"Great. I can help you," the enthusiastic voice responded. "What is it?"

"Geostar Biotechnologies."

"Okay." In a moment he came back. "Are you sure of the name? I checked the New York, NASDAQ, even American exchanges, but I don't see it."

"That's what I was told. Oh, wait. He said something about over the counter and GBST. Does that help?"

"It sure does. One moment." He found it selling at two dollars a share. The broker nearly choked as he asked her if she wanted to "actually" buy any of it.

With a shudder, she said no.

What kind of fool did Max Squire take her for?

She'd fumed about him all day, and maybe that was why she'd only sold a single item—a twenty-dollar porcelain flower and vase to a woman looking for a small gift for a hospitalized friend allergic to real flowers.

Not only that, Dennis hadn't called, either. What was with him? He should at least have apologized for not saying good-bye when he ran out on their lunch. He was making it mighty hard for her to keep him high up on her stud rating chart. Right now, he was a whisker below Russell Crowe, and sinking fast.

A minute before closing time, the shop's bell rang. Connie froze. If the customer was returning the vase, she'd run into the back room and hide until she gave up and left again. That sale was important. She needed to eat.

When she gathered her nerve and glanced up, Max stood in the doorway.

"What are you doing here?" she demanded. She

could feel her face redden—God, sometimes it was awful being blond—as anger and frustration warred. "Looking for more money?"

"I was desperate, as I told you," he said, approaching her. He hesitated, then said gruffly, "I'm sorry about the way I treated you yesterday. It was uncalled for. I also want to thank you for not saying anything about it to Dennis. What I did was embarrassing enough without him knowing."

Now he wanted to apologize? "It embarrassed me, too, to have been such a patsy!"

"I've known Dennis a while," he continued, his voice calm. "I saw you with him—the way he looked at you. He's a good guy. A good woman is exactly what he needs, and you're a good woman, Connie. I feel bad about involving you in my problems at all. I'll try to do something, when or if I'm able, to remedy it."

None of this made any sense to her. "You feel bad about me?"

Dark eyes captured hers. "Hell, woman, do you think I'd be here if I didn't? I couldn't get you out of my mind, even though I tried. Believe me, I tried real hard."

That gave her pause. She swallowed, then asked, "Why?"

"Why couldn't I forget you?"

"Why did you want to?"

He shook his head. "Your kindness. Your trust. I didn't think women like you existed anymore."

She didn't know what to make of him, only that he was hurting and desperate. She'd been there herself at times. Slowly stepping around the counter toward him, she lifted her hand to touch his arm, but then dropped it again and drew in her breath. "We met, we talked, and to my amazement, we seemed to enjoy each other's company. You were hurt, and I helped you. It was all good . . . until you made it turn ugly."

"I know," he said, his voice filled with pain. "I know."

She stamped her foot. "You make me so *angry!*"

A hint of a smile touched his mouth. "Hit me, why don't you? A slap in the face or a good hard sock in the stomach—your choice. It's what I deserve, and it'll make you feel a hell of a lot better."

She smacked her arms against her sides. "I can't hit you! I'm mad enough at you, that's for sure, but I can't."

Gently, he touched her cheek. "I'm so sorry, about everything." With that, he turned away.

She watched him walk toward the door. Under his beaten-down, trying-to-be-jaded, trying-to-be-tough exterior, she saw a good man, a lonely, sensitive man, someone who had been damaged badly. She moved toward him. She wasn't sure why; she was never impulsive. "Constant Connie," as Angie had said. Angie was the impulsive one. Not her; never her.

"Max, wait!" she cried. He turned.

She stopped, unsure what to say. How could she forgive him? But somehow she had. "What would you say to a bowl of Campbell's vegetable soup and a couple of hamburgers for dinner? Chef Connie's cooking might not be exciting, but it's filling."

He blinked as if not sure he'd heard her correctly. "It would be better if I just left."

"No," she said, despite herself. "It wouldn't."

With the engine running, Veronica sat parked in a loading zone and watched Max enter Everyone's Fancy. She couldn't imagine why he'd taken a taxi across town to go to a cheap little gift shop. She hadn't intended on following him, but merely to check up on him: to keep him in her sights, so to speak.

But curiosity had gotten the best of her.

This morning, Dennis had called her cell phone sounding agitated. He'd just heard that Max had learned she was out of jail and wanted to kill her. She had to be careful, Dennis said, to get out of town. He also suggested she stay away from him, his house, even Wings, because Max could find her there.

She didn't know what to make of the phone call. Although she didn't trust Dennis, something about his words, the fear in them, rattled her. And strangely, she had felt watched; as if someone, something, was moving ever closer to her. Something dark and deathlike. Perhaps death itself.

She hated such thoughts, didn't believe in them. They meant nothing. Shoving them aside, she concentrated on Max.

By following him after he'd left Wings, she discovered he was living in a homeless shelter. She was shocked.

He used to be a Hugo Boss suit man, his casual wear nothing less than Armani or Polo, with three-hundred-dollar loafers and fifty-dollar haircuts. He liked imported red wine, gourmet meals, classical music, and Broadway shows—and treated her to the same, when he wasn't working. Too much work had been Max Squire's biggest problem. He had spent so much time involved in his business, expanding it and finding new clients, that to say it made Max a dull boy was an understatement.

At first, he'd considered himself far above her. Eventually, he swore undying love for her, but when it came to a choice between his money and reputation or her, he'd chosen the former.

He could have let her get away. He was smart enough to make back the money she'd taken and no one would have been the wiser. Instead, he turned her over to the police. That wasn't love; it was betrayal.

She'd gone to jail, and instead of working, he'd obviously spent the last three years wallowing in self-pity, a loser.

Now, she was stuck in this city with another loser—Dennis. As soon as she got her hands on the money, *her* money, she'd be out of here. No one was going to get in her way.

She sat a little higher in the seat when the "OPEN" sign in the door of the shop flipped to "CLOSED." A moment later, the door opened, and a blond woman, a bit too heavy in the waist and hips, stepped out of the shop, Max right behind her. Veronica had seen the woman before—with Dennis.

She locked the door and took Max's arm as they walked down the street. Who was this two-timing broad?

Max always was a sucker for blondes. She touched her hair, the long strands brushing her shoulders, as she studied the woman.

Her hair had been short, just like *hers*, when she and Max had their affair. He liked it; used to rifle his fingers through it. She wondered if he pretended the blonde was her when they kissed, when they made love. Max had sworn his love to her, and now was proving himself to be as fickle as all men. It was good the only lust she ever felt around him was for his clients' money.

Veronica abandoned her car and followed them to a corner, then onto Wawona Street. Two blocks later, they entered a building. She crept close and managed to grab the heavy main door to the apartment building before it locked again.

She waited a moment, then entered. No elevator; the stairs carpeted. A woman's hand glided along the banister near the top, three flights up. Silently, she climbed the stairs, practically running. Those prison workouts had paid off well for her.

On the top floor a door opened and then a light came on. She angled herself to see which apartment they'd entered. Soon, the door closed again and all was quiet.

She paused on the stairs, remembering the many times Max had taken her to his home—an immense, professionally decorated place that he lived in alone. He'd been a good lover, one of the best, in fact. Much better than Dennis, who was more in love with himself than anyone or anything else. *Too bad things went so wrong, Max.*

It was tempting to simply burst into the apartment and have it out with him. To think that while she'd rotted in prison, he'd been out enjoying life. Bad enough that he was rutting, but doing it with women who looked so much like her infuriated her even more.

Her breathing grew heavy as her fingers twisted in her hair and she tugged on it hard. Damn them both! If her hair were short, her eyes blue . . .

An idea, a wonderfully pleasing idea, struck her. Could she do it? Tomorrow was the big day. But if she hurried, she would have time.

As she faced the apartment door, her plans for the next day's adventure grew a bit more complicated . . . but far, far more satisfying.

Chapter 14

Max sat in Wings of an Angel, the income and spending records in shopping bags all around him. He'd never seen such a mess. All of them, Earl, Butch, and even Vinnie, thought nothing of reaching into the till whenever they needed cash, mixing tips with receipts, credit card payments with cash, even payables with receivables in ways he'd never imagined were possible. He didn't even want to think about what they'd done to state sales tax, let alone liquor and cigarette taxes.

Where to begin puzzled him. He might not have taken the job at all except for Butch's statement about too many from the past showing up, first *her*, then him. Had Butch meant Veronica? In that context, who else could he have meant?

If she'd been to Wings, that meant Dennis was lying to him. Max needed to stick closer than ever to Dennis and Wings both, and this job was one way to do it.

He was trying to decipher scribbles on a receipt when Earl called him to the phone. "For you."

Assuming it was Dennis, Max answered.

"I'd know that voice anywhere," a woman said.

His blood turned hot, then cold. He'd know *her* voice anywhere as well. "Veronica."

"You remember. How sweet. I was sure you'd forget after you sent me away. Three years, Max."

"It was your doing," he said, trying his best to keep his voice hushed and steady. Your doing, he wanted to say, and then ask *Why?* Why did she do that to him when he loved her so much? Why had she caused pure love to turn to black, soul-crushing hatred?

"I'm out now," she said. "It's over."

His hand gripped the receiver. It wasn't over for him. "I want to see you." He struggled to keep his voice soft and friendly, but could hear it quiver.

"Why? Do you think I want to share?" She laughed.

"I know you better than that," he said. "I just . . . want to see you again."

"I'm sure you do. Maybe we can pick up where we left off, is that what you're thinking? Except now, I'm the one with the money."

Every word was another stab to the heart. It was already broken, how could it continue to hurt? "You do have it, then?"

"How could I? I served time. You don't think they let you keep money you've embezzled, do you?"

He knew she was toying with him, the same as always. He'd followed the case as closely as humanly possible. No one knew where most of the money she'd taken from his clients had gone. She claimed it went to gambling and drugs—all eight million. He knew, though, that she didn't gamble and rarely touched the hard stuff.

He knew far too much about her.

The image flashed in his mind of the day she'd first walked into his financial consulting office holding a folded *San Francisco Chronicle* with his help-wanted ad circled. The business was growing more quickly than he and his secretary, Mrs. Hendricks, could handle. He needed a part-time office aid.

She looked like a schoolgirl, her hair pulled back into a ponytail, face scrubbed and make-up free, wearing a sweet dress buttoned up to the neck and hemmed below the knees. Her intelligence had shone through, and she quickly learned and understood everything Mrs. Hendricks explained to her.

Even then, behind the innocent smile, there was a knowingness, a sexiness, that Mrs. Hendricks didn't recognize, but his male hormones did.

Before long, Veronica was coming into his office after Mrs. Hendricks had gone home for the day, pointing out to him how incompetent his secretary of the past seven years had been, and how much more efficient she was. During those times, they'd relax, and she would often unbutton the top few buttons of her dress or blouse to breathe more easily, or remove the band from her ponytail so her long blond hair could swing freely.

When confronted, Mrs. Hendricks's protests sounded weak, and the more she complained about Veronica, the more Max found himself defending her. Three weeks after Veronica began working for him, she came into his office after hours and didn't stop with unbuttoning just a few buttons. Their affair began, and almost immediately after that, Mrs. Hendricks quit.

Veronica took over her job. She was amazingly intelligent. He trusted her completely. His little protégée, he'd called her, and promised to teach her all about financial counseling. They had dreams of her bringing in her own clients and having the business grow larger and more prosperous than ever. She made a goal for herself—a goal to hire a secretary for them both.

They say love is blind, and he was more blinded by Veronica than ever a man should be. She cut her hair short and sophisticated—much the way Connie wore hers—threw away her cotton dresses for business suits, and got to know his clients' affairs as well, or better, than he did.

A few times he walked in unexpectedly to hear her talking cheerfully to one of them. He didn't question her, though, and pushed aside his suspicions, especially when she'd tell him how magnificent he was and that the luckiest day of her life was when he hired her.

He wanted to get married, practically begged her, but she refused. He didn't know why. Only much later did he learn she'd had lots of lovers, including several of his clients, like Dennis Pagozzi. Ironically, if she'd married him, he wouldn't have been able to testify against her.

It was his deposition that had caused her to plead guilty and bargain her way down to a three-year prison term, with five additional years of probation. The case never went to trial.

He'd been furious. Three years was a slap on the wrist for what she'd done to him, to his business and reputation. To his heart. He'd loved her with a passion and intensity he'd never felt for anyone before and hadn't felt since. The day he realized she'd betrayed him was the day he'd lost interest in life, along with his faith and self-respect.

Although she was the embezzler, and he wasn't criminally guilty, since she'd been in his employ, civil lawsuits against him were very real. At first, he'd cared about his clients, even though they were so rich their losses wouldn't have mattered that much. Hell, with the tax write-off it gave them, they might have made a profit, for all he knew. But instead of showing him support or understanding, they sued him. They ruined him. He would have worked hard for them, too, had they not been like sharks at a feeding frenzy, taking all they could, destroying any sense of regret, obligation, or even basic humanity he felt for them.

Everything he'd worked for, everything he owned, went to pay his lawyers and pay off the clients. He'd been insured, but what he owed was far more than the insurance and much more than he had saved, so a lien was placed against his future earnings as well. Since his capital would be taken away from him the minute he amassed any, he soon realized he would never be able to build up his assets. He was, in a word, screwed.

A few of his clients, like Pagozzi, stuck by him for a while, but he was changed. Long before the creditors lined up at his door, long before the last of his clients took their business elsewhere, he'd ceased to care. Some days, he would find oblivion in a liquor bottle so that he didn't have to wonder why she'd done it, and if she'd lied about everything. For months after the betrayal, he would wake up out of a nightmare with her name on his tongue and tears in his eyes. He hated her then as he hated her now. It was the only honest emotion he'd felt for the past three years.

The life he'd known, his business, his love, were gone, all destroyed by the woman on the telephone.

And damn it, as much as he wanted to kill her, he also wanted to see her again.

"If you don't have the money," he asked, "where is it?"

"I didn't say that, exactly. In fact, that's what I want to talk to you about."

"I'm ready."

"Good. Let's meet at Ghirardelli Square, under the

clock tower. Be there at three o'clock, and no funny business."

"That's a great one, coming from you."

"It's *perfect*, coming from me. And . . . I suggest you don't tell your new girlfriend anything about this. I'd hate to fill her in on what you're really like. It could ruin a good thing for you, don't you think?"

He hung up the phone, hating her even more than he thought possible.

Was she referring to Connie? How could she possibly know anything about Connie? Maybe it was just a stab in the dark.

He hurried out of Wings and dashed along the city streets to Ghirardelli Square. He'd be early, but that was okay. He wanted to be sure he saw Veronica before she saw him, just to get ready to face her again.

He didn't want her spooked, didn't want her to do anything other than trust him and talk to him about where she'd put his damned money!

He wanted it back for himself. He wanted enough to live somewhere that wasn't squalor. He deserved that. Didn't he? Well, didn't he?

He also wanted to know why Veronica had contacted Pagozzi when she got out of jail. What did they mean to each other?

Suddenly, he staggered as a completely new thought struck him.

Was it mere chance that Veronica had walked into his office when he needed clerical help three years ago, or had something else been going on between her and Pagozzi even then?

Paavo tried to bury himself behind his computer and ignore the chaos going on around him as Elizabeth and Bo Benson made lattes and cappuccinos for Homicide, Robbery, and any other inspector who wandered into room 450, following their noses and the aroma of good, strong espresso. Angie had rented an espresso machine and sent it over, along with biscotti and cannoli, as afternoon coffee-break treats.

"Inspector Smith."

Paavo started at the sound of Lt. Hollins's voice. Hollins was the head of Homicide. Age fifty-plus, gray-haired, heavyset, and usually found holding or chewing on an unlit cigar. Right now, his tone was harsh and his expression a severe frown. And he never used his men's title unless there was a problem.

Paavo jumped to his feet. "Yes, sir."

"Come into my office." He marched off, and Paavo followed.

The office was no more than a partitioned section in the corner of the bureau. For several years, the lieutenant had been promised a real office, but whenever he'd get one, the mayor would create a new commissioner or department, and the boss—usually a friend—would, of course, need his own office. People would be juggled around to accommodate the political appointee, and Hollins would be booted out of his new office, the supposedly temporary partitions put back in Homicide.

"Have a seat," Hollins said.

Paavo sat down.

"I don't know quite how to put this." Hollins didn't sit, but walked around the little space, then stopped in front of the window. "I appreciate that you've just gotten engaged, and that your fiancée is thrilled by it, and she has money . . . but she's going too far."

"She is?"

"Nothing's getting done. The inspectors are all hanging around the office waiting for their daily delivery of food rations." Hollins's face began to redden. "Is this an office or a soup kitchen? The problem is, the food she's sending is great. I can't pass it up either. It's delicious, and fattening. I've gained five pounds just this week!" Each word was more agitated than the last. "I can't keep this up. I won't be able to fit into my clothes. My wife is wondering why I don't eat much dinner anymore. She thinks I'm stepping out on her or something. I can't take it!"

"I'm sorry. What do you want me to do?"

"Stop her!"

Paavo kept silent. He'd have more luck locating Jimmy Hoffa. He wondered grimly what would happen when the lieutenant found out Angie had match-making plans for his fellow cops as well.

"You don't understand temptation!" Hollins cried. "That's what's going on. Many of us, er, them, are weak around such temptation. Especially the pizza." His eyes rolled heavenward. Instead of agony or anger, he almost seemed to be in bliss. "And the Italian deli foods—the coppa, galantina, Gorgonzola, pepperoncini—"

"I understand, sir," Paavo said, standing. "I'll talk to Angie soon."

"The caponata, dry olives, bruschetta." Hollins raised his handkerchief to the corner of his mouth, aware that he was starting to drool. He blinked, forcing himself back to the task at hand. "Good, Smith. I expect you to take care of it."

Paavo hurried out of the office and back to his desk.

Chapter 15

Sid Fernandez sat in the van's passenger seat and watched as a young female courier drove into the Sutter Street building's underground garage. She looked bored. This was just a job, one she'd done over and over, despite the supposed danger of it, and the danger in becoming blasé about it.

She should have listened to her boss's warnings, because as she shut and lock the truck's door, Julius Rodriguez stopped the van, sprang out, and hit her on the head with an iron bar. He caught her as she crumpled.

In under ten seconds, Julius had lifted her into the van. While he broke the courier's neck to make sure she wouldn't wake up and cry out, Veronica changed into the uniform stripped from the woman.

Fernandez watched as the two double-checked the company's ID to confirm that the one made for Veronica was the same as the IDs currently being used by Couriers Unlimited. It was.

Veronica took the courier's package, carefully removed the mailing label, and taped it onto a large padded envelope with heavy cardboard inside so it

148

wouldn't bend. She had to be sure Isaac Zakarian would open the door to receive it.

Zakarian's, a very exclusive diamond jewelry shop, was located on the third floor. It had a small public area, where customers could view the unset diamonds and settings, and a back room where the diamonds were stored in locked display cases. Each day, the office closed between twelve and two, and between one and one-thirty when his assistant went to lunch, the owner was alone. The only people he would open his doors for were couriers. And one or more came each day with a package for him.

Initially, Julius was going to handle the robbery, but when El Toro found out Veronica would be getting out of prison, he thought she would be less likely to arouse any suspicion on Zakarian's part. Their scheme required him to relax enough to open the door from the public area to the back where the diamonds were kept.

He and Julius would wait until she was in—giving her exactly one minute from the time she stepped onto the elevator. She'd send the elevator back down to the basement, and they'd hold it there, waiting, until the minute was up.

If they showed up on the cameras that scanned the hallway outside the shop, the owner would never open the inner office door for her. Once she knocked him over, they'd enter, clean out the store, take out the cameras, and simply ride down in the elevators, leaving the way they'd got in.

It was a simple, straightforward plan, and in his experience, that was the kind that worked best. Too many of his compadres came up with complicated robberies only to have some little something go wrong and end up in jail. Just like what had happened to Veronica three years ago.

Once, he'd thought he could trust her with this job, but now he questioned that. She'd changed her hairdo—cut short and dyed a light blond—and she wore blue contacts over the gray of her eyes.

He didn't like to question the loyalty of his people. He didn't like it at all, but the robbery was set, and to change plans now would only create more delays.

Delays always brought bad luck. El Toro hated delays.

He'd also lined up an airtight alibi and made sure his fingerprints would be nowhere at the crime scene. Afterward, if she and Julius were being as disloyal as he thought, as he'd seen with his own eyes, he'd take care of the problem. Permanently.

They waited until Zakarian's assistant walked through the garage to his car and drove off. They now had a half hour to complete the job.

Veronica gave Fernandez a backward glance, then stepped into the elevator.

Veronica walked to the entry room and rang the bell. An older man with a round face atop an equally round body, receding gray hair, and oval glasses perched on the end of a nose with enormous, fleshy nostrils came to the bulletproof window.

"Delivery," she called.

He didn't say a word, but opened the slot. "Give it here," he ordered gruffly.

When she placed it against the slot and it wouldn't fit, she tried to fold it with no luck. "What the hell did they send me?" Zakarian complained. "Let me see it."

She held it up to the window so he could read the label. "Okay, okay! Bring it to the door." He stood. "Hold it, you! Show your ID. Don't you know procedure?"

She held the ID against the glass.

"Cut your hair," he said. "Looks better now."

She kept her expression taut as she tucked the card into her back pocket.

He opened the door just a crack and was waiting for her to slip the package through when she hit the door hard, knocking him backward onto the floor. As soon as she did, she drew her gun. "Don't touch a thing!" she ordered, knowing there were panic buttons all over, on the floor as well as the walls. She grabbed the shoulder of his shirt, lifting and spinning him around so he didn't face her. At the same time she pulled him to his feet. "Keep your head down. Don't look at me!"

He raised his arms up even though she didn't tell him to. He'd seen lots of movies. "What the hell is this?"

"Unlock the cases and grab those trays." She handed him a pillowcase to put them in. "We're going out the back way. Fast!"

"Okay," he squawked. "Anything you say."

She knew he was thinking about the alarm on the back door, which, if opened when not deactivated, would cause the office to be surrounded with security, and soon after, the police.

It was all right. She'd be out of there by then. With the diamonds. And if Fernandez and Julius were caught lurking around the hallway, so be it.

He stuffed a bunch of trays into the pillowcase. She looked at the time. Fifty-five seconds had gone by.

"That's enough. Move it!" She shoved him toward the back of the store. "Listen, old man. My friends expect me to kill you then let them in, but I'm not. I'll let you live. Got it?"

He nodded, quivering.

"I want you to run right down the stairwell to your

car. If you don't run fast enough, my friends might catch us. Then we're both dead. Understand?"

He turned a pale shade of green and nodded again.

"Now. Run!"

He ran, faster than she thought he could, literally jumping from stairs to landing as he descended the three flights to the garage. She stopped him as he got there, stuck her head out, and didn't see El Toro or the others. They should be riding up on the elevator by now, or even waiting in the hall.

"Now!" she ordered, and he ran, dripping sweat, to his car, a blue Buick.

They jumped in, and he tore out of the garage, using his key card to open the door and get out.

One good thing about silent alarms even in jewelry shops was that so many people tripped them by mistake, nobody took them as seriously as they should. There was always a delay—an "is-it-real-this-time-or-just-another-false-alarm?" moment—which she was counting on to give her the additional seconds she needed to escape.

"Hey!"

She didn't know if it was a security guard or one of El Toro's men who yelled, but she ducked and told Zakarian to head for Ghirardelli Square.

He kept staring straight ahead, gripping the steering wheel, his foot like lead on the gas pedal. "Slow down!" she yelled. "Do you want to get a ticket?"

"You've got the diamonds. Let me go," the old man pleaded as they neared Ghirardelli Square.

"Shut up and drive."

Max stood beneath the clock tower, just as he'd said he would. "There. Stop the car in the bus stop," she ordered.

"The bus stop? But what if a bus comes?"

She waved at Max, and he nodded back. She watched Zakarian stare unblinking at Max while not daring to glance at her again. He remembered her warning. His voice quaked as he whispered, "Please let me go."

"Ask him—he's the boss." She swiveled toward the jeweler and smacked the butt of her Smith and Wesson hard against his temple. He slumped against the driver's door.

Clutching the bag with the diamonds, she jumped out of the car and ran down the hill. Max stared in horror at the old man, the blood now gushing from his head, then ran after Veronica.

People in the busy tourist area began to put together what had happened, and several yelled for Max to stop. Veronica reached her Ford Escort and in seconds was pulling away. She wove around the busy traffic, ran a red light, and somehow managed to find enough space open on the roadway to leave quickly. In the rearview mirror, she could see Max's diminishing figure, and she started to laugh.

The idea came to Angie from weddings in which each table of guests was given a disposable camera to take pictures—their point of view, so to speak. A number of people who worked with Paavo had witnessed his proposal to her in an old abandoned church after an insane killer had been stopped. To them, she had sent inexpensive tape recorders along with a blank tape, instructions, and a return envelope, and asked that they tell her what they saw, from the time Paavo proposed and she fainted, until she woke back up and her *compos* became *mentis* again. She hoped for a lasting memory of that wonderful moment since, unfortunately, she'd missed most of it.

They did as she'd asked, and now, the tapes were in front of her. With great anticipation, she picked up the first one, Yosh's, placed it in the tape recorder, and hit "Play."

"Paavo rushed off without me. When is he going to learn not to do that? We're partners, damn it. Supposed to depend on each other, not go it alone. I should have been with him the whole time. You tell him, Angie. You want me there. If he'd told me what he was going to do, I could have had a glass of water in my hand, then when you passed out, I could have splashed it on you, right? But did he ask my help? No! He went and asked all by himself, and look at how it ended up. When will he learn? I give up."

Whew! She put on Calderon's tape.

"You keeled over, then you woke up. So what?"

Next, she picked up a tape from Officer Crossen, a cop Paavo had asked to protect Angie. She wondered about it when he wrote "to Angie" and instead of a dot over the *i*, there was a ♥. She hit "Play."

"Your big brown eyes fluttered shut like a butterfly folding its wings. You slowly sank to the floor and stretched out over the hard ground before anyone could save you, looking like a real-life Sleeping Beauty waiting for her handsome prince. I guess you've settled for Smith, but if you ever get tired of him, give me a call."

She gawked, tempted to listen again, but instead went to Bo Benson's.

"I was pretty cool that night. Caught a serial killer and all. He was dead before I got there, but he knew I was real close. Mean sucker, wasn't he? I was talking to the coroner when you hit the floor. She was interested in how the killer died. I explained it to her. When people finished asking for my help, you were awake. Oh, yeah. Congrats."

Angie put the tape recorder away. Some ideas just didn't work out.

Chapter 16

Kevin Trammel rang the bell to Connie's apartment. He had to see her, to talk to her alone, and she should be off work by now. It couldn't really be over between them. She'd give him a second chance; hell, she always had before.

If not, having an ex-wife who hung out with a Forty-Niner team member might not be such a bad thing. She always did have a soft spot for him, and if suddenly she was rolling in dough, she wouldn't be too selfish. It wasn't in her nature to be.

He waited, but there was no response. He rang again.

Maybe she was out with her jock. He probably had a fancy car, fancy house, fancy servants. He wondered, had the guy learned yet how much she enjoyed making love in the morning, when the house was chilly, but the bed toasty warm? Or the way nibbling on her ear and neck turned her on?

Hell, but he missed her.

Still no answer. Damn it!

From deep in his pockets, he pulled out a ring of keys. He tried a couple before finding the one he'd been looking for. He unlocked the main door, then quickly climbed the stairs to the third floor.

Kevin Trammel wasn't born yesterday. The last time Connie had tried to make up with him and he'd stayed with her over a week until she decided it just wasn't working out, he'd had copies made of the keys she'd given him.

He knew they might come in handy someday. Like today.

He let himself into the apartment.

Nothing had changed since the last time he'd been there. Same old furniture, same pictures on the walls, same old-fashioned dolls junking the place up. She'd thrown out his beer-bottle collection, he noticed. He'd been trying to save bottles from all over the world. They looked really cool, or so he thought. What did she know, anyway?

He walked into her bedroom. She'd made the bed. Now, he couldn't tell if it had been slept in on just one side, or two. It was the queen-sized bed they'd used. Damn thing nearly filled up the whole room.

He turned away. There were some memories he didn't want to have. He walked into the kitchen and found a beer in the refrigerator. Bud Lite. It figured. Connie was always worried about her weight.

When he had money, he was a Heineken man. Today, Bud Lite would have to do.

He picked up the beer, then settled down in the living room to wait for his wife, ex-wife, to come home.

Julius kept his head facing straight ahead; only his eyeballs swiveled toward Fernandez. El Toro was still red-faced and sweaty with fury. Julius had never seen him so out of control as when he realized Veronica had somehow gotten away with the jewels.

They'd stepped onto the elevator, expecting to ride up to the third floor, when it stopped on one. Someone

in a wheelchair had to get in, but the person pushing
the chair kept getting the wheels skewed in the wrong
direction. The space was tight, and by the time they'd
gotten it squared away, the security guards had rushed
in and stopped the elevator. There'd been a robbery at-
tempt in the building.

El Toro and Julius simply stepped off the elevator,
walked out of the lobby, and left.

They abandoned the van they'd stolen for the job in
the garage and waited at the end of the block to see
what happened next, expecting to see Veronica under
arrest.

It didn't happen. She'd gotten away . . . with the diamonds. El Toro's diamonds.

As terrifying as Fernandez's anger was, the ensuing
silence was worse.

Julius didn't know where they were going. They
were still in the city, but in the southwest corner, near
the Pacific.

Raymondo stopped the car by the sand dunes.

"It's peaceful out here, isn't it, Toro?" Julius said.

"Peaceful. Yes, that is one word for it."

"We'll find her," Julius added quickly. "She can't
hide from us."

"She can't hide. That's true. Not from me. You can't
either."

His nerves jumped. "Me? What do you mean?"

Fernandez's eyes were harder and blacker than coal.
"Where are you planning to meet her?"

Sweat beaded on Julius's forehead. "Boss, what do
you mean? I had nothing to do with this!"

"Get out of the car, Julius."

He quaked. "No! I mean, Toro, you've got to believe
me."

"You *will* tell me where she is. Don't doubt it for a minute."

Raymondo opened the door beside Julius and waited for him to step out of the limo.

Max dashed into Connie's shop a half hour before closing time. "Are you all right?"

"What are you talking about?" she asked.

"Nothing." He looked around the shop, then stepped outside and searched the street.

"What's going on?"

He tried to appear nonchalant. No sense scaring her more than he probably already had. "It's all right. Just . . . nothing. Why don't I take you to dinner? There's a Chinese restaurant down the block. I was paid a little yesterday for helping with some tax forms."

She studied him, and he was afraid she'd refuse. They'd spent a pleasant evening together the night before. She'd cooked a simple dinner, and they'd talked. He asked about her marriage, and about her sister, and how she'd coped with losing both. She didn't say much about her ex-husband, and that troubled him. He even was surprised at a pang of something—could it have been jealousy?—that made him want to say the guy had been a complete jackass.

It had been a long time since he'd sat and talked, as a friend, with a woman. He'd enjoyed her company, her humor, her good nature. He thought she might ask him to stay, but she didn't do that either, and he left a little before midnight.

He wouldn't blame her if she tossed him out again, now. Who was he to ask anything of her? But then she smiled and his heart lightened and lifted.

He stayed as she counted and wrote up the day's receipts, then locked up the shop. They went to dinner at a nearby Chinese restaurant and then decided to go for a walk. Max had never been to Lake Merced, so they drove over to it, a lonely stretch of parkland tucked into the southwest corner of the city by the sand dunes and the Great Highway. No businesses or tourist attractions were in the area, put off by the nearly perpetual cold wind and fog and lack of public transportation.

Max held Connie's hand as they strolled along the path that circled the lake. He should have felt carefree and happy; instead, his mind kept going back to the afternoon at Ghirardelli Square, and he was worried.

Although he hadn't seen Veronica in three years, he was shocked when he saw her. She looked just like Connie.

It couldn't be happenstance; something more was behind it.

Veronica and Dennis had a lot more going on between them than he ever imagined, and Dennis knew Connie. Was that the connection? Something involving Dennis?

His instinct told him Connie had no idea about any of this, and he wondered about Dennis. Still, if Veronica was involved, it meant danger—and he was afraid the danger could extend to Connie.

In the distance, a loud report, sounding like a gunshot, rang out.

Max's grip on Connie's hand tightened and he turned off the pathway, plunging into a forest of tall pines and pulling her with him.

"Was that a gunshot?" Connie asked, eyes round. "It sounded far from us, Max. Why are we running?"

He stopped, confused. "You're right. I'm just a little tense after . . ."

"After what?"

He ran his fingers through his hair. "Damn her to hell! The gunshot wasn't meant for us this time . . ."

"Damn *who*? What are you talking about?"

He glanced at her, but his eyes were clouded, his mind elsewhere. "I'll make sure she doesn't get me, or you, if it's the last thing I do," he whispered.

Connie grew even more desperate. "You're scaring me, Max. Am I in some kind of danger? What's wrong?"

"Be careful, and don't trust *anyone*, Connie. Do you hear me? Don't trust anyone."

He rode back to her apartment with her, and after seeing her safely inside and checking to be sure the apartment was empty, he left.

She immediately called Angie, needing to talk to her about what had just happened, to ask if she could make any sense out of it and to get some advice. But Angie wasn't home.

She hung up without leaving a message and rubbed her chilled arms as she glanced over her silent apartment.

When Max told her not to trust anyone, that included him.

Chapter 17

Angie spent a good part of the morning watching for the mail truck. When she saw it, she raced down to the third floor, grabbed her neighbor, a sweet though gawky and timid thirty-year-old, and almost bodily dragged her down to the foyer. The girl needed help. *Angie* kind of help.

Just yesterday she'd been chatting with the mailman and learned the handsome young fellow was not only going to San Francisco State at night, but was also single and unattached. Well, it didn't have to jump up and bite her for Angie to know a match made in heaven.

The elevator doors opened as the mailman finished depositing letters into the bank of boxes.

"Hello, Tim!" Angie cried, tugging her neighbor along beside her. "Wait a sec. I'd like you to meet Samantha McGregor. Samantha, Timothy Collins." Angie beamed from one to the other. "Timothy is studying landscape design and Samantha is a master gardener. Since you're both single"—she gave a pointed *ahem*—"I thought I should introduce you two."

As she smiled, they spoke pleasantries to each other,

including a little botanical shoptalk. Almost immediately, though, Timothy caught Angie's eye. "I don't want to mislead anyone here," he said, "but the fact of the matter is, I'm gay."

"In that case," Angie said, not missing a beat, "I should introduce you to Frank up on six. He works for the city's Recreation and Park Department."

Connie kept one eye firmly fixed on the door to her shop, wondering if Max would show up, and then wondering why she cared. She'd scarcely slept last night after his nervousness at Lake Merced and his frightening words about some woman possibly wanting to shoot him. Or her. It was as if she'd found herself part of the cast of some horror movie. Zombies at Lake Merced or something. What was with him?

In the light of day, however, she decided he was just being melodramatic. No one was after her, and if Max was in trouble with a woman, that was *his* problem. The less she heard from him, the better off she'd be.

Still, she had to admit, two nights ago at her house, and even yesterday, during dinner, before it had all catapulted into the Twilight Zone, she'd enjoyed his company more than any man she'd met in a long, long time. He was, of all things, a good listener. Sometimes, just having someone listen with no criticism and no advice was of more benefit than all the well-intentioned suggestions in the world.

Curiosity caused her to call another stockbroker. To her amazement, Geostar Biotechnologies was now selling at six dollars a share, a three-hundred-percent increase over the last report.

If she'd put two hundred dollars into Max's recommendation two days earlier, she'd have six hundred now. As she contemplated how many porcelain figurines she'd have to sell to make four hundred dollars, she felt a little queasy.

How could he have known the stock would soar that way?

Helen Melinger stuck her head in the door. "I'm closing up early today. Got a crick in my shoulder, can't get nothing done. If anyone comes by upset, just tell them to keep their shirt on, and I'll be back tomorrow." She looked from one end of the shop to the other.

"What are you looking for?" Connie asked.

"Want to make sure Angie's not here with any more male friends. The last one should have been pinned like a bug on a display board."

Connie grinned. "Stan's not really so bad."

"Not if you like someone with the personality of kitty litter. Anyway, I noticed your sister hanging around," Helen added. "That must be nice for you."

Thoughts of Tiffany rocked Connie. "What are you saying? My sister is dead."

"I'm so sorry!" Helen looked abashed. "She looks so much like you, I'd assumed . . . a cousin, maybe?"

"I don't have any cousins, either."

"Hmm. Well, whoever she was, she looks enough like you to have fooled me. Like I said, I'm out of here. Stay cool."

"So long, Helen."

The door chimed throughout the day as more customers than she'd seen in ages came in. But Max wasn't one of them.

Paavo couldn't take much more of this.

Angie varied the time of what was becoming her daily food contribution to the SFPD Homicide Division. Today, it was afternoon—around break time.

Now, as he and Yosh returned to Homicide from testifying in court, the bureau was empty. On the desk at the front of the room stood an open pastry box and a cake box.

Both had been picked clean. Yosh scoured each one, as if hoping a piece of napoleon had been stuck under the lid or in the folds. No such luck.

Paavo looked around for Lt. Hollins and was relieved when he didn't see him. He quickly broke down the boxes, making them as small as he could and stuffing them into a wastebasket. If Hollins hadn't spotted them, maybe no harm done. Or, less harm.

While Yosh made a fresh pot of coffee, Paavo returned to his desk. On it was a thin slice of Italian rum cake. He pushed it aside as he picked up a message from the Robbery detail.

The counterfeit autographed sporting goods they'd found matched items Robbery had gotten complaints about from people who'd been scammed. They'd been able to lift some prints off the boxes and would soon go after whoever was behind it.

"Good news," Paavo said, giving a quick rundown as Yosh headed for his own desk. He realized that not only was Yosh paying little attention, but that his head had bobbed from his desk to Paavo's at least three times. No Italian rum cake graced his desk.

Yosh, who loved sweets more than anyone he knew—except maybe Angie's neighbor Stan—looked so crestfallen Paavo wouldn't have been surprised to see tears start to roll down the big man's cheeks. "You take it, Yosh," he said, handing Yosh a plastic fork and the cake, which had been placed on a napkin.

"No, Paav," Yosh said with forced dignity, raising

his hands so Paavo couldn't hand him the cake. "It's your engagement. She sent the cake to you. Gee, I wonder what else she sent."

"I'm too full to eat any cake now." Paavo placed the slice down on Yosh's desk. "It's got cream; it won't keep. Enjoy it."

"You sure?" Yosh asked, his eyes bright.

"Positive."

Paavo was relieved of any more argument when a call came in. A young woman had been killed, her partially clad body found in a van in the basement garage of an office building on Sutter Street.

Earlier that day, Zakarian's, a jewelry shop in the building, had been robbed. No one knew yet what the connection was.

Connie hurried home from Everyone's Fancy, glad to be there. All afternoon she'd felt a strange nervousness in her stomach, a prickling on her neck, as if just waiting for something terrible to happen. A couple of times she thought someone was watching her. Thank God, no phantom stalker came in search of porcelain figurines or stuffed toys.

She locked the apartment door, checking the deadbolt to make sure it was strong and secure. Damn that Max Squire! He'd done this to her with his creepy ways. Why did she have to get involved with him, anyway?

At least she'd had the good sense not to let it go too far. A couple of times, she'd been tempted. But common sense had prevailed.

For dinner, she dished out a big bowl of Safeway's own cherry-vanilla ice cream. Too much common sense was no fun.

She curled up in front of the TV and watched

Friends, to which she paid scant attention, while scarfing down the ice cream with Oreo chasers, which she barely tasted.

Her mind wouldn't let go of Max. He was making her crazy. If she didn't watch out, she might become as insane as he was, then what would she do?

On an impulse, she went to the window and looked out. But there was nothing out there in the dark. She sighed and turned back to the couch.

That was when she realized that one of her best dolls, one with a hand-painted porcelain face and that was fairly old, from the 1940s or so, wasn't on the shelf near the front door. What had happened to it?

She remembered showing Max some of the oldest and most intricate of them, but she thought she'd put them all back where they belonged, or close to it. He couldn't possibly have—

A loud knock sounded at her door. That was strange, because normally she had to buzz people in.

Her heart pounded as she stepped slowly toward the door. "Yes?" she called, praying the deadbolt was as secure as she believed.

"Connie? Open up. It's me—Mrs. Rosinsky."

She recognized her landlady's voice and, relieved, unlocked the door.

Her landlady huddled off to one side, and two uniformed policemen stood in front of her. "Connie Rogers?" one asked, to her surprise.

Surprise immediately turned to fear as thoughts of all the horrible things that could possibly have happened to someone she was close to assailed her. Her mouth dry, she said, "Yes."

"You have the right to remain silent . . ."

Chapter 18

Angie raced along beside Paavo as they entered City Jail, Connie's panic-stricken phone call still playing in her mind. The jail shared a parking lot with the Hall of Justice, whose back door was near the jail's front entrance. "I just hope my father's attorney has already been able to bail Connie out," Angie said, huffing a little as she kept pace with Paavo's long-legged strides. "What in the world is going on?"

"We'll know soon enough." Paavo showed his ID to get past the night guard, then they rode the elevator up to the jails. He quickly located the clerk for the night magistrate.

"She's here," the clerk said, checking his logs. "In fact, if you hurry, you'll catch her in a lineup in 7-C."

"A lineup!" Angie glared at Paavo as if it were his fault. "What are they trying to do to her? Let's get her out of here."

"I'll run down the arresting officer. We'll know more in a while." He'd been in the field with Yosh investigating the murder of twenty-four-year-old Janet Clark, who had worked for Couriers Unlimited, when the message had come in that Angie needed to talk to him immediately. He left Yosh on the scene to help Angie find out exactly why Connie had been arrested. Angie's version from Connie was muddled, to put it mildly.

"I want to see this lineup." Angie whirled on the clerk. "Which way is 7-C?"

He pointed toward the right, down a long hall.

"Angie, why don't you wait here?" Paavo suggested, ushering her toward one of the benches lining the hallway.

"No!" She dug her heels in. "Connie's my friend and I want to know why the police arrested her. It just doesn't make sense."

Paavo led her close to the room where the lineup was being held and found her a seat, explaining that she couldn't go inside. He could, and would let her know all about it.

She didn't like it, but there was nothing she could do.

Paavo had turned to enter 7-C when Robbery Inspector Vic Walters stepped out. He looked at Paavo, and a smug expression crossed his face. "Hey, you Homicide boys are fast. Guess you heard we might have solved your case for you."

That wasn't what Paavo was expecting. "My case? What do you mean?"

"The courier. Hold on a minute." Walters began to make a call on his cell phone.

A sick feeling gripped Paavo at Walters's words. A thought struck him, but it was impossible. "I'm going into the lineup," he said.

"It's ended. Just a sec." Walters quietly said a few words into the phone. As he spoke, they stepped aside as a man in his sixties or so, with a thick gauze bandage on one side of his head, was led out of the lineup room, accompanied by a robbery inspector and a uniformed cop. As soon as the door opened, Angie was on her feet in search of Connie, trying to see around the men leaving the room.

"That old guy isn't Isaac Zakarian, is he?" Paavo asked.

"He sure is."

His impossible idea was beginning to look more probable. "And the lineup was for him to identify the woman who stole his diamonds?"

"You Homicide boys sure are smart," Vic said.

"What makes you think the woman you arrested is the right one?"

Vic pushed back the sides of his jacket and put his hands on his hips, his chest puffed up like a peacock's. "Other than the fact that Zakarian made a positive ID right now, you mean? She killed the courier, dressed up in the courier's clothes, and stole half a million worth of diamonds."

"Impossible!" came a furious shout behind them. "Connie's no murderer!"

They spun around as Angie stormed toward them. "She's no thief, either! Anyone with half a brain can see that! What's wrong with you?"

Vic raised his eyebrows at the angry woman. "This must be your fiancée," he said. "I've heard a lot about her."

"Yes. Angie, this is Vic Walters, Robbery. Vic, meet Angie." As the two shook hands, Paavo couldn't help but think how incongruous it was to be introducing Angie to a peer as his fiancée, while her best friend was being charged not only with a robbery she didn't commit, but possibly of a murder he was investigating.

"Connie Rogers is my dearest friend," Angie explained to Walters, visibly trying to calm herself. "This has got to be some horrible mistake!"

"I'm sorry." Vic's expression said he'd heard that one before. "But if the lineup confirms our case . . ."

"Angie's right," Paavo said coldly. "Connie doesn't have it in her to do any of this."

"There's a man involved," Vic said out of one side of his mouth, angling his shoulder to try to cut Angie out of the conversation. "You know how nutso some dames get around a guy. She might be one of them."

"No way!" Angie said, once again proving how sharp her hearing was. "Not my friend." She was so annoyed she was practically hopping.

"Who's the guy?" Paavo asked.

"The jeweler called it. Six-one or -two, a hundred eighty or so, sandy hair, longish, curly, said his eyes seemed 'dark,' but he was too faraway to see their color. His clothes apparently seemed pretty grubby— jeans and an old black overcoat."

Paavo turned to Angie. "Does Connie know anyone like that?"

She paled, and then shook her head. More subdued now, she slid closer to Paavo as if for protection. "Let's talk to Connie, see what she says."

Paavo's eyes narrowed, but he turned back to Vic. "How bad is it?"

"Looks cut and dried to me."

"You know how unreliable eyewitnesses are. Any evidence?"

"We're sending a team over to search her place right now for the diamonds. Half a mil worth."

"You have people going through Connie's things?" Angie shrieked. "And she's not even there to watch them? Paavo, you've got to stop them! What if they break something? Or steal it?"

"Angie, they're cops," Paavo said with a you've-just-gone-too-far warning tone to his voice.

"I don't care who they are! She has rights. Cops can't just go barging into her place and—"

"We got our search warrant approved when Zakarian ID'd her. That was the call I made," Vic explained.

"You did?" Angie quieted down considerably.

"How did you know to search her place?" Paavo asked.

"A phone tip. Anonymous, from a phone booth downtown, next to Union Square. They gave us the apartment to go to, said we'd find the robber, her lover, and the diamonds there. So far, we haven't found the stones or Casanova."

"So you've got nothing but some anonymous call and an old man who probably has a concussion," Paavo said. He didn't need to add what a good defense attorney would do with this.

"He was with the woman," Walters pointed out.

"And also scared to death."

"He doesn't seem like the type who'd say a thing and not mean it."

"You're talking five hundred thousand in diamonds. That can be pretty convincing."

Walters shrugged. "Maybe we've got something else, besides." With a Cheshire cat smile, he walked away.

Angie and Paavo went in search of the lawyer Angie had contacted after receiving Connie's desperate phone call. They found him talking with the Robbery inspectors. When he noticed Angie, his expression mirrored the grimness of Connie's situation.

Luciano Matteo had often worked for Angie's father and had known her from the time she was a little girl. He was a meticulous dresser, even at nearly eleven o'-clock at night, and his suit showed no wrinkles, his shoes were glossy, and his shirt fresh and starched. A fringe of black hair surrounded a bald crown, and he had a narrow Hitleresque mustache. As soon as he finished with the police, he held his arms out to her and they hugged. She introduced him to Paavo. "I'm so sorry this is happening to such a nice young lady as your friend," Matteo said.

"Can you get her out of here?" Angie asked, worried. She read the answer on his face and her stomach sank.

"There will be an arraignment soon, but until then, there's no bail. I'm frankly out of my league here. I do corporate and family law—civil cases—people suing each other, that kind of thing. She needs a good criminal lawyer. I have some people I can recommend."

"This case isn't going to be over quickly, then?" Angie asked.

He shook his head sadly. "Not without a break. Let's go see Connie. She'll be happy you're here."

Angie waited while Matteo and Paavo signed her in with them to the attorney's visiting room. Connie had already been made to change into an oversized prisoner's orange jumpsuit and paper slippers. With no makeup, she looked pale, confused, and frightened. When she saw Angie, she flew into her arms with a sob. Angie's eyes teared up as well.

"I don't understand any of this," Connie said as they hugged. After a moment, she backed away and turned to Mr. Matteo. "Can I go home yet?"

His gaze was gentle. "The jeweler said you robbed him."

Angie was holding her hand, and Connie nearly crushed her fingers at this news. "How can he do that? I was at work!" she searched their faces, bewildered. Tears spilled down her cheeks.

"Let's all sit down," Matteo said, "and discuss this calmly."

Except for a wooden table and four chairs, the beige-colored room was bare. Wired glass faced the hallway, allowing the guard to view everything that happened inside.

"Since she's got to spend the night here," Paavo said, "you need to request that she be put in the ASU."

Matteo nodded. "Right. I do know about that, at least."

"ASU?" Angie asked.

"Administrative Segregation Unit. Isolation. It's not great, but it'll keep her away from the general population. It's for her protection."

Connie and Angie both blanched and scooted closer together.

At the lawyer's tacit consent, Paavo asked Connie, "Do you have proof you were working yesterday afternoon between one and three P.M.?"

"Yesterday? Today I had a lot of customers, but yesterday . . . The store was open. I was in it," Connie said helplessly.

"Did anyone see you there? Any customers who could testify for you, if necessary."

"What about later? Around six o'clock, does that help?"

Paavo shook his head.

She thought a moment. "Anyone walking by could have seen the OPEN sign on the door."

"What about Helen Melinger?" Angie asked. "Did you have the door open? Did you talk to her?"

"Actually, the door was shut. The heating system isn't working well, and I was freezing."

"Connie, how many times have I told you that you need to make your shop inviting for people to walk into?" Angie cried.

Connie looked at her as if she'd lost her mind. "And

find me sitting there blue with my teeth chattering? I don't think so!"

"Now isn't the time for this," Paavo interrupted. "What about the phone? Did you make any phone calls?"

Connie nervously flexed her fingers. "Between one and three? I doubt it."

"E-mails?" he asked.

"I don't have a computer in the store."

"How can you run a business without a computer to help with inventory?" Angie put her hands to her head in frustration.

"People have been doing inventory for centuries without them, and so do I!" Connie was growing more hysterical with each question she couldn't answer. "Anyway, what good would a computerized inventory do now?"

Angie rolled her eyes. Paavo frowned at her to keep quiet.

"What about this fellow who was supposed to be with you in this?" Mr. Matteo asked.

"Why do they keep asking me about—" Connie abruptly shut her mouth.

"About who?" Paavo asked.

Connie faced Angie, her eyes wide. Angie faintly shook her head. "No one," Connie said.

"Do you know what's going on, Angie?" Paavo asked, his jaw tight.

Angie stared at Connie, desperate for her to say something. She didn't. Angie glanced at Paavo. "How could I know?"

He faced the attorney. "Miss Amalfi seems to have lapses of memory at times."

"Yes." Matteo stroked his mustache. "It runs in the family, I'm sorry to say."

"You need to think twice before protecting anyone, Connie," Paavo warned, "because in the course of the robbery, the female courier was killed."

"Killed? You mean I could be up for murder?" Connie's voice rose so high she could have broken the sound barrier. She looked ready to pass out. Angie jumped up and pushed Connie so that she was bending forward, her head between her legs.

"I didn't tell my client that part of the proceedings yet." Matteo sighed. "She was already so upset, I didn't think it would help matters any if she fainted."

Paavo was not so sympathetic. Both Connie and Angie were hiding something. They had to know how serious this was. "She had to find out sometime."

"I suppose she did," Matteo responded, eying Paavo with new respect.

At this point, Connie was crying harder than ever, and Angie burst into tears with her. The two men escaped.

Once outside, they stood in the hallway in mutual sympathy. The nature of the charges against Connie Rogers meant that if she were convicted, she'd spend the rest of her life in jail. The only thing Paavo was sure of was that she was innocent. Angie wasn't wrong there.

"There's nothing we can do tonight," Paavo said. "I'll talk to the DA first thing in the morning."

"Then?" Matteo asked with some professional curiosity.

Paavo looked at the closed door of the waiting room. "Then, I'm going to take apart the case point by point, and find out who really stole the diamonds and killed the courier."

Chapter 19

The San Francisco District Attorney's office was located on the third floor of the Hall of Justice, right below Homicide. The DA had a walnut-furnished office to the right of the reception area, and the assistant DAs—the ones who handled ninety-nine percent of the casework—were in a cubicle-lined room to the left.

The Zakarian robbery and Janet Clark murder case had been assigned to Assistant DA Hanover Judd.

Paavo had worked with Judd on many occasions and knew him to be a hard-nosed by-the-book guy. File folders, message slips, briefs, and a half-eaten bagel with cream cheese cluttered his desktop. After shared greetings, Paavo said, "I'm here to talk to you about Connie Rogers."

Judd offered a chair. He didn't answer right away. Handsome, ambitious, and in his early thirties, a few years out of Hastings Law School, he was cautious to a fault, seeing the DA's office as his most promising route to a political career. "We'll be pressing charges for the Zakarian robbery. I assume you'd like to add in the murder of the young courier as well. You weren't thinking special circumstances, were you? To go after a woman with the death penalty—"

"I'm asking that you take a little time before you indict her on anything," Paavo said. Judd put his pen down on the desk and regarded Paavo as if he'd lost his mind. "I know Connie Rogers. I have no idea, yet, what's going on here, but there's no way she could have been involved."

Judd tapped his fingers and Paavo noted his suspicious look. "Sounds like some guy took part as well," Judd offered. "Maybe he masterminded it and she just went along. An accessory to murder, though, is equally guilty."

"Did Robbery find any diamonds in her apartment?" Paavo asked.

Judd's face closed, but meeting Paavo's direct look, he relented. "No. But she could easily have stashed them somewhere else. Or the guy got to them before we did."

"The jeweler's identification was weak," Paavo added. He was only guessing, but based on past experience, it was true in about two-thirds of the cases. "He 'thought' she looked a lot like the robber, but he couldn't say positively, right?" When Judd didn't protest, he added, "Something about her face bothered him."

Judd didn't deny it. They were both old hands at this, and there was little need for subterfuge or mind games. "What do you expect? Zakarian has a slight concussion from where she clobbered him. Plus he was under stress. And his vision isn't great."

The identification sounded even weaker than Paavo had imagined. He pressed his point. "Connie Rogers is as clean as they come. She's never been involved in any crime. Probably not even a traffic ticket. I'll bet she doesn't even fudge on her tax return. You're saying that someone like that committed murder and robbery?" Since Judd didn't stop him, he pulled out the big gun. "Someone whose own sister was murdered, by the way. Tiffany Rogers. You remember the case. It involved our very own former district attorney, Lloyd Fletcher." Paavo watched the ADA's face turn gray.

"She's that sister?" Judd's voice cracked. He remembered the case. He should. It had rocked City Hall and San Francisco politics for months.

"That's right. It has no bearing on this case one way or the other, except for me to tell you that Connie is a law-abiding citizen. She certainly wouldn't stand around and let some boyfriend kill an innocent woman."

"There's the phone call—"

"Called in anonymously. How much can you rely on it? A good lawyer could say it'd been called in to throw off a bunch of cops too eager to close a case."

"But if so, he'd have to answer why Connie Rogers?" Judd mused. "There's got to be something going on there. Her name wouldn't have come out of a hat."

"She looks like the real robber, obviously."

"Hmm. Next thing I know you'll tell me the robber is a third sister. Or maybe Tiffany, come back from the dead. Look, Robbery had enough on her to bring her in."

"I don't know what the connection is," Paavo said. "I'm working on it. The courier's death is my case. I'll find out who killed her, but I don't want my investigation stalled or the whole case going off on the wrong track if you indict Rogers and only later learn it was a mistake. I'm here to stop you from ending up with egg on your face."

Judd smirked. "Nice guy, aren't you?"

"We're on the same side in this."

"I know. Hell. Let me think about it."

Paavo wanted Connie out of jail. She was separated from the other prisoners, but ASU was no suite. The walls were padded, the toilet a hole in the floor, and the bed a block of concrete with a mattress on it. Instead of bars, the door was heavy steel with a peephole and a slot for food on the bottom. "She's not a threat to run, Judd. Let her go. She's innocent."

Judd's secretary buzzed him, and he picked up the phone. "It's Robbery with some new information," he explained to Paavo. "I'd better take it."

Paavo waited, listening to Judd's "yeses" and "I sees." Finally Judd hung up and cast a stony glare at Paavo.

"Well, well." He rocked back in his chair, one foot up on the edge of his desk. "Robbery just got the security tapes from the Sutter Street garage. The tapes that Homicide had taken and were holding in connection with the courier's murder."

Paavo just stared at him.

He dropped his foot and jumped to his feet. "Damn it, Paavo! How could you come here and plead for Rogers's innocence when you saw those tapes? You know they show Connie Rogers leading the jeweler away at gunpoint."

"Paavo will get you out of here," Angie said tearfully.

She sat at the visitor's chair on one side of a glass partition with Connie on the other, a small mouthpiece embedded in it for them to converse. This was much worse than the lawyer's meeting room, which had been fairly decent and in which Connie could freely move around. Here, armed guards watched them, and

Connie, her sweet friend who could never hurt anything, had been brought in wearing shackles.

"I hope so," Connie said. Glassy-eyed, she appeared numb with shock.

"He's at the district attorney's office right now. It should be only a couple of hours." Angie prayed her words would be prophetic.

Connie nodded glumly. She seemed to have aged ten years overnight. The jumpsuit hung from her shoulders as if she were no heavier than a scarecrow. "He believes I'm innocent, doesn't he? He looks so hard sometimes."

"He knows you. He gets that stone face when on the job. Don't worry. We're going to find out who's behind this. That's the best way to clear your name."

"If anyone can, it's you," Connie whispered.

"Connie, I need you to be honest with me. From the description of the man involved, he sounds like Max Squire," Angie said sternly. "I want to know what this is about. Who is he and what's going on between you two?"

Connie slumped in the chair, as if she could scarcely hold her head up. "There's nothing going on, not really. I thought he was a nice guy. Troubled. Interesting. What can I say?"

"You can say he's no good for you! You can tell Paavo about him!" Angie waved her arms in frustration. The guard noticed and stepped closer. "It's okay. I'm Italian." She smiled demurely, then quickly sat on her hands. The guard didn't smile back.

"Do you think he pulled this robbery?" Angie continued.

"I'm sure he didn't," Connie said.

"Why?"

"I know him, that's why!" Connie cried.

Angie lowered her voice. "Then tell me who he is. Why is he hiding? Why doesn't he have a job?"

Connie thought a moment, then told Angie everything she knew about Max, including the money he took from her and his reaction to the gunshot near Lake Merced just hours after the robbery and murder took place.

Angie couldn't believe what she was hearing. "He stole from you when you tried to help him, and later you saw him, scared and nervous, just hours after someone had been murdered, and you still don't believe he was involved?"

"He's hiding something, yes, but I don't think he committed those crimes," Connie said, not sounding wholly convinced herself.

Angie sighed in exasperation. "The jeweler who was robbed identified Max as an accomplice of the woman who looked like you," she repeated, and then firmly stated, "You've *got* to answer Paavo's questions about Max."

Connie pressed her hands to her temples. "I'm so confused. None of this makes sense. He seemed troubled, as I said, but honest. A good man."

"You could be wrong about him, Connie," Angie urged.

Connie nodded, even more dejected. "Okay, I'll tell Paavo whatever he wants to know. But I still think Max is innocent."

The guard moved closer. Visiting time was over.

When Paavo stepped off the elevator on the fourth floor of the Hall of Justice, Angie stood in the hallway waiting for him. She looked worried and scared and terribly sad. "There you are!" she cried. No kiss, no flowers, no café lattes or French pastry. He almost wished them back.

She rushed toward him. "Where have you been? Can we get Connie out of here yet? I can't bear the thought of her having to spend another minute in that jail! It's so horrible, Paavo! I feel so bad for her."

"Calm down." He put his arm around her and drew her into the elevator. No sense taking her into Homicide with him. Not with the mood Lt. Hollins was in. "I was just talking to the ADA. He's not willing to let her go yet."

"But he's going to, right?"

"Eventually. Because she's innocent."

They left City Hall and went to her Mercedes.

"He doesn't believe it's simply mistaken identity? That Connie and the robber look a lot alike?"

"Not yet."

"What can we do?" Angie stopped walking.

"One thing you can do is tell me who the man is that's supposedly involved. I hope your memory's improved over last night."

Angie was taken aback by his harshness, then realized he was right. She nodded. "I talked to her. She's ready to answer your questions, but she insists he's as innocent as she is."

He took her keys to unlock the car, then held open the door. "I'll go see her. I'm doing what I can, Angie. Just go home and don't worry. We'll get her out. I'll call you as soon as there's a break in the case."

He kissed her hard and walked away.

Angie wasn't about to go home and bake cookies when her friend was in jail. She drove to Wings. Earl stood by the entry stand. "Earl, I've got to find Dennis's friend Max. Do you have any idea—"

Earl pointed toward a far corner. Max sat at a table

with piles of paper around him. "He's doin' our books. Tax time. Butch said he's good at dat stuff."

"Thanks." She marched past Earl and got in Squire's face. "All right, mister. You tell me what's going on, and I mean now."

He stood. "Now? I don't . . ."

"Connie's been arrested," she shrieked.

He sank back into the chair. "Arrested? For what?"

"Murder . . . and robbery."

He looked dumbfounded. "Is this a joke?"

"I wish! She supposedly killed a female courier and then robbed a jewelry wholesaler, a little old man. She nearly killed him—she hit him on the head so hard she caused a concussion."

"She . . . oh, my God!" He said nothing for a moment, then asked, "Why do they think Connie did it?"

Angie told him about the wholesaler's identification.

"Don't they realize there can be other women who look like that?"

"Who?" Angie asked, eying him closely.

"Well . . . anyone."

"No," Angie said. "You're thinking of someone in particular, aren't you?"

"I was just speaking in generalities," he replied quickly.

"The jeweler said Connie had an accomplice—a man who fits your description exactly. Now, frankly, I don't think you'd be here shuffling papers if you'd just stolen a half million dollars in diamonds, but the police might not be so rational. Tell me what you know, work with me on freeing Connie, or I swear, I'll call them and tell them you're here."

"An accomplice? Ah . . . now I see. It makes sense." He was ashen, his hands shaking as he rubbed his chin, deep in thought.

"See what? What do you mean?" Angie was so frustrated she could have clubbed him with the receivables register.

"Give me time, Angie. I know who did it. I'll get Connie out of there."

Angie was shocked. "You know? You were involved?"

"No, not me." He shook his head.

"Why should I believe you?" she cried.

"Good question." He slammed down his pencil and rushed out the door, leaving Angie gaping.

She spun toward Earl. "Have you ever talked to Butch about his nephew's friend?" Angie asked. "Did Dennis ever tell Butch why Max is so strange?"

"Butch don't talk to me," Earl answered.

"What about Vinnie?"

"Vinnie had to go down to Chin . . . I mean, to da bank. Nobody knows nothin'."

Another stall job, and she wasn't about to put up with it. "Well, Butch will talk to me." She headed toward the kitchen.

"Stop! Miss Angie, you can't go in dere!" Earl's stubby legs pumped fast as he ran to the swinging double doors that led to the kitchen and hurled himself, arms stretched out wide, in front of them.

"Why?"

"Uh . . . da Board of Health says we can't let nobody in but da cook and da waiter."

"I've been in a number of restaurant kitchens. Besides, who taught Butch how to cook half the items on the menu?"

"I know, an' we 'preciate you. But you still can't go in dere. Anyway, you're a customer!"

"Not now. Now I'm a consultant. Dennis has asked for my help, you may recall. I suggest you let me in there, or I'll help him expand this place to the size of Candlestick Park!"

He dropped his voice to a whisper. "I'll tell you da trut'. Dere's a problem."

"Do tell!"

"We got a couple cockroaches, and Butch put powder all around to kill 'em. He don't want nobody to see what's going on. Not even you. I'm sorry."

She put her hand to her throat. "Cockroaches? In the kitchen?"

"Shhh! He just saw a couple, so he's acting real fast. He's standin' dere wit' a can of Raid, and if he sees one, he shoots it. Bam! We don't want 'em to tell deir buddies to come over. An' you don't wanna see dem layin' on deir backs, wigglin' deir little legs in da air, an' strugglin' with deir last breaths."

Her mouth curled in disgust. "This is the truth?"

"Miss Angie, would I lie?"

"Then ask Butch to come out here and talk to me. It's about Connie. She's been arrested, and I've got to help get her out."

"Miss Connie? Arrested? Wait here."

He was back in a minute. "Butch is gone. He put all da pots on simmer and took off."

Chapter 20

Paavo lived in a bungalow in San Francisco's Richmond district, a neighborhood of small middle-class homes, not too far from Ocean Beach, but without the ocean view that would have raised the prices of the homes even higher than inflation and lack of expansion space in San Francisco had already done.

Paavo had bought his house some years earlier, when the economy took a slight dip, and he could afford it. It was also affordable because it consisted of only three rooms and one bathroom, needed work—much of which he did on his own—and didn't have a garage, which wasn't too bad, since neither rain nor snow nor sleet nor hail could do any more damage to his Austin Healey than old age had already done to it. Nevertheless, he loved the house. So did Angie.

To an extent.

Angie's biggest concern about their marriage was where they were going to live. She wouldn't be able to fit her clothes into Paavo's place, let alone anything else she owned.

They had time; they'd work it out . . . somehow. He had a good-sized backyard. The house could always be expanded into it. Or, have an entire second floor added. Or possibly raise it to fit in a garage and basement room or two. Or do all three.

Angie sat and watched while he chopped and stirred and seasoned. She offered suggestions when he wasn't sure about the instruction in the recipe. It was hard to concentrate on food, though, when Connie was still in jail.

Paavo was cooking a Finnish dish for her called Karelian Hot Pot. It was a simple stew made with equal parts chuck steak, pork shoulder, and stewing lamb, onions, salt, and allspice. Since discovering that he actually was part Finnish, Paavo had been learning all he could about his heritage. Aulis Kokkonen, the man who'd raised him and whom he regarded as his father even though Aulis wasn't a blood relation, told many stories about Finland, Finnish history and legends. Paavo now wished he'd paid more attention to those stories as a boy instead of doing the usual kid's stunt of tuning him out, thinking Aulis was dull and that Finland was "totally uncool."

Paavo was a good cook in that he could follow a recipe with the diligence of Jonas Salk developing the polio vaccine. Angie didn't tell him that the recipe he struggled with was about as simple as any she'd ever seen. Since he was preparing the main course, she volunteered to make a Caesar salad and a Finnish dessert. After much searching, she found one, a kind of cheesecake that was more spicy than sweet—the manly dessert, according to Connie's ex. The crust was made with dry breadcrumbs and butter, and the custard in the center was a mixture of flour, cottage cheese, and eggs, seasoned with brown sugar, cinnamon, cardamom, ginger, butter, and orange and lemon rind.

She made the cake while Paavo worked on his stew.

As he cooked, he began talking about Connie's situation. Hearing her friend referred to as a "case" infuriated her. Hot tears of anger and frustration that the system she believed in could be making such a horrible mistake sprang to her eyes, and it took all her willpower to compose herself again.

He told her that surveillance cameras had shown the courier being hit by a figure wearing gloves and a black sweatshirt with a hood. It could have been a man or a woman. She was dragged into the van where the police later found her.

A bit later, a woman wearing the courier's uniform—who, in fact, did look a lot like Connie—left the van for the elevator bank. She kept her face averted so that none of the pictures were terribly clear, and none straight on. A minute later, two men, one thin, the other fat, got out of the van. Both wore gloves and hooded sweatshirts and kept their faces down.

Suddenly, the Connie look-alike reappeared, pushing a scared, panting Isaac Zakarian to his car. He drove away in obvious panic.

The van had been stolen that very day. It was a maze of fingerprints, but the only ones they could identify belonged to the owner and the dead courier.

Finally, Paavo placed the Karelian casserole in the oven. His work done, he put his arms around Angie, studying her face and the unshed tears he saw there. "Relax, Angel. We'll get her out. She's innocent. There's no way they could prove otherwise."

She shut her eyes and leaned into him. As much as she wanted to enjoy the comfort he offered, all she could think about was the fear and loneliness Connie was enduring at that same moment.

* * *

Veronica walked toward Wings of an Angel. She was feeling good. Connie Rogers hadn't shown up at work that day. A little birdie told Veronica why. Now, all she had to do was get the police off their fat asses to arrest Max. If he was at Wings, she'd call them now; if not, she'd watch the homeless shelter where he'd been staying. They could pick him up there.

Footsteps were fast approaching. She turned but saw no one behind her. Odd.

She kept going, suddenly irritated when she thought of the stupid cops who hadn't managed to pick up Fernandez or Julius. Robbers and murderers at the scene of the crime—and they just let them walk away. What idiots!

Now, she had those two losers to worry about. But she could handle them. No problem.

She heard the footsteps again. Stepping into a doorway, she reached into her purse and clutched her gun. The street was empty.

Nerves. That's all it was. Maybe because of El Toro, or one of the others . . . out there . . . looking for her.

Or maybe because of the courier. When she'd put the woman's uniform on, it was still warm from her body. She hadn't known Julius would kill her like that. Tying her up should have been enough . . .

She shook away the image and proceeded down the block. Some cars went by, but no other pedestrians were near. This wasn't a touristy area, but usually someone was out walking.

She concentrated on her situation. Dennis was the one who bothered her. She had to come up with a way to—

From the corner of her eye she saw a hand reach for

her. She spun around fast, and he ended up with only the strap of her shoulder bag.

"You!" she yelled, jerking on it. He didn't let go and the bag flipped over, the clasp opening and the contents falling to the sidewalk.

She fell to her knees and lunged, but he was faster. In one quick movement, he picked up the Smith and Wesson and pointed it at her.

Drawing herself to her feet, she saw the cold, icy fury in his eyes. "You can't be serious," she said. She glanced from side to side, thinking that he would back off if she could get someone to notice them, but the streets were empty. Even the cars seemed to have vanished. Her heart pounded, and her throat went dry. "Put it down!"

He slowly neared, and she backed up, scared now. "Hey, let's talk about it, okay?" She tried to modulate her voice, make it low and husky, the way he liked it. "I know you're disappointed. In me. Us. We can fix that."

She looked around, searching for some means of escape. Behind her was an alley and what looked like an open door at the bottom of a flight of stairs. She needed to get down there, shut the door, and lock it. She could do it.

"Talk to me," she said. "We were always able to talk." As she began stepping backward, he followed.

He was blinking fast, and tears filled his eyes. A cold certainly descended on her. He was going to kill her. "You wouldn't do this to me. Not to me," she whispered.

Her hand touched the railing that ran along the steps to the basement door. She grabbed it and spun around, starting to run.

He fired, and fired again, even after she fell.

* * *

The phone rang in the darkened bedroom. Angie un-
wrapped her arms from Paavo's chest and rolled to
one side as he sat up. "Hello."

He glanced at Angie. "It's okay, Rebecca. What's up?"

Angie raked her fingers through her hair and fluffed
it as she listened. Why was the homicide inspector
calling Paavo?

Whatever it was, the shocked look on Paavo's face
made Angie's blood run cold. Quietly he hung up the
phone.

"What is it?" she asked, imagining the worst.

"Probably just a false alarm, but I've got to go." He
got out of bed and stepped into briefs—Angie once
gave him black silk Tommy Hilfigers, but he was a
white cotton Hanes man and nothing else—and then
his trousers. "If all goes well, I'll be back in an hour. If
not, I'll give you a call."

"You have to go?"

"Yes." He shrugged on a shirt.

"But what about the dinner you worked so hard to
prepare?" Angie protested.

He picked up his shoes and socks, padded out to the
kitchen, and faced the stove. "How do you put this
thing on pause?"

Paavo hurried into the morgue on the bottom floor of
the Hall of Justice. He didn't want to tell Angie why
he'd been called here until he was certain about the information Rebecca had given him.

He knew Connie's lawyer had been working on getting her bail since receiving the bad news after his talk
with Judd. That was why the story might be true. And
that was why a part of him believed Rebecca when she
called to tell him the victim of a shooting—the dead

woman with no identification on her—was Connie Rogers.

He could have just called the jail, gone through a lengthy rigamarole, and found out if Connie was still there. But he didn't want Angie asking questions. Also, if the victim wasn't Connie, he wanted to see her for himself. Something about a spate of Connie clones in the city just didn't sit well.

If his worst fear was true, however, he'd return to Angie immediately. He didn't want her to hear it on the news or to be alone at such a time.

Rebecca saw him and waved him over. "Thanks for coming by. I hope I'm wrong, but you need to see this."

He nodded.

"She was still alive but unconscious when the cops found her. The paramedics reached her, but she died on the way to the hospital, so they came here. She'd been shot in the back and shoulder."

The body lay on a gurney awaiting autopsy, covered by a plastic sheet.

As Rebecca glanced at Paavo, she gripped the edge of the sheet, and slowly, carefully slid it back.

Paavo's heart nearly stopped when he saw the short, blond hair. "Good God!"

The face was slack and colorless in death. "I see I was right in calling you," Rebecca said. "Is she Angie's friend?"

He looked at the jawline, the shape of the brow, and let out the breath he'd been holding. The victim wasn't Connie, but someone who bore an unsettling resemblance to her. "It's not her."

"Thank God!" Rebecca answered, also sighing in relief. "We've got her prints. If they're on record, we should have a match soon."

The woman's clothes were askew, some blood was

on her fingers, and her knees were scraped. "Any evidence?" he asked.

"Nothing much. The CSI has already bagged what they could. The only strange thing was in her hand. It might be a factor, though it could be just trash found on the street, and she clawed at it just by chance."

"What was it?" Paavo asked.

"A matchbook. It was from a restaurant I've never heard of."

"Do you remember the name?"

"Sure. A weird name for a restaurant, frankly. Bill Sutter said it reminded him of an old, old song about prisoners wanting to escape. I don't know if you've ever heard it. It went something like, 'If I had the wings of an angel, over these prison walls I would fly.'"

Paavo nearly choked. "Yes, it is familiar to me."

Chapter 21

When Paavo returned to Homicide in the morning, the fingerprint identification Rebecca had requested on the murder victim had come in. Rebecca placed a photocopy on his desk as well as her preliminary homicide report on the victim and the victim's prior file. Paavo turned to the prior file first.

Veronica Maple. Ex-con.

He studied the mug shot taken three years ago when she was arrested. An attractive woman despite her hard, cynical smirk, with features surprisingly similar to Connie's, except that her hair was longer and darker, and her eyes gray. He quickly read through her record. She'd been sent to prison on a three-year term because of embezzling from her boss, one Max Squire. She'd recently been released, on parole, from the Women's Correctional Facility at Chowchilla.

On parole . . . he called over to Benson. "Where's Calderon? Your partner has been making himself scarce around here lately."

Benson grinned. "Last I heard, he was going to lunch with that tall, skinny blonde Angie brought over here. She calls every hour on the hour to talk to him.

He's either fallen for her, or he's going to kill her."

Paavo cringed. Knowing Calderon, he had an idea which it was. Calderon was divorced. His wife had taken the kids and moved to New Mexico, saying she couldn't handle being married to a cop any longer. He was bitter about life and everything in it, but Paavo couldn't say that that bitterness had come about because of the divorce. He'd been bitter before the divorce; after, he'd turned completely toxic.

Paavo turned back to the reports on his desk and read Rebecca's findings. At times, handling a homicide investigation was like putting together the pieces of a jigsaw puzzle. This was one of them.

Maple's eyes were gray, but she wore blue contact lenses. Her natural hair color was a dark shade of blond, yet she'd dyed it light ash. Her resemblance to Connie Rogers, as far as he could tell, was no accident.

A woman who looked like Connie had robbed a jeweler. Was it this woman?

According to the jeweler, a man was also involved in the robbery—a man whose description fit Max Squire.

Connie had met Max Squire at Wings of an Angel. The victim was found with a Wings of an Angel matchbook in her hand when she died.

A parole officer had shown up in Homicide looking for a woman who'd skipped and allegedly killed a man in Fresno. The woman's name was Veronica Maple.

This puzzle was trickier than most.

Continuing with her file, he turned to her younger years. One of her cohorts back then was Sid Fernandez.

He knew about Fernandez from the Gang Task Force. They'd come to him a couple of years ago, hoping to find a way to pin a homicide on El Toro, since they'd so far failed to tie him to any drug dealings.

Fernandez was smart, though. He covered his tracks well.

Two of his underlings were picked up, one for robbery, another for murder, but there was no solid evidence linking them to Fernandez, and the men wouldn't talk. Paavo figured they both had families to protect.

Paavo also noticed that back in those early days with Fernandez, Maple sometimes stated she was married but separated, and other times said she was single. Nowhere in the file did she give her husband's name, if there ever was a husband.

Maple was her maiden name.

Strange. No one had questioned her on it; no husband had ever shown up.

He had to wonder if Veronica Maple was the true victim, or if someone had wanted to get Connie Rogers out of the way. If word went out that Maple was dead and Connie was the real target, her life would be in danger.

Whoever had shot her had probably run, but might also have hidden and watched as the paramedics picked her up. They would have seen she wasn't dead.

A strange cat-and-mouse game was going on. If the cat knew the mouse was dead, it would go away, but if it didn't and kept hunting . . .

Paavo walked into Wings of an Angel.

"Hello, Inspector," Earl said. "Can I get you somethin' to drink?"

"No thanks," Paavo said. "I'm here on business." He took out a photo, Veronica Maple's mug shot, and handed it to Earl. "Do you know this woman?"

Earl looked at it. "Who is she?" he asked, not meeting Paavo's eyes.

"I was hoping you could tell me something about

her. We were given information that she had some connection with this restaurant."

"I see." Earl swallowed hard and studied the photo
a little longer. "If you got da case, it don't mean she's
dead, does it?"

"Not everyone I investigate is the victim." Paavo
carefully chose his words.

Earl grew increasingly nervous and handed the
photo back. "I don't know her."

"I'd like to go back and talk to Butch and Vinnie,"
Paavo said.

"Wait, Inspector. You don't hafta do dat. Dey'll come
out an' see you."

"No need. It's just a couple of questions."

"You wait right dere!" Earl dashed away. Paavo
frowned and sat down to wait for Vinnie and Butch.
When he two men arrived, they didn't look pleased to
talk to him.

"I'm here about a case," he began. Although no customers were in the restaurant at the moment, he added
"If you'd rather go into the kitchen, or someplace more
private, that would be fine."

Vinnie glanced balefully at the other two. "Right
here is okay." The three eyed each other, then each
took a seat. Earl wiped a drop of perspiration from his
temple.

"Do you recognize this woman?" Paavo asked,
showing them the mug shot. "Her hair may be lighter
and shorter."

Butch was the first to back away, followed by Vinnie,
then Earl. "Is she dead?" Vinnie broke the team silence.

"We're investigating her," was as far as Paavo
would go.

"I already tol' him I never seen her," Earl said
quickly.

Vinnie scowled at him, then at Butch. "I've never seen her neither," he responded.

"Ditto," Butch added. "Why you askin' us, Inspector?"

"Something was found at a crime scene that might link her to this restaurant. We're trying to find out why."

"Sounds like a coincidence to me," Butch said, standing. "We don't serve no criminals here. An' if a dame what looks like her came in here, Earl would remember—right, Earl?"

"Sure," Earl said, also getting to his feet. "Sounds like one of dem coincidences, don't you t'ink, Vinnie?"

"Sure. It's a big coincidence. Nothin' else." Finally, Vinnie also stood. "If that's all you want, Inspector . . ."

He stopped talking as he watched Dennis stride into the restaurant.

"Hey, looks like the gang's all here!" Dennis chuckled and patted his uncle as he traded hellos.

"We ain't got nothin' for you today," Butch frowned. "You may as well go home. *Now!*"

"Go? I just got here. I'm hungry." Dennis said, then paid closer attention to the expressions of the three owners and Paavo. "What's wrong? You guys look like you lost your last friend."

"I'm trying to find out about a woman."

Dennis froze.

"Here's her picture," Paavo said.

He looked at it, his face drained of color. "Did . . . did something happen to her?"

"I'm just asking about her. Do you know her?"

Dennis's smile was sympathetic, but without any warmth or brightness now. "Can't help you, I'm afraid. Well, I, uh . . . I better be going," he said, backing up. "I didn't mean to intrude. I was just going to say hi to my uncle. In the neighborhood and all. Later. You'll be around, Butch?"

"Sure, kid. I'll be here for you."

Paavo didn't answer. He watched the vanished Dennis with cold speculation, then said good-bye to the three owners huddling nearby.

Dennis stood alongside his Jag, lighting a cigarette as Paavo left the restaurant. He walked with Paavo to the old Austin Healey Paavo drove when no city-issue car was available.

"What brought you to Wings looking for information about that woman?" Dennis asked. "My uncle and his friends aren't connected with anything, are they?"

"Just following up," Paavo said. "You had an interesting expression when you looked at the photo."

"Not every day I look at a mug shot. She a felon or something?" Dennis asked.

Paavo stared Pagozzi straight in the eye. "If you know anything about her, you should tell me."

Dennis toyed with his car keys, then grabbed them, as if making a decision. He faced Paavo. "Some years back, a guy I know had a girlfriend. She ended up doing time. Some kind of money scam. Embezzling, I think. I didn't really understand it."

"And?"

"And . . . I'm not sure." He studied Paavo a long moment. "It might be her. But that doesn't mean Max is involved. He's not that kind of guy."

"Max who?" Paavo asked innocently.

"Max Squire." Dennis looked at him curiously. "I thought you knew him. Angie and Connie both do."

"Is that so?" Paavo said, trying not to grit his teeth. "Tell me about this Squire."

"He's a good guy. Down on his luck right now, so I helped him out, got him some bookkeeping work with my uncle, a few free meals, that kind of thing. In fact, the woman in the picture—I think she was the one who ruined his career. Heck, ruined his whole life. If it's her, she's bad news. Real bad. I don't know why a guy like Max got involved with her."

"What does he look like?"

"Tall, medium build, I'd say. Dark blond hair, long—needs a cut bad, brown eyes." The description was getting too familiar.

"How did you know Max Squire?"

Dennis sighed heavily and gave Paavo a you-aren't-going-to-believe-this look. "He was my financial advisor."

Angie spent the day hovering near her telephone waiting for Paavo to tell her Connie was being released. When she heard a knock at her door, even though it was lighter than Paavo's usual hard rapping, she hoped it was him with good news.

Instead, she found Nona standing there with a glass bowl filled with chocolate-orange trifle. Nona was blinking back tears.

"What's wrong?" Angie asked.

Nona shoved the trifle at her. "You and your big ideas!"

They went into the living room, where Angie tried to calm her sometime friend down.

"It's bad enough that I once went to meet Luis for lunch—"

"Inspector Calderon?" Angie asked, stunned.

"That's right, and he showed up reeking of disinfectant and God-only-knows what from an autopsy room; then, when I thought we were going out on a hot date, we ended up at the morgue because he had to witness someone identifying a body, but today, when I worked so hard to make that dessert, he came by just long enough to say he couldn't stay because he had to go to question some people about an old woman found dead in her bathroom. She'd obviously died of natural causes. I mean, she was *old*!"

"That's the life of a homicide inspector," Angie said.

"His questions could have waited until after he ate dessert. I told him so—me or a meaningless investigation. And"—she sniffled—"he said, '*Hasta la vista*, Toots'? Can you imagine?"

Angie just shook her head.

"How could I have wasted my time with a man old enough to be my father—almost—with creaky knees, overly pomaded hair, a cranky personality . . . and who uses a word like 'Toots'? This is just too mortifying."

Angie got out a couple of bowls and spoons. They drowned Nona's sorrows with layers of chocolate custard, whipped cream, orange slices, and chocolate génoise.

For Angie, though, not even Nona's trifle could take away her constant worry about Connie and the heaviness in her heart.

Chapter 22

"I need to ask you a few questions about the day of the robbery, Mr. Zakarian," Paavo said as he stood in the doorway of the jeweler's home.

"Of course. Please come in."

Paavo walked into a beautiful Presidio Terrace home, in one of the most exclusive parts of the city—the area where U.S. Senators, a chain of former mayors, and other top politicians lived. It was a part of the city that Angie had her eye on.

He couldn't see living in a place like this. He'd prob ably feel he should wear a powdered wig and brocade jacket just to go to breakfast.

The opulent living room was a riot of gaudy French furniture and oversized gilt-framed paintings and mirrors. Angie's parents also liked this very ornate furniture that cried "money." Paavo, on the other hand, preferred rustic and comfortable. Right now he liked Angie's taste: refined and not overblown. He could only hope it stayed that way.

Zakarian showed Paavo to a sofa framed in cream-painted wood and upholstered in beige with gold thread embroidered in the pattern of leaves. He was unsure if he should sit on it, until Zakarian plopped himself into a matching armchair. Between them was a delicately carved coffee table that looked like it might fall over if heavy cups were placed on it. "I want to know if this man is familiar to you," Paavo asked, placing a mug shot of Max Squire on the table.

After talking with Pagozzi, he'd pulled up Max Squire's arrest records. Around the time Veronica Maple was put in prison, Max had gone on more than one rampage of bad temper. He'd even once threatened to kill her when being questioned by the police. Later, he'd been arrested a couple of times for assault, but both times the charges were dropped.

What had he been doing these three years? Pagozzi's own story had checked out—he'd lost money when Max was caught up in Veronica's scheme, but had recouped most of it. Squire's finances, though, were a different story.

From all Paavo had learned about the situation, he couldn't say that he blamed Squire for being furious. Nonetheless, the arrests had left a trail of violence that had to be accounted for. Coming face-to-face with the woman who had caused him all this trouble might have driven him over the edge.

Zakarian crossed the room to a cream-and-gold-edged sideboard and pulled a pair of reading glasses from the drawer. "I need these, I'm afraid."

Sitting back down with the wire-framed glasses perched on the end of his bulbous nose, he studied the photo a moment. "Yes. I'm quite sure this is the man I saw. He looked a bit shoddier—his clothes were close to rags, and his hair was long and shaggy. When he and the robber nodded at each other, I was shocked."

"They nodded?"

"Yes. As if they were expecting each other. She said

he was her boss. That was when I relaxed, and I thought she'd just get out of the car to meet him. Instead, she knocked me out. I never even saw the blow coming." He complained and touched the bandage still around his head.

"You identified a woman in the lineup as being the robber."

"Yes," he said hesitantly.

"I want you to look very carefully at this next picture, and tell me what you think."

Paavo handed him Veronica's death photo. It was the only one showing her with short, dyed hair. Zakarian stared at it a long moment, then handed it back to Paavo with a shake of his head. "I'm not sure. She looks a lot like the robber, but so did the other one."

"What are you saying?" Paavo asked. "They can't both be guilty."

Zakarian regarded Veronica's death pose again, then placed the photo on the table. "There was something about the woman in the lineup that made me unsure. I don't know why. I've been trying to convince myself it was her. And now that I see this one, I don't know anymore."

"Are you unable to distinguish between them?" Paavo eyed him closely. "This is a murder case, remember, as well as a robbery."

"I was scared." Zakarian rubbed his hands as if they were still chilled from all he'd been through. "The woman ordered me not to look at her. She had a gun! I tried not to, but there were flashes. When I saw the young woman in the lineup, she looked scared. The one who robbed me didn't have a frightened bone in her body. So, I don't know. It might not have been her. I need to see this woman in a lineup."

"That's impossible."

"Ridiculous! There was a murder, as you said. I need help identifying the right woman. She—"

"Mr. Zakarian, the woman in this picture is dead."

With this latest information, Paavo decided to go back to Wings with Yosh. They had the good cop/bad cop routine down pat. All he knew was that something was going on in this restaurant. He just hoped it wasn't murder.

Paavo didn't like the increasingly complicated Squire–Maple connection he was learning about, nor did it make sense that Butch didn't know about Max's background. He surely would have heard if his nephew's finance counselor had lost a bundle of his clients' money due to an embezzling employee. Butch must have known a lot more than he pretended to. This time, Paavo was determined not to take no for an answer.

The lights were out as Paavo and Yosh passed by Wings in Yosh's Ford Galaxy. It was eight o'clock on a Wednesday night. The restaurant was usually more than half filled on a night like this.

Yosh parked in a white zone and put an SFPD placard in the windshield. A CLOSED sign hung in the window, and the door was locked. Angie had told Paavo the three owners lived in the flat over the restaurant. No one answered there.

Yosh decided to call it a night. After the last couple of all-nighters on the courier's murder, then Paavo's involvement with Veronica Maple's, Yosh wanted to go home to his wife and kids.

Paavo realized how much he wanted to be with Angie. He knew she was home alone, worrying about Connie, and he hated that she was anything but happy during this special time in their lives.

Right then and there he decided the heck with Lt. Hollins's concerns about her gifts. Hollins would have to deal with his inspectors enjoying the treats Angie sent to them. He wasn't about to stop her. He was proud of her, her generosity, her good heart, her fine taste.

She was the woman he loved; and she'd actually agreed to marry him. He should have been used to it by now, but he wasn't. Each time he looked at her, the wonder of it filled him all over again.

Instead of going to see her, though, he called Hanover Judd. The ADA was still at the Hall of Justice, and he agreed to meet him.

Paavo filled him in on everything he'd turned up since Veronica Maple had entered the picture. Maple was a known thief and felon who had made herself up to look like Rogers. She knew Max Squire, who Zakarian had identified as an accomplice, and knew Sid Fernandez, who could easily have been the fat guy on the security camera tape. And she herself had been murdered. On top of that, Zakarian wasn't sure if the robber had been Rogers or Maple. The evidence made a lot more sense if it pointed to Maple. The case was getting complicated.

Judd agreed. If no new evidence against Rogers showed up, he would let her go in the morning.

Paavo called Connie's attorney and Angie with the news. Then, he drove faster than the law allowed to Angie's place.

"I knew you could do it!" she cried, throwing her arms around him and kissing him.

He held her tight, enjoying the way she felt in his arms. "She's not out yet," he cautioned.

"She will be." She stepped back. "Stay right there. Don't move. I'll be back, and we'll talk."

He sat on her yellow petit-point sofa in shirtsleeves, his jacket, tie, and shoulder holster discarded on the antique Hepplewhite chair, waiting for her to rejoin him. Talking was the furthest thing from his mind at the moment.

She walked into the living room carrying a big, colorfully wrapped present. "For you." She wore red satin lounging pajamas and matching slippers with high heels. She kicked off the slippers and curled up beside him.

"A present? But why?"

"Just for fun. I ordered it before Connie's troubles began, and it arrived today. Anyway, it's just a little thing until . . . or, I should say, I'm having a such good time buying you things, in case you hadn't noticed. The French meringue cake is one of my favorites, so I just had to share it. And wasn't that pizza absolutely adorable? I was just joking about making it heart-shaped—and then they did it for me!"

"Adorable," he mimicked, with a grin. And it was, in an Angie sort of way. He was getting to like heart-shaped things. He even discovered he liked roses. He tore off the fancy gift-wrap.

Inside was a football. He pulled it out and saw it had been autographed. "What does it say? It all looks like consonants."

"I think it's upside-down."

He turned the ball over and studied it. "Elvis Grbac?"

"Remember when he was a Forty-Niner quarterback?" Angie said enthusiastically.

"Barely."

"That's right. It was just a short while. Back-up, I guess. Anyway, that's why this autograph is so rare."

"I see."

"That means it's quite valuable. I mean, Montana and Steve Young autographs are a dime a dozen. But how many Elvis Grbac autographs are there?"

"I don't know. But he was a quarterback for the Baltimore Ravens for some time."

"Oh. Oh well. This is a Forty-Niner football."

"This wasn't from Dennis, was it?" Paavo asked, carefully inspecting the ball and the signature.

"Yes! Did I tell you Connie once met his partner, Jonesy, in what Dennis hopes will be a lucrative business? I don't know, though. He knocked off over fifty percent for me. Not a great way to make money, though it still wasn't cheap by any means. Anyway, he said he was quite sure my fiancé would be stunned and amazed by such a gift."

"He's right about that."

Chapter 23

Remembering Paavo's careful instructions of the night before, Angie raced to City Jail first thing in the morning. Two hours later, Connie's lawyer walked into the waiting room and joyously waved a sheet of paper. "She'll be out any second. I've cleared her record. But she has to stay in town in case they want to talk to her again."

"Wonderful!" Angie cheered.

As promised, the door opened and Connie stepped into the room, a free woman once again. Angie gave her a crushing hug. Connie thanked her lawyer, holding Angie's arm like a lifeline.

Just then, Paavo entered. Connie's face fell when she saw him.

"Don't worry," he said. "I just want to explain to you and Mr. Matteo what's happening."

In a private interview room, Paavo told them about Veronica Maple's murder, and that he was going to keep her death quiet as long as possible. Hanover Judd had agreed to forty-eight hours, but no more. Judd was a man with good law-enforcement instincts, and he trusted Paavo's judgment on this. Unfortunately, he had bosses, and newspapers could get nasty if they thought the news was being covered up.

He explained Veronica's connection to Max Squire, and her prison term for embezzling from his clients.

"This woman really does look like me?" Connie asked, incredulous.

"She dyed her hair, cut it like yours, was even wearing blue contacts," Paavo said.

"That's creepy." Angie shuddered.

"I have a picture of her," Paavo said to Connie. "It's a mug shot from some years back, but I was hoping you might recognize her and give us some idea why she wanted to look like you."

Connie nodded and he handed her the photo. "Does she really look like me?" she asked, studying it. "I don't think she does."

Angie took it from her. "I've seen this woman." She glanced from one to the other. "She was at dinner with Dennis Pagozzi."

Without another word, Paavo put the photo back in his breast pocket. They all stood. "Listen carefully, Angie," he said. "Do *not* go near any of these people. Connie, you stay at Angie's place until this is over. Don't go home."

Connie gasped. He didn't have to explain.

Paavo walked with them to the parking lot and then took his leave.

The two women got into Angie's car.

"Before we go to your place," Connie said, "let me just stop at my store a minute. I've got some money in a safe there, some extra checks, and a change of clothes."

"I'll lend you money," Angie replied. "Aren't you tired?"

"I'm exhausted, but I need to make sure everything is okay."

Angie could understand that. Connie was a businesswoman, the store her livelihood. Of course she'd want to check on it, and Angie couldn't deny her that.

Unlocking the shop's door, Connie stepped inside, Angie behind her.

Connie froze. "My God!"

The first thing Angie saw were rows and rows of empty shelves, followed by shattered figurines on the floor. Stuffed toys had been shredded, and the stuffing lay in clumps throughout the room.

"Oh, Connie!" Angie whispered. She grabbed her friend's arm, but Connie shrugged her off and walked directly to the phone. Somehow holding herself together, she called the police first, then her insurance agent. That done, she stared numbly at the mess around her.

Angie chewed her bottom lip, unsure what to say or do. Connie was emotionally and physically exhausted. This was sure to drive her over the edge.

It didn't. By the time the police arrived quickly she was beside herself with fury. The insurance agent soon joined them. Reports were made and pictures taken, the only snag coming when Connie told them she'd been in jail at the time of the robbery. Angie practically dared them to make an issue of it. They didn't, and all but backed away from the two murderous sisters-in-arms as they left the store.

"Why do I *know* this has something to do with Max Squire?" Connie fumed, when she and Angie were alone again. "First he stole my money, then I was thrown in jail because I resemble some floozy he knew, and now the shop I've put years of sweat and blood into has been destroyed. I've had it with him!"

"That's the spirit!" Angie affirmed. "You have two choices: to cry, or to kick ass."

Connie's eyes narrowed. "Where can I find a pair of combat boots?"

Angie high-fived her. "Watch out, Max Squire. We're coming, and we want answers!"

"Answers, hell." Connie put hands on hips. "I'm going to beat the crap out of him!"

They tore out of the shop, commandos on a mission, and jumped into the Mercedes. "Put your seatbelt on, girlfriend," Angie said through gritted teeth as she cranked the motor. "This is going to be quite a ride."

Forty minutes later, they shuffled back toward Angie's car. Max hadn't used the Vallejo Street shelter facilities for several nights.

"Now where?" Angie asked.

"I'm not sure." Connie sulked, disappointed, while Angie phoned Wings.

"Earl said Max hasn't been there for days," Angie reported.

"If I find him and kill him, it'll save the taxpayers all kinds of time and money."

They got into the car. "Someone called the police and said you robbed a jeweler." Angie ticked off the items on her fingers. "The police searched your apartment looking for the diamonds, but found nothing. Now, someone has gone through your shop. What if whoever did that is looking for the diamonds? That would make sense, wouldn't it?"

Connie glanced at her. "Max? Could he have done that?"

"It goes back to the woman, that Veronica Maple," Angie said. "And she knew Dennis."

Connie yawned, and Angie could see that the adrenaline that had kept her going up to now had fizzled. She needed rest, but Angie didn't. It was up to her now to help her friend no matter what it took.

* * *

"What do I know about cleaning carpets?" Stan whined. He sat in the passenger seat of her Mercedes and pouted. The big coward didn't want to get involved, but Connie needed their help, and Angie wouldn't take no for an answer.

"You don't have to know anything," Angie said as she drove. "Put water in the tank, cleaning solution in the dispenser, flip on both the brush and suction switches, and then push the machine around the room. Just remember, you have to do the talking. He might recognize my voice."

Earlier, Angie had taken Connie back to her apartment and given her a bowl of Tuscan bread soup, which she made by laying thick minestrone in a baking dish with sliced day-old Italian bread, topped with thinly sliced red onions. She baked it until it was warm and then served it topped with a drizzle of olive oil and Parmesan cheese. The meal was comforting and heavy, and Connie soon fell asleep on the day bed in the den. Angie removed her shoes and covered her with a warm afghan.

She would probably be asleep for hours, which gave Angie time to act.

The fact that Dennis had known Veronica Maple and lied about it was important. As she dwelled on that, inspiration struck. Luckily, Stan hadn't gone to work today, because she couldn't have managed alone.

"What if he recognizes you?" Stan griped. "Then what?"

"If he does, I may have to shoot myself." She glanced at herself one more time in the rearview mirror and shuddered. A light blue satin tablecloth wrapped to look like a Muslim chador covered her head, shoulders, and the bottom half of her face. She pinned it into place so it wouldn't fall off. She then left off her mascara and heavily colored her brows and eyelids with a thick black eyebrow pencil. As a final distraction, she made a big, black beetle-like mark by her left eye.

Under the chador, she wore a long-sleeved white blouse and a full-length baggy black cotton skirt that she borrowed from her neighbor Samantha.

"What if he's not home?" Stan asked hopefully.

"Look, I called a little while ago, and he was. He wouldn't give me any information about him or Max—claimed he knew nothing. He's lying again. This is the only way I can think of to get inside the house and look for evidence of what he knows or doesn't know. You clean the carpet. I'll do the rest."

"I don't know, Angie . . ."

She parked down the block from Dennis's house. She didn't think it would be believable for carpet cleaners to drive up in a Mercedes CL600. Besides, veil-wearing women didn't usually drive their men around, but there was no way she'd let Stan behind the wheel of her new car.

"This is heavy!" Stan complained, as he lifted the Bissell out of the trunk and onto the sidewalk.

"Don't put it down! We don't want the wheels and brushes to get dirty."

"Maybe you don't . . ."

Angie grabbed a couple of old sheets she'd put in the trunk, and then picked up two handfuls of dirt from beneath a Japanese maple near the sidewalk. "Shut up, Stan, and follow me."

Dennis answered the doorbell.

"It's Happy Carpet Time!" Stan said, handing Dennis a business card Angie had run off on her computer. He lifted the carpet cleaner into the house. "We'll be in and out in a jiff, just like we promised."

Angie stayed hidden behind Stan's back, her head bowed, her arms around the sheets.

"Hey, what is this?" Dennis demanded. He was a few inches taller than Stan, but about twice as wide, and a hundred pounds of pure muscle heavier.

As Stan tried to explain that he was there to improve Dennis's life, Angie darted past them and sprinkled dirt over the pure white carpet, then she twisted her engagement ring around on her finger so Dennis wouldn't see the distinctive blue diamond.

"You paid for it, man," Stan said, finally. "Like, I'm just doing my job."

"I didn't pay for this."

"Yeah, you did. It's on our records." Stan pointed to a folded-up piece of paper sticking out of his pocket. "Anyway, this place is a mess. Look at all the dirt you got in here. You're going to ruin your rugs if you leave it there. Don't worry, we're fast."

Dennis looked where Stan pointed, then up at the Arab-looking woman standing demurely by the wall, pulling her headpiece down further over her forehead.

"How long did you say this would take?" he asked.

"Just about twenty minutes," Stan answered.

"You said I already paid for it?"

"That's right."

"I never noticed all this crap on the carpet before."

"That's always the way it is. You don't notice until someone else points out the filth you've been living with. It's kind of that way in life, wouldn't you say? In and out. Twenty minutes, that's all."

Angie cringed at Stan's sudden philosophical pronouncements, and started to spread a sheet out next to the stairs to the bedroom. Dennis looked at her, and scratched his head. "I guess, since it's paid for . . ."

"Good."

As Stan plugged in the machine, Dennis escaped to the den.

Angie continued to spread sheets over the stairs. When her parents had their wall-to-wall carpets cleaned, the place was always covered with sheets so that no one would step on a still-damp carpet. It didn't make sense to put them on top of dirty carpets, but she was pretty sure Dennis wouldn't know that and was definitely sure Stan had no idea what she was doing.

She snuck into Dennis's bedroom and quickly looked around for anything that might tell her about Max. Nothing.

Another bedroom door stood open. Angie crept toward it, not wanting anyone to suddenly appear and find her snooping.

The room didn't have the unused look or musty smell of a guest room. The closet door stood open, one bureau drawer wasn't quite shut, and the bedspread looked mussed. What if this had been Max's room? What if he was staying at Dennis's house? Worse yet, what if the two of them had set up Connie?

The closet was empty. Opening the bureau drawers, she saw they were all empty as well. A bathroom was attached, and she entered.

A hairbrush lay on the washbasin. Twisted in its bristles was blond hair. She saw some clothing tags in the wastebasket and lifted them out. Two Liz Claiborne tags from Nordstrom's, size six, $149.95 and $79.95.

Connie hadn't worn a six since high school, if then. She was a snug eight on a good day. What was wrong with all these people who said the two women looked alike?

So, Dennis had Veronica Maple staying at his home at the same time as he was making goo-goo eyes at Connie. The two-timing cad! And to think, she'd encouraged them! Why, oh why had she ever gotten involved in anyone else's love life?

A cordless telephone was on the nightstand by the bed, a pen and paper beside it. It had a digital display and several special features. When she hit the "last number redial" button, a number popped onto the display. She jotted it down.

A quick look in what would have been a third bedroom revealed a room filled with football trophies, footballs with dates and special achievements marked on them, photos, and memorabilia from Pop Warner to the Forty-Niners. Dennis Pagozzi, this is your life.

She pulled the door shut and headed for the stairs.

Stan wasn't sure how to fill the Bissell tank with water or where to add the cleaning solution, so he simply got a glass of water from the kitchen and poured it on the dirt. He then flipped a switch. The brushes spun and he pushed the carpet cleaner. Water and dirt swirled around and formed mud. More water, Stan thought, and ran to the kitchen for another glass full.

The now diluted mud began to spread, the white carpet taking on a peculiar brown tinge. Back and forth he went adding more water. The mud puddle grew, engulfing even more carpet.

Frantically, Stan rolled the machine furiously back and forth over the carpet. The slop only spread further. He then ran with the cleaner up and down the length of the carpet, pushing down hard, his gaze darting every so often to the stairs Angie had taken and feeling like Cinderella being watched over by her evil stepmother.

He leaned heavily on the machine, hoping that would cause the cleaner to slurp up the mess like milkshake through a straw. It didn't. He must have pressed down too hard, because the Bissell suddenly shrieked, gasped, and died, refusing even one glug of the gelatinous mess.

Now what? Stan wiped perspiration from his brow, then headed for the kitchen, flinging doors, drawers, and cabinets open and shut as he searched for a cure-all. Panic grew.

Angie was going to kill him.

"Finally!" Relief and triumph filled him. He reached for the aerosol can labeled "Easy-Off—Industrial Strength."

Exactly what the doctor ordered, Stan thought, snatching the container from the shelf and holding it close to his heart.

He sped back to the mud and sprayed the entire contents of the can onto the oozing mass. "Gotcha!"

He waited for the brown color to lift up and away, leaving the carpet clean and new again. Easy off, right?

Carpet fibers began to quiver and shake. The mud started to bubble ominously. He watched aghast as Easy-Off plus water plus poly-this and poly-that fabric, and God-only-knows what components in the dirt, caused a chemical reaction. A cloudy vapor rose from the swamp. The stench was unbelievable.

Triumph turned to horror.

He'd created a gas chamber.

Holding his breath, he flung open windows and the front door, praying Angie wouldn't come downstairs and the football player wouldn't turn him into a pigskin. Then he ransacked the kitchen for paper towels and anything else he could use to scoop up the toxic dump site.

On his hands and knees, he desperately scooped the molten muck into a light plastic bucket he'd found under the sink.

The center of the rug was gone, and in its place lay a crater. He peered down it. In some spots it was bare all the way to the hardwood floor.

The few surviving carpet threads at the edge of the crater appeared to be writhing.

His hands and knees tingled ominously and he jumped to his feet and looked down at himself. His shoes were pockmarked with fissures, and his slacks were shredded around his knees. He was being eaten alive!

"Stan!"

Angie's cry barely cut through his shocked numbness.

"What did you do here?" she whispered, pulling on his sleeve, and looking toward the den as if praying Pagozzi hadn't heard her cry.

"Thank God you've found me!" he wailed. "Quick, take me to Emergency. I'm rotting!"

"But the carpet—"

"Who cares?" He waved his red, slightly swollen hands. "My pants are disintegrating. My knees are on fire. My shoes are frying off my feet!" He started to cry.

"Okay, okay. But how?"

"I found a spray—Easy Off, it said. I thought that sounded good."

"That's oven cleaner!"

"So?"

Angie didn't answer. Instead, she stared slack-jawed at the plastic bucket, at the hole that formed at the bottom, and the muck that was starting to ooze out and eat its way toward them.

Just then, they heard movement in the den.

Stan grabbed the Bissell, Angie wadded up the sheets, and the two fled in terror.

Chapter 24

 Paavo arrived at Wings of an Angel before the dinner customers. He marched up to Earl. "I'd like to talk to Butch now. In the kitchen."

"In da kitchen? Why, sure, Inspector. No problem." He waved his arm toward the swinging double doors and pushed one open wide. "Go right in, Inspector. It's okay."

He gave Earl an odd look. Butch was stirring a pot of spaghetti sauce.

"I want to ask you a little more about Veronica Maple," Paavo said.

Butch flinched. "Who's that?"

"The woman in the photo I brought you."

"I told you, I don't know nothin' about her." He set the wooden spoon on the counter.

"Your nephew knows her," Paavo said.

Earl walked to Butch's side as he washed his hands. "Dennis knows lotsa people."

"He tried to deny it," Paavo added.

Butch's entire body began to twitch. "Maybe he forgot."

Paavo wouldn't let up. "She used to work for Max Squire."

"The guy helpin' with our books?" Butch's voice squeaked. He looked ready to faint and turned imploringly toward Earl.

"Can you imagine dat?" Earl cried, a suspiciously astonished expression on his face. "I didn't t'ink Max could've had somebody woikin' for him. He acts like woik is poison."

"And he ain't been around here for days," Butch added, now that he could breathe again.

"In fact," Earl said quickly, "we'll tell Dennis. We don't want his friend to come back here no more. How's dat? In fact, why don't you go tell him right now, Butch?"

Butch grabbed his jacket. "Sounds good. You hold down the place. I'll go find Dennis."

"Wait a minute," Paavo said. These guys were acting peculiar, even for them.

"I'm sorry, Inspector," Butch said, fidgeting and studiously avoiding Paavo's eyes. "I got no information for you. Absolutely nothin'."

Paavo climbed up the steep sandy soil to the street above. He was on the dunes edging the Pacific.

When he stepped over the concrete guardrail between the roadway and the oceanside drop, Yosh joined him. Lying at the bottom of the dunes was the body of a man, thin with black hair. They couldn't tell much more at the moment. The body lay hidden under shrubs, sand, and rocks until a combination of buzzards and bad smells aroused the curiosity of some residents.

When the body was found, word had quickly

spread through the nearby neighborhood of middle-class homes, and a crowd formed. A dead body discovered in that part of town was rare, one that had obviously been a murder victim rarer still. The uniformed cops had cordoned off the hill, and now Homicide, CSI, the coroner, and her staff were all over the area.

"God, but I'm getting sick of this," Yosh said, disgust marring his usually cheerful face as he scanned the area and the crowd. When it was clear the victim wasn't known to any of them, they were able to relax and treat it almost as a TV show come to life, creating a neighborhood block-party atmosphere. "Sometimes it seems they kill them faster than we can catch the perps. It's a losing battle, Paavo."

"What choice do we have?" Paavo's voice was coldly rational. "We need to try."

"Maybe it's time for me to quit this job. I think I'd like my next job to be at Disneyland. Someplace where I can work with kids all day long—kids who still believe in joy and fantasy and goodness in life. Wouldn't that be a change? Man, listen to me. I need a beer."

Paavo nodded. "You and me both. Maybe after we get through with the prelims."

His partner grumbled grudgingly, but followed him toward the crowd. "That should be about six A.M. tomorrow morning, the way these things usually go. What a time for a brew."

As the CSI continued their search for blood, hair, clothing fibers, and any other physical evidence, Paavo gave the medics the okay to remove the body from the murder scene. They slowly carried the body bag up the hillside.

A hush fell over the landscape.

The time had come for Paavo and Yosh to take

names and talk to people. They had to interview the neighbors, onlookers, and anybody else who might be able to give them a clue as to who had killed this man, who he might be, and if they were very, very lucky, why he'd been targeted to die.

Suddenly, the tune "Here Comes the Bride" began to chime. Paavo stared at Yosh a moment, whose head was swiveling back and forth with the alarm of one searching for inescapable doom, before he realized the sound was coming from his pocket—from the brand new Nokia 8860 cell phone Angie had given him, to be precise. He yanked it out and flipped it open, to the amused curiosity of the crowd.

It was Nona Farraday, wanting to know if Inspector Calderon was with him. He wasn't.

"Would you pass on a message?" she asked sweetly. "Just tell him, I'll try to be more understanding in the future. All is forgiven. Call me." With that, she hung up.

Paavo stared at the phone. Angie had turned him into a dating service.

Chapter 25

Connie was awake when Angie returned home, pushing the carpet cleaner ahead of her. Connie opened her mouth to say something about Angie's clothes and makeup, but Angie shook her head. "Don't even ask. You're better off not knowing."

Connie snapped her jaws shut.

Angie took a piece of paper from her baggy skirt and phoned the number on it, listened, then hung up.

"Veronica Maple stayed at Dennis's house. I phoned the number she'd last called from his phone," she explained. "It was a small hotel called the Madison. Since none of her belongings were at Dennis's—and if we can assume he didn't kill her and burn her things—she might have moved there. If we can get our hands on her stuff, it might have some answers for us."

"How do you propose we do that?" Connie asked with a frown.

Angie pulled a pair of Armàni sunglasses out of her purse and handed them to Connie. "Easy."

Connie approached the desk of the Madison Hotel wearing dark glasses, Angie at her side, the two deep in conversation. "I think I locked my room key in the room," she said, only half facing the desk clerk as Angie blathered. "Can you give me another? Veronica Maple. You know me, don't you?"

"Of course, Miss Maple." He quickly created a new key card.

"You have the room right, I hope?" Her tone was sharp. Angie had convinced her that this was the sort of hotel where patrons expected to be recognized and remembered. So far, she was right.

"Room 15," he said proudly.

"Thank you." She took the card, pretending to be paying far more attention to Angie than him.

The two women hurried to the elevator and rode up, scarcely able to contain giggles and squeals of joy at how easily their plan had worked.

When they reached the room, Angie knocked. They didn't want any ugly surprises. After a moment of silence, Connie unlocked the door.

Cautiously, they entered. The place scarcely appeared inhabited, as if Veronica had dropped off her clothes and left. Opening drawers and closets, they began a meticulous search of the few jeans, the T-shirts, one blouse, and a couple of bras and panties. It wasn't as if the owner were going to come waltzing in and find them there.

"Hey!" Angie was on her knees, peering under a dresser drawer she'd opened. Taped to the bottom was an envelope.

She yanked it free. Inside was a ticket from Bay Pawn Shop and a torn sheet of paper with about twelve numbers on it. "I wonder what these are."

"Whatever, they must be important," Connie answered, still rifling through the closet. "Keep them."

"I sure will." Angie put the envelope in her purse.

"What could she have pawned. She had nothing, it seems."

Connie reached into a jeans' pocket and pulled out a scrap of paper. A phone number was written on it.

"It was a phone number that got us this far," Angie said, picking up the phone and dialing.

After several rings the phone switched over to an answering machine which gave no identifying information.

"A dead end?" Connie asked, then with a chill, glanced around the too-silent room, remembering who it belonged to. "Sorry." She put the jeans down quickly.

"Where there's a will . . ." Angie replied thoughtfully, ignoring Connie's sudden squeamishness. "Let's go to the bank."

Max watched Angie and Connie enter the Madison Hotel. He was trying to find Veronica's room. He knew her taste. Back in the days before she could afford to stay in posh four-star hotels, she'd favored the small upscale ones, the Madison in particular.

He'd come here on a hunch, and apparently it had paid off. What did they know about Veronica? Why were they at her hotel?

He walked up to the desk clerk, who drew back at his scruffy appearance. "Does Veronica Maple have a room here?"

"I'm sorry, Miss Maple just left."

"Was that her? The blond lady? A short brunette was with her?"

"Yes, sir. Now, if you would be so kind as to leave . . ."

Max didn't bother to listen, but headed out the door.

How much did they know about Veronica? How much were they onto him?

Much to everyone's amazement, especially his employers', Stan Bonnette was in his office at Colonial Bank's headquarters when Angie and Connie arrived. He had the title of assistant director of supply maintenance, an honorary title if ever Angie'd heard one, because the guy never did any work. That his father was one of the bank's largest stockholders, however, gave him job security.

Although there was a secretary's desk in front of his office, it wasn't being used. Angie knocked on his door.

"Come in," he called.

She walked in to find him with his feet on the desk, cleaning his fingernails with a letter opener. His desk was almost as spotless as the secretary's. One manila folder was on it. In back of him, his computer was on, the screen showing a game of solitaire. He had lost.

"Angie!" He jumped up. "And Connie. What a surprise. Did you two come to take me for a late lunch?" Suddenly his face fell. "You didn't bring Connie's neighbor, Paula Bunyon, along, did you?"

"Relax, Stan. We're too busy to eat. We need your help."

"No one should ever be too busy to eat," he murmured, disappointed, as he sat back down in his chair and indicated guest chairs for them to sit on. "What can I do for you?"

Angie wiped the dust off the guest chair before she sat, then said, "We've got a phone number. I need you to find out who it belongs to."

He swiveled around to his computer. "You can do this on the Internet, you know."

"Not if it's a private number," she said.

He tried the Internet first, and sure enough, nothing came up. "You want me to go into bank records to find who this is?"

"Right. And, depending on what you find out, we might want credit reports and anything else you can tell us about the person." She glanced at Connie, who gave her a firm nod.

"And after that, how about doing the same for a man named Max Squire?" Connie added with a sly smile.

Angie high-fived her.

"All right," Stan said, "but it'll cost you. Let's say, a home-cooked meal of my choice."

"Agreed."

Angie and Connie nearly fell asleep as they sat slumped in their chairs, waiting. Stan wasn't good at finding his way around the bank's computer system, which was no wonder, considering how little he used it, but he was persistent. He loved Angie's cooking.

Finally, he turned and faced them. They pulled themselves up straight. "The phone number belongs to Sidney Edmund Fernandez. I've written down his address. The bank gives him a zero credit rating. He has no bank or saving accounts, but he does have credit cards that he uses infrequently. He pays them off right away, so I suspect the zero credit rating has something to do with him not exactly being a law-abiding citizen, but I'm not sure."

"Interesting." Angie tried to make sense out of the news.

"What about Max?" Connie asked.

"I have no address for him, zero credit rating here, too. But if you go back three years, he had superior credit. His bank account had over fifty thousand dollars in cash, plus a couple of CDs. He obviously had a lot of stocks, bonds, and real estate. The mortgage on his house was for over six hundred grand, and he never missed a payment. He often put ten thousand on his credit card in one month, and paid it in full the next. Then he filed for bankruptcy and everything disappeared. I show no credit history for him after the bankruptcy."

"Mercy," was Connie's only comment.

"That explains a bit about his attitude, doesn't it?" Angie murmured.

Stan looked from one to the other. "Ready for lunch yet?"

Chapter 26

The sand dunes murder victim was an ex-con named Julius Rodriguez. He'd been killed by a bullet to the back of the head. Before that he'd been castrated. Rodriguez had done time for dealing drugs and was said to have been the right-hand man of Sidney Fernandez.

Fernandez might have been a player in the Veronica Maple heist, and now his top man was dead. What was the connection?

While pondering this, Paavo noticed a bald man working his way around desks, printing stands, fax machines, and file cabinets, but he was so bland and colorless, Paavo paid no attention until he stopped in front of his desk.

"Paavo Smith? Inspector Paavo Smith?" the man asked.

Paavo stood. "Yes. What can I do for you?"

"The name's Chuck Lexington. I was Veronica Maple's parole officer." With that, he held out his hand to shake Paavo's.

Lexington . . . he was the first one who'd brought Fernandez's name to Homicide's attention when he'd talked to Calderon about Veronica Maple. The case was going around in circles in more ways than one.

"Have a seat." Paavo indicated the chair by his desk.

"Thanks." Lexington settled in. He took a breath, then let his words flow. "I talked to Calderon but haven't heard anything back from him. I've been trying to find out Maple's whereabouts. I don't know if you heard, but she got out of prison and killed a man."

Paavo looked at him questioningly.

"Me and her, we talked a lot before she left prison," Lexington said. "It was kind of strange. I liked her. Now"—he shook his head—"I want to bring her in myself, if I can. I hate to see her get hurt. I know, she's a killer. Still . . . have you heard anything about her at all?"

"I do have some questions about Maple," Paavo said. "Let's go to the interrogation room. It's more private, less noisy." He nodded at Yosh, who followed.

The room had a metal table with two chairs. Lexington took one, Paavo the other. Yosh stood near the wire-glass window at the far wall.

"Why did she come to San Francisco?" Paavo asked.

"I think she had some unfinished business here. Something she needed to take care of. Maybe involving her old boss, Max Squire. The two absolutely hated each other."

"Enough to kill?"

"Him kill her, or her kill him?" Lexington asked. "He came to see her a couple of times in Chowchilla, and the guards said they thought he was going to go through the glass wall to get at her."

Paavo and Yosh's gazes met. "Anyone else?"

"I told Calderon about Sid Fernandez's gang. The two of them go back a long way. I was worried that she might try to contact him, since he's in the city. She swore she was through with that kind of thing, but after what she did, who knows?"

"So it seems," Paavo said. "Anyone else?"

"No. I don't think so," Lexington said with a sigh. "It's weird, her disappearing without a trace. I thought she might be dead. No such luck. I guess I'll keep looking."

"What about Dennis Pagozzi?"

"How do you know about him?" Lexington asked.

Paavo shrugged. "As I said, we're trying to be helpful."

Lexington gazed suspiciously from one to the other. "When they were young, she was married to Dennis Pagozzi."

Both inspectors froze.

"Holy Moses," Yosh muttered.

"Are you sure?" Paavo asked.

"They were only seventeen, and went down to Mexico. Rosarita Beach. Dennis apparently claimed the marriage wasn't legitimate, but the United States recognizes Mexican marriages. His family got involved and it was annulled. After she realized half the money he'd earned playing football could have been hers, she fought the annulment, saying it was invalid. It didn't work, though."

"How did you find that out?" Paavo asked.

"I told you, we used to talk. I didn't think she was a bad person—just misguided, especially about money. I never imagined she was a killer. Nothing in her background pointed to it." Lexington swore. "If it had, I'd have watched her a lot closer."

"Maybe she didn't kill the guy in Fresno," Yosh offered.

Lexington shook his head. "It had to be her. There's no other suspect."

* * *

Angie and Connie rode to the Excelsior Street address Stan had given them, parked down the block, and sat in the car, doors locked.

"What now?" Connie asked as they stared at the house. "We can't just walk up and say, hi, tell us about Veronica Maple. We're running out of time! This day is almost gone. Only one more day and word will get out that Veronica Maple is dead, then who knows what will happen?"

"All we need to do is find out what this Fernandez is all about. We know he's shady and single. He liked Veronica. There's got to be a way. Whatever it takes, we're going to find out what's happening and dispense some justice!"

"That's what I'm afraid of."

Angie gave a long glance in Connie's direction. "Of course! You look like Veronica Maple, and she was his friend, possibly his *girlfriend* . . ."

"Not again, Angie. No! I won't do it. No way, no how!"

When Lexington left, Vic Walters from Robbery was waiting for Paavo. He had a description of the guy who'd tried to fence Zakarian's diamonds—tall, broad shouldered, scraggly blond hair, wearing ragged clothes. Sounded like Max Squire had struck again. The usual fences wouldn't touch the diamonds—too hot to handle, they said.

Paavo found information about Dennis Pagozzi on the Internet due to Dennis's position with the Forty-Niners. Born and raised in San Francisco, attended Galileo High School, was given a football scholarship to USC in Los Angeles, and signed with the Forty-Niners as a third-round draft pick.

He then turned to Veronica Maple's background. She was born the same year as Dennis, but in Sacramento, California. Moved to San Francisco when she was fifteen. From the address on her juvenile arrest records, she would have been in Galileo High School's jurisdiction. Although it was a good-sized city school, the odds were excellent that Dennis and Veronica, both in the same grade, had known each other.

Veronica left San Francisco in her eighteenth year and went to Los Angeles. It would have been the same year Dennis went to USC. Another connection?

In LA, her problems with the law began again, and the name "Sid Fernandez" showed up in her file as someone who'd been arrested with her.

Five years later, the same year Dennis joined the Forty-Niners, Veronica was back in San Francisco.

It looked like Chuck Lexington was right about Pagozzi and Veronica— whether they had a legal marriage or not, they had a long and complicated past.

Pagozzi, Squire, Fernandez . . . and Julius Rodriguez could be thrown into the mix. Rodriguez, who was as thin as Fernandez was heavy. Just like the two hooded men on the basement-garage security tape . . .

He grabbed his files on the courier's murder and went in search of Robbery Inspector Vic Walters.

"I don't like this one bit," Connie said, tugging with dismay at the hem of the two-sizes-too-small glittery purple sweater she was wearing. How did she let Angie talk her into these things? They sat in her car, a half block from Fernandez's house. "All I want to do is find Max."

"One leads to the other," Angie insisted, picking lint from the red midriff-baring angora she wore.

"I should be so lucky!" They'd gone to the Stonestown mall and bought short skirts, tight sweaters, spike-heeled boots, frosted turquoise eye shadow, and bright orange lipstick—the kind that turned practically fluorescent after a while. Angie ratted her hair so that it stood out from her head in gnarled splendor. Connie's was too short to rat, for which she was grateful.

They changed clothes and put on makeup in the ladies' room at Macy's, then ran like crazy to Connie's car just in case someone who knew them was in the store.

"Now," Angie began, "remember, all we have to do is saunter up to his house, knock on the door, and say we were told he was having a party and that we're there to party, *big time*. Got it?"

Connie looked sick. "Yes. Unfortunately."

Angie couldn't be more pleased with her brainstorm. "Well, when he sees a couple of 'ladies of the night,' so to speak, and with one of us—you—looking so much like Veronica, he's going to be hot and horny and curious, right? So he'll invite us in."

"Lovely."

"Don't worry, I'll be right there—I'll protect you. But first you've got to play up to him, sweet-talk him, charm the pants off him—but not literally. And then just *sli-i-i-ide* in a question here, and a question there, until you have some idea what the connection is between him, Dennis, Veronica, and Max."

"And what if he's trying to *sli-i-i-ide* you-know-what in me while I'm doing all this nicey-nice stuff?"

"If things get scary, I'll just say our pimp is outside, and he's livid. Then we'll leave."

"At least say he's 'pissed,' Angie. I don't think 'livid' is a pimp kind of word."

"Whatever. Let's go."

"Wait!" Connie said, clutching a door handle with

one hand and rubbing her stomach with the other. "I'm scared. I feel sick. I can't do it!"

"There's nothing to be scared of. I'm sure he's harmless. Just some creep Veronica hung out with, a little shady, but aren't most people?"

"What if I throw up on him?"

"That'll work even better than my threat about a pimp."

Just then, a limousine turned onto the street, and the two stared, their mouths agape, as it pulled into Fernandez's driveway. The limo looked nearly as big as the house.

A large man, as wide as he was tall, got out and thumped up the stairs to the front door, the limo driver behind him. The first one unlocked the door, and they went inside.

"Fernandez," Angie whispered. "He must have a lot more money than we thought."

"What does he know about a deadbeat like Squire?" Connie asked, hunkering down behind the wheel. "All the more reason to get out of here."

"Chicken!" Angie cried. With that, she was out of the car and sauntering sexily down the street.

With a groan, Connie caught up, and then began to saunter as well. They would have gotten there a lot faster if they'd simply walked, but Fernandez might have been watching from the window.

"Let's just take a look at the limo before we knock on the door. I wonder why he uses it," Angie said. The windows were darkened. She and Connie cupped their hands against the glass and tried to see inside with no luck.

"Where the hell have you been?" A voice bellowed. "I'm going to kill you!"

The two spun around. Fernandez huffed down the

stairs toward them, waving a gun. It looked like a cannon.

"Don't shoot!" they screamed in unison. This wasn't the kind of greeting Angie was expecting.

"We're just looking at your car," she explained.

"Yeah," Connie said, too scared to add another word.

"Hey," Fernandez said as he stepped closer. "You're not Veronica." He faced Angie. "What the hell are you two made up for, Halloween?"

Angie was taken aback. "We're here to party," she said indignantly. Had she gone a teensy bit overboard with the clothes? Must be the eye shadow.

"Is this some kind of game?" His voice was low, dangerous.

The driver stepped to his side, eying the two women. "Hey, they ain't so bad, boss. Maybe they are what they say. They just wanna see the limo, maybe meet the driver. Party." He faced Angie. "The name's Raymondo."

"You drive this monster? How cool," Angie said. "And you're right. We just wanted to look at it and meet you guys."

Like a puppy on a leash, Raymondo's eyes begged Fernandez to let him go play.

Angie peered up at Raymondo and smiled. His tongue was too busy hanging out to form words.

She moved closer to him and turned so that he faced away from Connie. "Why don't you tell me about the . . . drive shaft," she purred.

This time, he didn't even wait for Fernandez's okay, but started talking. She paid no attention, simply wanting to get him out of the way so Connie could talk to Fernandez.

Connie's eyes widened with obvious terror as Angie

glided away from her. She glanced from Fernandez's gun to his fat face and back to the gun again, and gulped. In a herky-jerky motion, she pointed at the gun. "I'm glad I'm not Veronica," she said with a forced laugh.

His eyes narrowed, but he lowered the gun. She smiled, and his gaze went to her very snug sweater. "You just came out of nowhere to party with me, huh?"

"Sure," she said. Angie's back was to her. "Uh . . . why do you hate Veronica so much?" she asked.

Big mistake. His fingers tightened on the gun. "Who are you two?"

Connie jumped back, grabbed a startled Angie, and pulled her close. "We're nobody. Just being friendly. Forget it, okay? Let's go, Angie."

"Hey, I'm friendly," Raymondo offered loudly.

Fernandez stepped to the side, blocking their way. "How did you two get here?" he demanded.

Connie turned to Angie to answer. It didn't make sense to say they drove there, but if she said they were neighbors, he might ask where they lived, and he might know she was lying. Her lips were dry. "The bus?" she offered.

"Get in the limo!" he ordered.

Raymondo, a lurid sneer on his face, opened a door. "Come on, ladies." he said, then laughed.

"No . . . no, we're leaving," Angie said. "Our . . . our pimp . . ."

Even Fernandez laughed at that statement.

She and Connie backed up, holding each other securely. When Fernandez stepped toward them, they bolted and ran into the street, hoping to get around him, the limo, and the driver.

Raymondo easily grabbed Connie's wrist, and a second later, his arm went around Angie's waist, lifting her off the ground even though her feet kept moving.

They screamed and tried to break free, but he was able to handle both with no problem and tossed them into the limo.

The next instant, the street turned into a sector of hell.

Sirens blared, car wheels screeched, and a force of men wearing black head-to-toe SWAT uniforms, Kevlar body armor, and shields appeared out of nowhere barking orders to Fernandez to drop the gun and freeze.

Feet pounded the pavement, there were shouts and the sound of scuffling . . . then all was silent.

Angie and Connie untangled themselves from each other and stuck their heads out the passenger door, Connie's below, Angie's right above hers.

Fernandez and Raymondo stood with their hands up, surrounded by police.

Chapter 27

"I knew it was a set-up!" Fernandez yelled.

Robbery Inspector Vic Walters walked up to him. "You're under arrest, Fernandez. We've got you this time. Not only for the diamond robbery—"

"*What* robbery? *What* diamonds? I don't have no diamonds!"

Paavo was right behind Walters. "Also for the murder of Janet Clark, a courier employed by Couriers Unlimited."

"Hell. I don't know what you're talking about."

"And for the murder of Julius Rodriguez."

Fernandez's face fell. "Where'd you get that shit?"

Paavo glanced toward Raymondo, who had also been cuffed. "I'm sorry, boss. They said I was an accessory. That I could get the chair just for driving you!"

"Shut up, damn you! So this was a set-up! I'll get out, and when I do, you're all dead men! *All of you!*"

"Did you also kill Veronica Maple?" Paavo asked.

Fernandez's eyes went wide with shock. He clearly wasn't acting. "What? She's dead? Where the hell are my diamonds? I thought she ran off with them—that Julius was going to meet her!" Suddenly, his mouth began to quiver as the full import of Paavo's words struck him. His voice was small. "I thought they'd double-crossed me. I thought . . . I cared about her, dammit! She can't be dead!"

"Take them away," Paavo said to the uniforms who were there with a paddy wagon. He started back toward his car.

"Excuse me, Inspector Smith," said Officer Crossen, the young policeman who had helped Paavo several times over the years. "Wasn't that your fiancée in the limo?"

Paavo stared at him. *"What did you say?"*

"In the limo." He pointed toward the passenger door. It had been pulled nearly closed, but not latched.

Paavo frowned, walked over to it, and swung it open.

Angie and Connie cowered on the floor, curled up to make themselves as small as possible. Big turquoise-shadow-ringed brown eyes looked up at him.

"Hi," Angie said, her voice as meek as he'd ever heard it.

Angie nervously toyed with her engagement ring after Paavo left. She was glad she still had it. She'd never seen him as furious as he was with her and Connie for going to meet Sid Fernandez.

How was she supposed to know he was a murderous gang leader? Nobody ever told her anything! She'd assumed he was rich, had a few dishonest financial dealings, but was basically a harmless guy whom Veronica had scammed—sort of like Max Squire, but on the shady side of the law.

How was she to know Robbery and Homicide had, minutes before, worked out a deal with Raymondo on the limo's phone, and that was why he'd brought Fernandez back home, saying the limo was overheating? The SWAT team had been called in just in case other gangbangers were at the house, and Fernandez refused to go quietly.

If a shootout had happened, as Paavo needlessly pointed out several times over, she and Connie would have ended up more holey than Swiss cheese. Angie's imagination, as she and Connie had hidden in the limo, had been far more vivid and hellish than any words Paavo had used. Keeping herself from shattering into a thousand pieces was all she could manage as he ranted.

And Paavo never ranted—except when he'd been scared to death, such as this evening, when he'd realized she'd been in the direct line of fire.

Finally, he left for Homicide to book Fernandez and to begin some of the paperwork.

Angie had to admit to being relieved by his departure.

Connie skulked out of the den where she'd been hiding. "Is it safe?" she asked, peeking around just in case.

"For the moment. Men can be so touchy."

"Well—"

"Don't start."

Angie went to the kitchen and got a bottle of Louis Martini Petite Sirah from the pantry, where she had a small wine collection. She'd been saving it for a special occasion. Surviving a potentially deadly situation was about as special as she could imagine.

The first glass was to settle their shattered nerves. They soon discovered it took the first bottle to settle them. With the second, they were finally able to talk.

"We're two logical, rational people," Angie began,

her head whirling. She put her glass down on the coffee table. "Surely we can figure out what's going on."

"Uh-oh." Connie drained her glass and poured herself another. "I don't want to hear it. I simply want to beat the snot out of Max Squire. Is that too much to ask? Nothing else. No more hotels, limos, or shootouts. Got it?"

Angie paid no attention. "You became involved in this because Veronica Maple made herself up to look like you in the robbery. The question is: why would she do that?"

"She was jealous of my good looks!" Connie took a long drink.

"She also framed Max—assuming he's innocent, which I think is a valid assumption."

"Innocent? When I'm through with him, his only use will be as a hood ornament! I'll pulverize him. Tony Soprano him. Flatline him!" Connie hiccupped and held her glass up for more.

"I hear he was quite good to her, fell in love, and then she scammed him. She went to prison, and when she got out, she came to San Francisco for God-only-knows what reason. Ah!" Angie sat up tall and faced Connie. "I've got it! What if she was jealous? Not of your looks, but of Max . . . of you and Max together?"

Connie forced herself to focus. "Helen Melinger told me about a woman she thought was my sister hanging around. That could have been Veronica!"

"*Now* we're getting somewhere." Angie staggered into the kitchen and grabbed a box of Godiva truffles. "This calls for the big guns."

They each took a truffle and ate thoughtfully. Then another.

"To Veronica," Angie said, licking her fingers, "it

must have been bad enough that Max was seeing another woman. Having you resemble her—somewhat—was that much more infuriating."

"But Max and I don't have that kind of relationship," Connie said. "At least, not yet. Now, not ever!"

They both ate more chocolate.

"That aside," Angie said, as she knelt down beside the coffee table and poured more wine to wash down the truffles, "Veronica needs money, right? So what does she do? She finds her old friend Sid Fernandez. They scheme to steal diamonds. She'll fence her share and get cash, and in the meantime, she'll set up you and Max to take the fall for the heist!"

"Me and Max. What might have been. Why do I fall for these losers?" Connie stretched out on the sofa, candy in one hand, wine in the other, and her head on the backrest.

"Max seems to think Veronica hid the money she embezzled, but he must be wrong," Angie said, sitting cross-legged on the carpet and munching another candy. "Or, for some reason, she couldn't get her hands on it. If I had millions, I'd own a lot more than one Liz outfit. And I'd be on the first plane to Rio."

"You're the big matchmaker. How about a match with a guy who'll take *me* to Rio!"

"I got it!" Angie waved her wineglass. "She was stuck, needed money, and was jealous, so she stole the diamonds, then called the police, and said you had them."

"I don't have any diamonds. Only a zircon or two. Kevin was too broke to give me an engagement ring. That should have warned me." She slugged back more wine. "I'm gonna kick his ass, too!"

"That's why Veronica made herself up to look like you," Angie murmured. "So Zakarian would identify *you* at the lineup." She backed up against the sofa, her legs straight out, ankles crossed, and then slid down so that her head lay on the seat cushions. She balanced the wineglass on her stomach, lightly holding it in place with one hand as she groped for the Godiva box with the other.

"Then, somebody killed her," Connie said, generously passing the box over after she plopped another truffle into her mouth. "Who would have done that?"

Angie noticed the edge of a piece of paper under the sofa. It must have dropped. She pulled it out and saw the letter from *Bon Appétit*. "Hey, look at this. I got a job offer." She sipped more wine as she read. "A *good* job offer."

"Max might have killed her to get even for ruining him," Connie reasoned, as best she could after so much wine.

The words seemed to jump all over the letter as Angie stared at it. "I kind of remember several good job offers, come to think of it. How strange"—she yawned—"that people seem to want my help now. Where were they when I needed them?"

"Or Dennis," Connie offered, also yawning. "He might have been jealous of her and Max, or angry that she came back."

"Or some other man in her life," Angie said, rubbing her eyes. "But *which*?"

"How could one woman have so many men, and here I am . . . the men in my life are so screwed up. Maybe it's me. I think I'll become a nun." Connie put the wineglass on the end table and rolled to her side, her lips smacking a couple of times.

"You haven't met the right guy, that's all," Angie murmured sleepily. "Anyway, you aren't Catholic."

"You're Ms. Matchmaker, and you came up with

worse losers than I did on my own." Connie suddenly giggled.

Angie was irked. "I wouldn't say that."

"I would!" She giggled again, then fell silent.

Angie, thankful she was no longer being laughed at, also set down her wineglass. "I was just thinking, I've got a cousin . . . Connie?" she murmured, her eyes shut.

Connie's answer was a snore.

Angie responded in kind.

Chapter 28

Angie awoke with a dry mouth, upset stomach, and splitting headache. The one eye she could open read 7:55 on her clock radio. All the ugliness of the past few days rushed at her and she sat up. This situation needed to be settled now. It was ruining Connie's life, it was unjust, and in part, she'd gotten Connie into it by her meddling.

She stumbled down the hall to the den and shook her friend awake. Connie sat on the edge of the bed in a stupor. Her eyes had dark circles, her skin was green, and her hair looked spiked. "We're going to go find Max," Angie declared. "Time to move it."

"I feel sick." Connie lay back down and pulled the covers over her head. "Anyway, I'd rather hear about your cousin," she murmured, then began to snore again.

"What cousin?" Angie asked, tugging at the blankets. "Let's go."

Connie held the blankets tight, twisting them around herself. As Angie tugged, Connie slid along the sheets and nearly tumbled onto the floor. "Okay, okay! I'm up already." She stood, blinked a couple of times, then gawked at Angie. "You look like hell!"

"Gee, thanks!" Angie's head felt as if drum majorette tryouts were being held inside it. "I'm just trying to help, here."

"Well, you'd have been more help if you'd listened to me earlier," Connie snarled as she headed down the hall. "I told you we needed to find Max, but would you listen? Nooooo. So we nearly got our hair parted by flying bullets!"

Her words stung. "Keep complaining," Angie said, "and I'll cook you some *soft-boiled eggs* for breakfast."

"Yuck!"

"With a great big glass of *buttermilk*."

"All right." Connie stuck her fingers in her ears. "I'm sorry."

"Topped with *extra thick whipped cream*!" Angie shouted.

"Stop!" With a groan, Connie ran toward the bathroom.

Angie rubbed her own stomach. Her irritation had backfired, and now she felt as queasy as Connie. In the kitchen, she made them both tea and dry toast. If she never saw red wine or chocolate again, it would be too soon.

After showering and downing several aspirin, they both felt a little more civilized. Each donned a pair of Angie's oversized dark sunglasses, more to ease their headaches than to be incognito, and then they were off in pursuit of Max—slightly battered guerrilla fighters this time.

Three homeless shelters and two food kitchens later, they sat in Angie's Mercedes, ready to give up.

"He must have changed his name," Connie said, adjusting the glasses to better protect her eyes from the sun's glare. "Max Shithead, maybe."

"He was going to do Wings's tax statements. Maybe

they gave him a few dollars in advance to get a room somewhere," Angie suggested. She wondered if wearing two pairs of sunglasses at once would help.

"He might be at Dennis's house," Connie said. "Let's call and ask."

Angie started the engine. "And take the chance he'd lie? No way."

"Go for it, girlfriend. Let's bust balls!" Almost immediately, though, Connie rolled down the window for a blast of crisp air. The rumbling of the car was playing havoc with her stomach. Angie rolled down the driver's side window as well.

By the time they reached Dennis's, both women were hanging their heads out the windows. It made driving difficult, but not as hazardous as the alternative. Anyway, their temporary misery would be well worth it if they could confront Dennis and Max.

Their spirits sank when they found the drapes closed at the house. It was nearly noon. Dennis might still be asleep, Angie thought. He seemed to keep pretty late hours.

She rang the ball, and after a wait, knocked on the door. No answer.

She and Connie stepped out onto the street. The windows were all shut tight. To the left of the house was a gate to the backyard, but it was solid wood and five feet tall. Neither was good at pole vaulting.

"We can come back later," Connie said, rubbing her temples, "and try again."

"That means we'd have to ride all the way back here," Angie wailed. Carsickness was nowhere on her how-to-have-a-good-time list. The potted ferns that adorned the front entryway gave her an idea. "Start looking," Angie said, lifting one plant and peering under it.

Three plants later, Connie found a key. She waved it at Angie. "Let's see if it fits."

"Try it." Angie watched Connie slide the key in the lock. "Only don't—"

She froze as Connie pushed the door open. "Don't what?"

Suddenly a loud shriek sounded, lights flickered, and an alarm clanged, making their already aching heads jangle so badly a guillotine would have looked like an angel of mercy.

"Don't set off the house alarm!" Angie cried, too late, as the two clutched their heads and scrambled to her car to make a fast getaway.

"Have a seat," Paavo said as he and Yosh sat across from Pagozzi in Homicide's interview room, a plain, windowless rectangle with only one four-by-eight table and four aluminum chairs around it.

They'd invited Pagozzi to visit Homicide—and then had given him an hour to get there. He'd made it in fifty-nine minutes.

"We have a few questions," Yosh said.

Dennis's face went white. "About what?"

"We want to ask you about Wallace Jones," Paavo answered for Yosh.

"Jonesy?" Dennis's Adam's apple worked, and sweat broke out on his brow. "Why? What's wrong?"

"He was arrested last night," Paavo said. "We looked at his phone records. Lots of calls between you and him."

Dennis looked as if his tongue were stuck to the roof of his mouth. "He's a friend. What's this about?"

"A stash of sports equipment was found not long ago and traced to him. Mr. Pagozzi, did you know his stuff was all counterfeit?" Yosh asked.

"My gosh!" Dennis cried.

Paavo had seen bad acting before, but this guy was beyond dreadful. "You thought it was real?"

"Sure."

"He was going to be your supplier for the sports bar you were talking about opening," Paavo said.

"Hey," Pagozzi was all wide-eyed innocence. "I wouldn't try to sell fakes in my uncle's restaurant, would I? I didn't know! If I ever found out, I wouldn't have gone through with the deal, all right? It's not against the law to trust a friend, is it?"

"That's what we're asking you," Paavo said.

"Tell us about your marriage to Veronica Maple," Yosh suddenly interjected.

Dennis's head whipsawed between the two inspectors, his forehead glistening. "Christ! Why do you want to know?"

"Why did you lie about knowing her?" Paavo asked.

"Is that what this is about?" His eyes clung to one, then the other. Finally he sighed. "It's ancient history. We were in Mexico. It was for fun, that's all."

"Not if there's a valid Mexican marriage certificate," Yosh said.

"It was annulled, all right?" Dennis cried. "It meant nothing. Nothing! I was only seventeen. I had a football career ahead of me. What would I want with a screwed-up pothead for a wife?"

"She did drugs?" Yosh asked.

"She sure did. Why do you think she spent so much time in trouble? She got mixed up with Fernandez and his gang. I couldn't handle it. I tried to get her off my back, but she kept coming around, and coming around . . ."

There was more to it. Paavo could tell he was holding something back. "She was under your skin, wasn't she?"

Dennis's lips tightened into a white line. "There was something about her. What can I say? I don't know the word, but almost . . . feral. Yeah, that's what you call it. Like a wild tiger. Or better, a leopard. Sleek, sexy, smart. And when she set her mark on a man . . ." He shook his head. "I've never met anyone like her."

"Sounds like you still love her," Yosh said.

"No!" he answered too quickly, too vehemently.

"You knew what she was up to with Max Squire?" Paavo asked.

"I never imagined she could do what she did! I was the one who told her about him. How he was handling my money, and lots of other guys. Before I knew it, she'd taken him for millions." Once he started talking, he couldn't stop. "She was good that way, using men. All men."

"Who else?" Yosh asked.

"How the hell should I know? She was in prison for three years. Ask the guards. She had all of them by the balls—literally. The same with Max and his clients." His mouth twisted. "Rich clients. Lots richer than Max or me. She could have had any of them, but she wanted money and independence, and Max saw to it she went to prison.

"She knew how to use you, all of you," Paavo said, pondering Pagozzi's words, Max's reaction to her, even El Toro's admission that he "cared" about her. "And then, she double-crossed you."

Dennis nodded, then shut his eyes against his memories.

"When she got out of prison, why didn't she just leave the country?" Yosh asked. "Everyone seems to think she had millions hidden."

"How should I know?" With his elbows on the table, shoulders tight, he leaned forward, his hands clenched.

"You spoke with her," Paavo said. The strange way Butch, Earl, and Vinnie had acted, it was a good guess that Veronica Maple had spoken with all of them.

Dennis started, clearly not expecting the cops to know that. "Look, we were kids together. When she got out of jail, she came here just a couple of days. Had to put her feet on the ground, you know? I let her hang out, then she split. I don't know more than that."

"Where'd she go?" Paavo asked.

Dennis chewed his tongue. "Why don't you guys ask Max Squire? Maybe he can tell you."

Paavo and Yosh stood. The interview was over.

"Thanks for your cooperation," Yosh said.

"Don't go too far," Paavo added. "I'm sure we'll have more questions to ask you."

After their visit to Dennis's, Connie developed a migraine and needed peace, quiet, and a dark room to lie down in. In just a few hours, Veronica's death would become public knowledge.

Angie decided to go to Wings and ask if Butch had any idea where Dennis might be. Earl stood at the maître d's stand, but no customers were at the tables. In fact, the tables weren't even set.

"What's going on?" she asked.

"Butch is feeling poorly, Miss Angie," Earl said. "We ain't got no food for customers, so we're only doin' take-out, not da full menu."

"What are you talking about? You need a cook for take-out."

Earl blanched. "Well, Vinnie can—"

"No. Vinnie can't," Angie said, brows crossed. "The

man has no sense of taste or smell. He'd eat cardboard. I've got to see this." She headed for the kitchen.

"No, Miss Angie. You don' wanna do that." Earl ran in front of her, his arms spread wide across the swinging doors.

She stared him in the eye. He wasn't about to budge.

She'd had it with people getting in her way, or trying to push her or Connie around. In one fast movement, she ducked under his arm, shoved the door open, and ran into the kitchen. "Hey!" Earl yelled.

On a table were four Styrofoam containers of varying sizes, each with a name written on it. No food was being prepared.

"Where's Vinnie?" she demanded.

Earl shrugged.

She headed down the stairs to the storeroom. Vinnie was surrounded by several wooden boxes stamped with Chinese characters.

He was picking items out of the boxes and putting them into a Styrofoam container.

"There you are!" Angie cried.

He raised his hands high in the air. When he saw Angie, he lowered them, wearing a sheepish expression. "Miss Angie. You scared me." He put his hand behind his back and casually stepped in front of his worktable.

"What's going on here?" Angie cried.

"You don't wanna do dis, Miss Angie," Earl said, now that he caught up with her.

"I'm afraid I do, Earl." She cast a steely eye on Vinnie. "Let me see."

Vinnie shook his head.

She stared, hard.

Vinnie and Earl exchanged glances, then Vinnie lowered his head and stepped out of the way.

She opened a box and lifted out a tube with a long fuse attached. "Fireworks?"

Vinnie and Earl showed no expression.

Suddenly, it all made sense and she slapped her forehead. "God help me. These are illegal! You three have been selling illegal fireworks from this restaurant. Are you *crazy*?"

"Da restaurant wasn't makin' too much money," Earl whined.

"We didn't do nothin' wrong, Miss Angie," Vinnie said. "I met a guy in Chinatown, and he needed help getting ridda some of his supplies. We're just helpin' him out, and getting a little extra money. It's not like we're doin' nothin' wrong."

"It doesn't wash, Vinnie."

"I was afraid you'd say that."

Angie looked at the six wooden crates, each about two feet across and three feet long. "Hasn't Paavo been questioning you? Walking around back here? How did he miss finding all these?"

"Remember dat night we locked up oily?" Earl asked.

"Yes . . ."

"We moved dis stuff. We carried it all back to Chinatown. After he questioned poor ol' Butch, we moved it all back."

"Without Butch wantin' to cook, how else was we gonna make money?" Vinnie asked. "You don't want we should lose the place, do you?"

No way could they claim they didn't know what they were doing was illegal. "Let's get these out of here, right now," Angie said. "This is our little secret, got it? You don't say a word, and you don't ever do this again!"

"But what about makin' more money?" Vinnie bellowed.

Angie could hardly contain her exasperation. "You won't be making any money at *all* if you're back in prison!"

"I guess you're right," Vinnie said woefully. "Maybe we can raise prices."

"Maybe you can add a few more items to the menu!" She began removing fireworks from the containers and putting them back into the correct crates. "We might have to pay a lot more attention to Dennis's sports-bar idea, although I don't know how we're going to do that and keep the ambiance."

"What's ambiance?" Earl looked at Vinnie. "Can we eat it?"

Vinnie gave him a shove. "Dummy. She wants to make sure the place stays pretty."

Earl harrumphed. "It's already purty. We can't eat purty."

"We'll figure out a way to increase foot traffic to the restaurant, but it'll be a legal way. Got it?" Angie asked, furiously sorting fireworks.

The two nodded, still just standing there.

"Pack!" she ordered.

"Can't we at least sell the ones we already promised people?" Earl asked. "Dey're comin' to pick 'em up—we don't wanna disappoint 'em."

"Get them out of here, right now!" Angie shrieked. The last thing she wanted was any more friends in City Jail.

All three of them were stuffing firecrackers back into crates when they heard footsteps coming down the stairs, and then Paavo's voice calling out. "Hello. I'm looking for—"

Angie launched herself at him, kissing him and spinning him as she did, so that he no longer faced Earl and Vinnie, then she grabbed his hand and hurried up the stairs to the kitchen, where she wrapped her arms around him again.

When she finally broke the kiss, Paavo was in the dining room. He looked a little dazed—pleased, yet confused—at what had just happened.

"You need to stay out of the back," she cried, leading him to a table. "They're having trouble. Butch is upset and won't cook. Let's sit down. How did you find me?"

He glanced at the swinging doors, then sat across from her. "Connie told me. I came by to let you know—"

Just then, a customer walked in, and up to the stand where Earl usually greeted people. Angie jumped up and stuck her head between the doors. "Earl! Get out here. Quick!" she roared, then faced Paavo with a sweet smile.

Earl plunged through the doors just as the customer began to speak. "The name's Agnos. I'm here for—"

"Yeah, I know," Earl shouted, cutting him off. "We ain't got no more."

"Oh? But I was told—"

"You was tol' wrong, buster."

The customer gaped a moment. "Will you get any more—"

"No! Never. Get lost!"

He looked from Earl to Angie, then Paavo, who regarded him and Earl curiously. "Go? But I was promised—"

"Can't you hear? I said out! We lost our cook. No more nothin' here. Leave. Sayonara! *Capisce?*"

"Cook? But I don't need any—"

Earl ran around the stand and grabbed the customer by the lapels. "I said I want you outta here, mister. You got a problem wit' dat?"

The guy raised his hands and backed up. "No, no problem. I'm going. See?" He turned and ran out the door.

Paavo stared at Earl as if he'd just lost his mind.

Angie tugged on his jacket sleeve. "I told you, nerves are a bit frayed."

He looked at her, his brows crossed. Earl straightened out his suit and waddled over to them. "Some people really like Butch's cookin'," he said.

Vinnie, who'd been peeking out of the swinging doors the whole time, came out when Paavo and Earl sat down. "I'll lock the door," he said nervously. "We don' want no more disappointed customers. They might decide to torch the place."

Angie gazed at Paavo, all wide-eyed innocence. "You wanted to talk to me?"

Whatever was going on at Wings, Paavo wanted Angie to have no part of it. He walked her back to her car after getting a promise that she would go home and stay there. After yesterday, he'd tolerate no more ugly surprises. "I want you to keep away from Max Squire and Dennis Pagozzi, both."

"Dennis? Why?" She held his hand as they walked.

"Dennis was married to Veronica Maple." He quickly told her the story. "They were just kids at the time, but still, it means he's a lot more involved in this than he let on."

"How did you find out?"

"Maple's parole officer gave it to me. He's in the city trying to find her for a murder down in Fresno. Also, Pagozzi was involved with fake autographed sports memorabilia. A lot of it's been showing up around town. A dealer was arrested—Wallace Jones. The guy Connie met. We've got reason to think Pagozzi was involved there, as well."

They reached the car and Angie hit the unlock button on her remote, then turned and faced him. "Did he know Jonesy's goods were fake?"

"Robbery's working on it. Just keep away from both those guys." He put his hands on her shoulders, wonder striking him as always at how small and delicate she was.

"What do you have on Max?" she persisted.

"It sounds like he was trying to fence the stolen diamonds." He told her all he'd learned. "If so, he's most likely Veronica's murderer."

"My God," Angie whispered.

He drew her close, and tilted her head toward his. "Be careful, Angel. I'll take care of this, all right?"

"I feel so badly for Connie, though," she whispered.

Not wanting to hear it, he kissed her. As he pulled her closer, his cell phone began to ring.

He answered, and she stepped back with a good-bye wave.

He didn't like the feeling that struck him as he watched her drive away.

"Where the hell is everybody?"

Calderon looked up at the gruff-voiced woman and scowled. "Probably working. Ever try it?"

Helen Melinger stomped toward him, hands on

hips. "Listen, you fatheaded bastard, I work harder than most men and all women I know, so watch your mouth."

Calderon's thick eyebrows nearly reached his pomaded pompadour. "What do you want? Somebody die, or you here to confess to murder? Maybe with an ax?"

"If you must know, I'm trying to find a wimpy little gal named Angie Amalfi. She skedaddled after leaving a shoe to be fixed. She hasn't returned, and her friend's closed up shop, but her fiancé works here, so I thought I'd give it to him."

Calderon waved his thumb toward the back of the room "That's his desk. On the right."

He watched as she swiveled her wide hips to fit through the narrow walkway between cabinets, chairs, and drawers left open.

"Is there a charge?" he asked.

"No. Payment enough will be if she keeps her single male friends out of my shop." Helen grimaced.

"Oh? Such as?"

"Stan something-or-other."

Calderon, who never laughed, suddenly burst out in a loud guffaw. "Stan Bonnette? She brought Stan Bonnette to meet you?"

"Most sickening experience of my life." Helen shuddered.

"You should have seen the anorexic blonde she brought to me." He shook his head.

Helen met his gaze, and then she too laughed. She touched her throat, so unaccustomed was she to the sound.

He liked her laugh. "Since you came all the way down here to deliver a shoe, I don't suppose you have time for a drink across the street? I was off work five minutes ago."

Helen eyed him up and down, not finding him hard on the eyes. "I might be, though I'm not one for wine or bubbly stuff."

"How about a boilermaker?"

She grinned. "You sound like my kind of man."

Chapter 29

"You can't imagine what I just learned." Angie ran into the den. Connie was lying down, an ice pack on her head. "Thank God you didn't get any more involved with Dennis Pagozzi. The man was married to Veronica Maple!"

"Married? And Butch wanted me to meet him?"

"It was annulled. Still, Dennis lied about her!"

It took a moment for Connie to absorb all this. She struggled to sit up, then lay the ice pack aside. "Does this mean Dennis is now a suspect instead of Max?"

"No, no, that isn't what I'm saying. Paavo is still convinced Max has the diamonds, and that would mean Max murdered Veronica to get them."

"What makes him think that?" Connie asked.

"Someone tried to fence them." She told Paavo's story. "But—"

"Max is the only one involved in this case who fits the tall, blond, and scraggly description," Angie explained.

"A lot of men fit that description, and Paavo knows it," Connie said.

"Why are you so ready to defend Max? The guy's scum."

"You're right. Still, when I think back on what he

was like when I was with him, it's hard to believe I was so fooled by him. Here I thought I was a good judge of character. Boy, was I wrong."

"Maybe you're just not a good judge of men to get interested in," Angie said jokingly, trying to lighten the mood and get Connie away from feeling any sympathy toward Squire.

"Isn't that the truth? Look at Kevin, and I was married to him! Come to think of it, he'd fit the fence's description, too, yet he and Max are nothing alike."

"That reminds me," Angie said. "Kevin came to my apartment one day. He'd heard about you seeing a Forty-Niner and wanted to know how serious you were about him."

Connie stilled. "Kevin wanted to know that?"

"He sounded very upset."

"When was that? He never contacted me."

"I'm surprised I didn't tell you . . . it was such a startling visit. Oh, I know why—it was the day before you got arrested! When I next saw you, you were in jail. Kevin was the last thing on my mind."

"The day of the diamond robbery, in other words," Connie said quietly.

"That's right." Angie gave it some thought. "You were with Max, dinner and Lake Merced, right? Someone tipped off the police that the diamonds were at your place, but the police never found them. No one would tip off the police unless they were fairly certain the diamonds were there . . ."

"Unless someone else took them . . ." Connie murmured.

Connie and Angie looked at each other. "Can Kevin get into your apartment?" Angie asked.

"Well, not that I know of. But I wouldn't put anything past him."

"Do you know where he lives?"

Connie nodded. "We can be there in ten minutes."

Kevin was home in his upper Mission district apartment when Angie and Connie arrived. The area had once been incredibly cheap, filled with warehouses and shabby apartments, until rents throughout the city grew astronomically, and ugly warehouses became artsy lofts. There was nothing stylish about Kevin's apartment building, however, or the battered door Connie knocked on.

"Who is it?" he called.

"It's me," Connie answered.

They listened as a series of chains, slide locks, and finally a deadbolt clicked open. When Kevin opened the door, he looked even shabbier than the apartment building—thin and unshaven, wearing a dirty T-shirt and grease-soiled jeans, generally a lot worse than when Angie'd last seen him.

"Were you inside my home last week?" Connie demanded as Kevin stepped backward, and she marched into the apartment nose-to-nose with him. A haze of cigarette smoke overlaid a sour smell coming from the tiny kitchen. Cheap, lumpy furniture reeked of a mixture of tobacco, beer, and sweat.

"Good to see you too, wife." He stood his ground, and she stopped short of bumping into him.

"Ex-wife, and don't forget it!"

Kevin offered Angie and Connie a seat. They both preferred to stand. He sat in the center of the sofa, leaned over the glass, ring-stained coffee table, and lit a cigarette.

"You got yourself into some deep shit this time, Connie," he said, his narrow blue eyes giving her a once-over and seeming to, almost despite himself, like what he saw. "And now, you've dragged me into it as well. What's wrong with you, woman?"

Connie's eyes shot daggers. "I've dragged you in? What the hell are you talking about?"

"Kevin," Angie said, trying to intervene before the conversation spun into a litany of age-old recriminations, "will you please tell us what happened?"

"You tell me." He glanced bitterly from one to the other. "Here I was, concerned about Connie being with some rich dude who was going to break her heart. I wanted to warn her, to tell her I'd be there if she needed me. And you will need me, babe. Believe it."

"You broke into my apartment, didn't you?" Connie screeched. "You prick!"

"I had a key." He glared defiantly.

"How the hell—"

"Go on . . . please," Angie said to Kevin.

Eying Connie warily, he proceeded to tell how he was in the apartment, heading for the kitchen, when he heard a scratching at the front door. Connie wouldn't have to do that to get into her own place. Suddenly uneasy, he hid behind a maroon easy chair in a dark corner of the living room. "Big, ugly sucker," he said. "Always has been. Nobody ever used it."

"Screw you," Connie said with a snort.

Kevin told them about the "chick" who entered. At first, he thought she was Connie. He almost stood up, planning to scare her and get a good laugh, but then he saw that her build wasn't Connie's. Neither was her walk. "You can't have been married to a woman and not recognize her walk or her shape, even in the dark."

"Cute," Connie sneered.

"You always thought I was," he said, catching her eye.

She rolled her eyes and turned away from him.

"Connie," he said, softly this time, his cocky expression suddenly vanished. "I'm sorry. You know I was just kidding around. I'm working; I've been clean for over a year. I'm trying, babe, but without you . . . what good is it?"

She pursed her lips and stared resolutely at the wall.

"Shit," he murmured, "why do I even try?" He gritted his teeth and faced Angie, a determined look in his eyes. "Okay, here's what happened."

He told of the intruder looking around, sneaking, peering at shelves, in closets, then sticking her hand behind the TV. There was something about her that spelled danger. She poked around a bit more, and as she was going out the door, she grabbed one of Connie's dolls.

After waiting a good five minutes to be sure she wasn't coming back, he looked to see what was so interesting behind the TV and found a small velvet sack. Inside were stones that looked like diamonds. He wasn't thinking clearly—only that he held a small fortune in his hand. He stuffed them in his pocket and ran.

"In your pocket? I heard about a hundred diamonds were stolen," Connie said.

"You're dreaming. There were ten. They were beauties, big and crystal clear. I tried to fence them, but no one will touch them. Somebody real bad wants them. I could see the fear in the fences' eyes."

"So you still have them," Angie asked, excited.

"That's why I'm staying locked in here. I don't know who wants them, but if they learn I have them . . ." He took the black velvet out of his pocket, opened it, and dropped the diamonds into his hand. They were eye-poppingly huge—two or three carats. Much larger than Angie's, to her dismay. But they were white diamonds, not exotic Siberian blue like hers, she thought smugly, glancing down at her ring once more.

"Give them to me," Connie said. "They aren't yours, and they're causing me all kinds of trouble."

"Give them to you?" Kevin looked shocked. "Do you know the trouble they've caused *me*?"

"Do I care?"

He glared at Connie, fuming. "That'd be a big change! Why start now? If you ask me, I deserve some recompense for my time and trouble. What if you had them? You might be dead! These guys are dangerous."

"I want them!" Connie yelled.

"What are they worth to you?" Kevin hollered right back.

"I'll show you." With that, she socked him in the stomach hard, and as he bent forward, she shoved him.

He toppled over, and the diamonds went flying.

Connie and Angie picked them up, and the two dashed out of the apartment.

Paavo was at work when Angie called on her cell phone to let him know she and Connie were heading for Homicide, and that Kevin was the one who'd taken the diamonds and tried to fence them. It wasn't Max after all. Max was innocent.

"You went *where*?" Paavo felt his blood pressure soar, and caught himself, biting his tongue. How many times could he warn her? "Don't be so sure about Max," he cautioned, working to keep his voice calm. "You said you have ten diamonds. There are a lot still out there."

"Everything points toward Dennis now—the dead woman is his wife."

"Maybe," Paavo said skeptically. "But why?"

"Maybe he has the rest of the diamond?" Angie offered. "Butch didn't like Dennis's idea to expand the restaurant, and if Dennis doesn't play football, he'll need money."

"It still doesn't fit," Paavo said. "Go straight home now. I've got a lead on Squire's whereabouts, and Yosh and I are just leaving. I'll come by later to pick up the diamonds."

"Can I leave them with Lt. Hollins?" she asked.

"Hold on." He made a quick call and got back to her. "Vic Walters is at his desk; Robbery is down the hall. Room four-eighty. He'll be waiting."

"Great. Be careful."

"Promise me you'll go straight home after you drop off the diamonds."

"Of course," she said.

Why didn't he believe her?

He was on his feet, putting on his jacket to find Max, when a small man wearing a green jacket, vest, shirt, and trousers, with green face paint, green pointy ears, a green bowler hat, and green suede shoes with up-turned pointed toes sprang into Homicide. A good-sized crowd chortled, clapped, and murmured behind him. "Paavo Smith?" he trilled.

Luis Calderon pointed at Paavo.

The green bean suddenly began to cartwheel down the aisle between desks, cabinets, and chairs to land on one knee at Paavo's feet. With his arms outstretched like someone about to propose, he announced, "I'm Larry the Leprechaun from Shamrock Motors. I'm here, Paavo Smith, because this is your lucky day!"

Paavo looked at him as if he were a giant green bug that needed to be stepped on.

"No, it isn't." Paavo barreled past the guy and marched out of the room daring anyone to say a word.

They didn't.

* * *

He couldn't believe what he was seeing. Veronica. Alive.

She was leaving the Hall of Justice, getting into a Mercedes.

They'd tricked him. He thought she was dead, but she wasn't. That was why there was nothing in the newspaper, no word of looking for her killer.

Was she working with the cops now? With Homicide? She must be.

The Mercedes pulled out of the parking lot.

He had to follow. He thought he'd killed her once. He wouldn't miss this time.

Chapter 30

Connie didn't know what to do. While Angie had delivered the diamonds to the robbery inspector, she'd stayed in the lobby and used a pay phone to check for messages at her home and business.

When she heard Max Squire's voice, she nearly fainted.

She returned his call. He'd gotten himself an inexpensive cell phone and was currently at the Main Library at the Civic Center. He was earning twenty dollars an hour to straighten out the accounting books for the organization that ran the shelter where he'd been staying. It was a bargain for them—a professional CPA could well charge ten times that amount, and it meant money for him.

He wasn't staying there any longer, though, because he knew the police had shown up looking for him. He'd been lying low ever since.

Still, he'd been worried about her, had checked on her apartment and business many times, but she seemed to have vanished. He wanted to see her, to try to explain.

She was angry with him—beyond angry—and

wanted answers. "Meet me," he said, "and I'll give them to you."

The Main Library was a busy place. She'd be safe meeting him there, and she wouldn't let him sweet-talk her into going anyplace where they'd be alone. This girl was no fool. She'd seen lots of TV shows and movies about murderers. No way was she going to let herself get into some dangerous situation.

She glanced over at Angie, now driving them back to her apartment.

Not most of the time, at least.

Why should she meet him? What she should do was call the police and have them arrest his ass! He was a sitting duck.

He'd trusted her, though; maybe that was why she couldn't do it.

She told him she just didn't know if she'd be there.

He said he'd wait all evening.

More trust.

God, but she hated it when people she hated decided to be nice. What was with that?

"Angie," she said as they neared the library, "I need to be alone for a while. Drop me off at the Main Library, okay? I'll take a cab back to your place later."

"The library? Are you joking?"

"No. I want to think. A lot has happened."

"You want to think about Kevin, don't you?" Angie said. "There's still an undercurrent between you two, you know."

She didn't want to hear that. "It's ancient history, nothing more. When I see him, the disappointment comes back all over again."

"Maybe this time he's straightened himself out," Angie suggested.

"Sure—like trying to fence diamonds he stole from

my place. If that's straight, I don't know crooked."
Connie turned away, staring out the window. "I'm
tired of hoping."

Angie nodded. "Are you sure you wouldn't rather
come back to my place?"

"I need to do this. Let me out at the corner."

Angie peered quizzically at her, but did as directed.

"Don't worry about me," Connie said. "I'll see you
later."

"Be careful."

Connie headed into the building. It was recently
built, with lots of glass, very modern. Frankly, she preferred the old Greco-Roman building that had served
as the main branch for decades. But, as she was learning, all things must change.

She went into the reading room and almost didn't
recognize Max. He'd gotten his hair cut short and was
wearing gold-rimmed glasses. Even his clothes were
fresh and clean. Hints of the high-powered financial
advisor were before her, a man he'd kept well hidden
up to now. Had he kept the side of himself who could
be a killer hidden as well?

He stood as she approached. "Shall we go outside so
we can talk?" he asked.

"No," she said too quickly. "No one is using the
table and chairs in the far corner. Let's go there."

He nodded, his gaze telling her he understood why
she didn't want to be alone with him.

They sat catty-corner on wooden chairs at a wooden
table, and Max slid his chair closer to hers, his demeanor sad. "You don't trust me at all, do you?"

"My store was trashed," she said. But he was right,
he seemed like a stranger now.

He shut his eyes. "I'm sorry. I had no idea."

She didn't want his sympathy. She was barely able

to contain her anger. "Tell me what the hell this is all about. Why am I involved?"

He relayed the story she already knew about Veronica embezzling from him. "So what?" she demanded. "You aren't the first guy who's ever trusted the wrong woman. She embezzled, she went to jail. Case closed. There's got to be more."

"She still has the money," Max said. "I thought that if I could get my hands on it, I could pay back my clients, get the lien against future earnings lifted off my back, and have a life again. I kept trying to find her."

"Why?" She spat the word at him. "Did you think if you asked, she'd just turn it over to you?"

He shook his head. "I thought that if I threatened, she might."

"Threatened to do what?"

"To kill her."

Connie stared at him. "And did you?"

"Did I what? I never saw her—except once. The time she used to frame us both. I still don't know where the money is. Or where *she* is."

She wondered if he was telling the truth. She wanted to believe him, and yet strangely, in cleaning himself up, he was no longer the scraggly, vulnerable man she'd been attracted to. He was more in control, more calculating and self-contained. She was always a beer-and-pretzel kind of gal, and he was suddenly chilled white wine and roasted Brie. An absurd sense of loss surrounded her, and she rubbed her arms.

"If she had those millions," she continued, "why didn't she just leave the country once out of prison?"

"That's what I can't figure either. It has to do with Dennis. She was hanging around him. He must know, but he pretends he hardly knows her."

"When they were teenagers, they got married in Mexico. His family helped him get it annulled."

Max stared at her a long moment, then he laughed bitterly. "Wouldn't you know it? God, what a fool I was."

"Do you think she gave Dennis the money, and now, he won't give it back? Could that be why she's here?"

"She wouldn't give it to him. I can't imagine her trusting anyone enough to give it to, but then"—another sullen chuckle—"I'm the last person to try to figure her out. I never could."

"If you had the money, how would you have hidden it?"

He picked up his pencil and tapped it, point, then eraser, then point again. "In offshore banks. That's what I did with a lot of my clients' money. That was the system she broke into."

"So, she understands offshore accounts. What would have stopped her from setting up one of her own?"

"I expect that's exactly what she did," he said with a shrug.

"How would she get into it? Could there be someplace in the city that she needs to go to?"

"It's easier than that. Any Internet account would get her in. It's just a string of numbers—a code."

"Numbers? Like, twelve or so?"

"Even longer. Plus, a couple of passwords."

Connie remembered the string of numbers she and Angie had found hidden in Veronica's room. It had been torn in a way that some of the numbers might have been removed. "What if she didn't have all the numbers?" Connie mused. "What if someone else had part of the code? She might have been here trying to get the rest of the code."

His gaze hardened. "What do you know?"

"Nothing!" she cried. "I'm trying to figure out what's going on. Why I'm involved; why some fiend is trying to ruin my life!"

He stared at her, trying to calm his suspicions. "You're right." He tossed aside the pencil and rubbed his forehead. "I've allowed myself to be consumed by her for so long, I can't think straight. You know what's the most ridiculous part of all?"

She shook her head.

"I don't really care anymore. Seeing her again, in that quick moment, I realized the woman I loved never really existed. I imagined her as what I wanted her to be, not what she was. The part that makes me the angriest is that I wasted three years of my life over her.

"I could have been working to pay off the liens against me, I could have gone back to court, had changes made in the judgment after the insurance companies paid off my clients, done something more than sit around brooding, lovesick and feeling sorry for myself." He caught Connie's eye. "I could have tried to find a good woman to love and worked to make myself worthy of winning her love in return."

"Nothing's stopping you," she said.

He bowed his head, and again the thought struck her that he might have killed Veronica. Her heart sank.

"You could have been a fine man, Max," she whispered, "a wonderful friend, and a caring lover."

"Not the way I was, not before I met Ronnie . . . and not after."

Ronnie? The night they'd first met, when he'd called out a name, she'd thought he was calling to her and she'd simply misheard. But he wasn't. It was Veronica he'd called. It was always about Veronica.

She folded her hands. "I'm so sorry, Max."

With great tenderness, he leaned over and lightly kissed her. She stared at him in shock, and he gently brushed a lock back from her cheek, his gaze studying her as if burning her face into his memory. "If I can ever become the kind of man you deserve, and if I'm lucky enough that you haven't found someone else—or if that ex of yours who you still care about despite your denials hasn't straightened himself out—I'd like to see you again, Connie. You've touched me more deeply than you know, with your serious ways and your good heart."

She wasn't sure how to answer, and the silence grew awkward.

He stood, understanding. "There's something I've got to take care of. When it's over, whenever that might be, I'll come back."

She nodded, and watched him leave.

Chapter 31

Vinnie stood over a kettle of boiling water. After finding a jar of Prego's Alfredo sauce in the grocery, he decided Fettuccini Alfredo would make a nice addition to Wing's menu. Since Butch wasn't interested in cooking these days, he'd do it himself. All he needed was to spoon the sauce over fat fettuccini noodles and add a ten-ninety-five price tag. Voilà.

And if it didn't work, he still had firecrackers in the basement. He'd just have to figure out a different way to get rid of them, since Angie was on a rampage about selling them from the restaurant. He didn't think she'd tell the cop, but he'd learned over the years, you just can't trust women. Not even the ones you liked. Once they opened their mouths, no telling what might come out.

When the water began to boil, he added a pound of fettuccini. The pieces were long and stuck out over the top. He smashed them down, breaking them into small bits.

He peered into the pot. The noodles were at the bottom and there was a whole lot of water to spare.

He added another pound of fettuccini. Since the

279

parts not covered by water wouldn't cook—he'd
learned that from Butch—he broke and scrunched the
noodles so water covered them.

The addition of the noodles caused the water tem-
porarily to stop boiling. He was able to see into the pot
even better now. It wasn't even half full! Two more
pounds went in before he had to ladle out some of the
excess water so the pot wouldn't overflow. Probably,
this meant a trip to the store to buy more Prego.

Finally, the kettle was filled almost to the top with
noodles.

The water that was there started bubbling furiously,
foaming, and boiling over the edge of the pot. He
turned the flame down to get it to stop bubbling.

Eventually, it did.

Angie paced around her apartment, her nerves frayed.
She tried to reach Paavo, but he wasn't at his desk, and
she didn't want to bother him in the field. Connie still
hadn't returned.

Angie had watched to make sure she went into the
library, then watched longer to make sure she didn't
pop right out again, until guilt for spying on her best
friend consumed her and she went home.

The phone rang and she pounced on it.

"Miss Angie, Vinnie's tryin' to cook," Earl cried.
"You gotta help."

"Vinnie? You're joking, right?"

"I wish I was. What am I gonna do?"

"I'll be right there."

Before she got to the restaurant, Connie called her
on her cell phone, saying she had interesting news.
They agreed to meet at Wings.

The restaurant was empty once more, Vinnie sitting

at a table with a glass of red wine. Angie went straight to him.

"I heard you were cooking," she said skeptically. "Haven't we been through this once already?"

"I'm serious this time, Angie," Vinnie said. "If a bozo like Butch can do it, so can I. In fact, I got something on the stove now. It was a breeze. No funny business this time."

"It's cooking in the kitchen and you're out here?"

"It's hot in there," he complained.

"Kitchens often are," she said. "Where is Butch, by the way?"

"He was wit' his nephew last time I saw him," Earl replied. "Up in the apartment."

Just then, Connie walked in. The taxi dropped her off right in front of the restaurant.

"Thank goodness you're safe." Angie jumped to her feet. "I kept imagining things happening to you, and it being all my fault."

"Not this time," Connie said. Not exactly the ringing endorsement Angie had hoped for, but it would have to do.

"I saw Max," Connie admitted, joining the others at the table.

"My God!" Angie cried. "Where is he? Did you call Paavo? We've got to catch him."

"I don't think he did it," she said. "I think he's innocent. He had no reason to kill"—she almost said "to kill Veronica," but realized that fact was still a secret—"to *do it* other than hatred, and he's well over that."

"Sid Fernandez wouldn't have *done anything* before getting the diamonds," Angie said. "So who did?" It all came back to Dennis, she thought. She didn't want to say it here, though.

Earl and Vinnie must have read her mind, because they caught each other's eyes and looked downcast. She wondered what they might know—what she was overlooking.

"Anyway, Max told me where Veronica may have hidden the money," Connie said excitedly. "Remember the torn piece of paper we found in her room with all those numbers? Max said offshore accounts use codes—even longer ones than we found. Someone else must have the other half of the code. She must have been here, in the city, trying to get it. Now, we just have to figure out who has the rest of the code, get the money, give it back, and Max's problems will be over."

Just then, the smell of something burning reached them from the kitchen, followed by a loud thud.

Max had been seen at a skid-row hotel on Third Street. When Paavo and Yosh got there, the room he'd been given was empty. It looked like he wouldn't be returning.

They were headed back to Yosh's Ford when the walking split-pea-soup guy appeared. "Larry the Leprechaun at your service, Inspector Smith. I'm here to give you the keys to your dream car." He pointed at a black Corvette parked across the street.

Paavo stopped and stared at the gorgeous car, then got into the Ford and locked the door.

"I've got to stop her," he said to Yosh, a tremor in his voice. "I didn't want to. I was hoping she'd get over it on her own."

"You got to be careful not to hurt her feelings," Yosh cautioned, salivating over the car. "Remember, your partner gets to ride with you."

"This is too much."

Yosh grinned at him. "You must have told her you

used to like *Miami Vice*. Didn't that guy drive a Corvette?"

"He sure did," Paavo said wistfully as they drove off, leaving Larry the Leprechaun standing slack-jawed in front of the car.

In no time they'd gone three blocks to another hotel, one Squire had stayed at a couple of days before. He might have returned.

When they walked into the shabby and urine-stained lobby, they found themselves in the middle of a drug deal. The dealer burst past them, hitting Paavo hard and knocking him into Yosh, who also toppled over.

They were running down the block after the dealer when Mr. Green Jeans jumped in front of Paavo. "Mister, before I can get paid, I've got to give you the damned car!"

Paavo didn't stop and the wayward elf flipped, head over heels, into a sidewalk trash receptacle.

Paavo and Yosh caught up to the dealer.

A paddy wagon was already on the scene before the little man came to. He stayed hidden until all the cops drove away.

Angie followed Earl and Vinnie as they ran into the kitchen. Black smoke made it hard to see. A strange white glob, like a temple of dough, jutted high over the kettle, listing to one side. The top of the temple had been broken off and lay splattered across the stovetop, part of it being barbecued by the flame from the burner. At the same time, smoke and the sharp smell of burning noodles were billowing up from the inside of the kettle.

"Turn the gas off!" Angie yelled.

Vinnie did so, then he and Earl each grabbed a

potholder and one handle of the kettle. They lifted it off the stove and into the sink.

"What is it?" Angie asked curiously, looking at the peculiar lump.

"It looks like it's alive," Connie said. "Like brains, squiggly things all mooshed together."

"We ain't never had not'in' like dat on our menu before," Earl said.

"What's wrong with you people?" Vinnie cried. "It's fettucini. Why did it stick together?"

"All you have to do to cook pasta is boil it," Angie said, disgusted. "For eight or nine minutes."

"Oh. So, maybe I overcooked it a little. Is that a crime?" Vinnie asked.

"What's a crime is your cookin' anyt'ing. We gotta get Butch back to work!" Earl cried. He spun around to open some doors and vent the room, and yelled.

Dennis stepped out from the far wall. He had a gun.

"What're you doing?" Vinnie asked, his eyes wide on Dennis's gun. "Whatsa matter with you?"

"I never wanted to hurt anyone," he said. "You forced me to do this."

"You're da one who's made Butch miserable," Earl scolded. "Why'd you wanna do dat to your own uncle? He was good to you. Didn't even tell da cops what a jerk you are!"

"Will you guys just shut up?" Dennis yelled. Angry tears glistened in his eyes. "I didn't do anything. Don't you get it yet? It was Veronica. She ruined everything. My football career, my plans for a sports bar, my life. All I needed was some of her damned money. My share, plus a little more to borrow, to get me out of debt and back on my feet. Do you know how expensive it is to live like a football star? To live the way everyone expects? And now my contract isn't being renewed. All my dreams, everything I've ever worked for, it's all finished. Give me the code, Angie."

"Where's Butch?" Vinnie asked, as the four of them slowly eased backward.

"He's upstairs in the apartment. I came down the back way and was going to cut through the restaurant to leave when I heard you talking. I need that code, then I'll get out of here." His voice was desperate.

"You have the other half of the paper?" Angie asked from behind Earl. "Why?"

"I . . . I saw her working in Max's office and we started talking. I knew a bit about the offshore accounts. We set one up for me—just to see if it'd work. I had no idea she'd go so far . . .

"In the end, I couldn't say anything about her because if word got out that I'd taught her anything, even though I was innocent, my career would be over. But also, if she said anything to the authorities about me, I'd tell where the money was. So she kept quiet, and so did I. Then, she came back here, expecting I'd give her my part of the code. She wanted nearly all the money, saying it was payment for the three years she did. But I needed it! I needed it more than she did!"

"You didn't ask how we got the code," Angie said quietly. "That must mean you know Veronica's dead."

He froze, searching Angie's face to see if this was another sick joke. "She's dead?" he whispered.

They said nothing, and the truth hit him hard. His whole body went limp, the hand holding the gun dropped to his side. "She can't be. Not Veronica. How? What happened to her?"

"Someone shot her," Angie said, studying him.

He shook his head. "Who did it?" His voice was thick with emotion.

"We don't know," Angie said.

"El Toro," Dennis whispered. "That bastard! I warned her!" Tears glistened in his eyes.

"He killed his partner, Julius Rodriguez, thinking Julius and Veronica scammed him out of the diamonds," Connie said. "But he didn't kill her—he wanted the diamonds too much to kill her before retrieving them."

"Then who?" Dennis demanded. His face drawn, he seemed genuinely heartbroken over Veronica's death.

"You knew Veronica," Angie cried. "Who else did she con? That's the murderer!"

"But that means it's someone who didn't take the money or the diamonds," Dennis said. "It doesn't make sense."

"It does," Angie said slowly, testing the theory, "if she was killed out of passion. Because of betrayal, not for wealth. Look at the reactions she's caused in you and Max. She knew how to wrap men around her finger—she acted on pure gut emotion, and the reaction she solicited was the same."

"You're right," Connie said. "What men did she know? Who was close to her?"

Angie tried to think of every man Paavo had ever mentioned who knew Veronica. Max . . . Dennis . . . Fernandez . . . Julius . . . Butch . . .

"Oh, my God!" Angie said. "I know who it is. I've got to call Paavo. He might be in danger!"

Chapter 32

While Yosh went back to the flophouse to check on Max's whereabouts, Paavo headed in the opposite direction across town. In lavish Sea Cliff, he walked up to the door of Pagozzi's home, rang the bell, and knocked, but there was no answer.

He stepped out of the front entry to see if he could get to the back door, or if there was any sign of movement in the house, when he saw a figure in jeans and a brown jacket dart from behind a hedge to scramble over a wooden gate to the side yard.

Paavo sprinted after him. The backyard was small, as is typical of even the most luxurious city homes, and the runner realized he had no escape there. One yard backed up to another, and another after that.

He raised his hands and turned around.

"We meet at last." Paavo's gun was drawn.

"You must be Angie's fiancé," Max said. "She talks about you incessantly."

"She does the same about you," Paavo replied, "trying to convince me I was wrong about your guilt, or trying to convince Connie that she was wrong about your innocence."

"I haven't done anything wrong here," Max said. "Except that I didn't want to be seen."

"Why not?"

"I came here to confront Dennis. I was convinced, for a while, after you learned he and Veronica had been married, that he was an accomplice of hers. That he worked with her to swindle my clients and ruin me. That the two laughed together over it. But as I stood here and waited for him to open the door, I realized I no longer cared."

Paavo studied the man, taking in the measure of him, of the truth behind his words. "Explain."

"It wasn't worth it. What I did to my life—waiting for three years for Veronica to get out so I could confront her—was pure, self-indulgent idiocy. Her and Pagozzi—to hell with them both. I want no part of either of them. So when I saw you pull up, I ran. It was foolish, not criminal."

"A pretty speech, but you could have been running for another reason." He paused. "Veronica Maple is dead, and you killed her."

A panoply of emotions flickered across Max's face—surprise, horror, relief, and regret. "No," he whispered, and then paused. "She was so very full of life . . . her mind always racing with ideas, big, exciting ideas." His lips tightened and his voice turned thick. "She could have done so much."

Yet another man Maple had double-crossed, and who seemed to love her. "If you didn't kill her, Squire, who did?"

Paavo's question snapped him out of his reverie. He shook his head. "I don't know."

"Dennis Pagozzi?"

"Dennis is no killer. And neither am I. The guys

Ronnie was involved with, in the jewelry heist—they were killers. But I find it hard to imagine they did it."

Paavo eyed Squire a long moment, then holstered his gun. "They're pros," he said. "It wasn't a pro hit, and they wouldn't have killed her until after getting the diamonds."

Max lowered his arms, then shut his eyes a moment in relief at being believed. "So," he said, when he was able to speak again, "the question is, who did it? There's got to be someone . . . someone else she conned into helping her. That's what she was best at— a real-life femme fatale, like the rotten women in the film noir of the nineteen-thirties and -forties. I've never encountered anyone like her before, and hope I never do again."

"Someone else she conned . . ." Paavo murmured, and suddenly he realized the suspicions he'd harbored for some time about her murderer were correct. He knew the identify. "You're right. We've been looking at this from the wrong angle. We've been looking at money and diamonds. But greed isn't always the motive for all that's bad in the world. Sometimes it happens for the most unlikely reason—like love."

"Love?" Max scoffed, but then his expression turned thoughtful and he nodded. "Yes, I suppose you're right. The pursuit of love can make men do all kinds of things quite out of character."

Paavo opened the side gate—it unlocked from the inside—and stepped out onto the sidewalk with Max. "It can cause them to change,"—he gave Max a hard stare—"cause them to rise above the trouble or injustice society throws at them. Or, other times, with other people, it can cause them to simply go bad."

Max said nothing.

"Give it some thought." Paavo turned away.

Just then, the leprechaun drove up in the black Corvette, stopped in the middle of the street, opened the car door, and started to get out.

Paavo pushed aside one flap of his jacket so his gun was visible. The Jolly Green Pipsqueak popped back into the car and drove off in a rush.

Paavo got into his city issue Chevy and picked up his cell phone to give a call to the Fresno PD.

As he drove, in the distance, he could just make out what might have become his very own gorgeous black sports car. He couldn't stop a heartfelt sigh.

Sometimes love did turn a man's life upside down.

"I think I get it, too," Dennis said, putting the gun in his jacket pocket.

"Well, I don't," Connie said. "All I understand is, it isn't Max."

"Tell her," Angie said.

He wiped his eyes. "I didn't think I'd be crying to hear Veronica was dead. I thought I'd celebrate such news. She nearly ruined my life. Did I tell you that? All . . . all because she loved me, and she just wasn't enough. I guess that means, in a way, I ruined her life even more."

The others said nothing as he tried to compose himself.

"I remember her telling me things, like how she was able to convince her parole officer that she was putting off her release until his day off 'to avoid suspicion.' Can you imagine? She'd told him about the money she'd hidden, and he thought the two were going to go away together, leave the country, and live off of it the rest of their lives. She used him the whole time she was in stir, getting him to move her to more malleable cellmates, to get her simple jobs—heck, the last six months she worked in the prison library, where he'd 'visit' her in the stacks. She had the jerk wrapped around her little finger. He thought she loved him," Dennis started to laugh, even as he cried because she was dead.

"God, Veronica thought she was such a genius, and she ends up killed by someone who was just plain stupid!" Dennis's sobs and laughter grew louder. "Is that funny, or what?"

A gunshot sounded, and in the shocked silence that followed, Dennis fell to the ground.

Then the lights went out.

Max watched Paavo get in his car and head after the leprechaun in the Corvette. He shook his head and smiled. Connie had told him about Angie's little surprises for Paavo. This one was a bit over the top.

Max breathed deeply, filling his lungs with fresh sea air.

He was free now. Free for the first time in three years. Free of the sickness he thought of as love; free of hatred; revenge; and now, free of the need to hide from the police.

When he was ready, he would go back to Wings and apologize to Earl, Vinnie, and Butch. Even to Angie, who, in the way she helped Connie, had shown him what true friendship was all about. And to Connie. Especially to Connie.

Puffy white cumulus clouds floated in a crystal blue sky. His heart swelled, and he started walking. As he went, his shuffling step turned springy, and soon, he began to whistle.

He'd take his time going to Wings. No need to hurry anymore.

* * *

Angie knew the layout of the restaurant like the back of her hand. As soon as she saw Vinnie hit the lights, she grabbed Connie's arm and led her to the stairway down to the basement storeroom, Earl and Vinnie right behind them.

They shut and locked the storeroom door, then switched on the light, while Angie frantically called nine-one-one on her cell phone.

Someone banged against the door. Earl and Vinnie lunged at it, trying to hold it shut.

Another thud jarred the door, and the lock sprang open, pushing the two small men back.

Connie screamed, and all of them leaped behind the crates of fireworks.

A stocky bald-headed man carrying a gun entered the room.

"Get up. Put your hands up!" he yelled.

"First tell us," Angie called, cowering ever lower behind the crate as she did so, hoping to throw him off kilter and buy time. "Are you the stupid parole officer?"

"Come out of there, Veronica. I won't hurt you. Not this time." He inched closer to the crates while Angie and the others frantically tried to find something, anything, to use to protect themselves.

"Please, Veronica. Talk to me. Tell me you're alive," he said.

"Stop! She's scared of you," Angie hollered. "Leave her alone!"

He froze. "Scared? Of me? Veronica, how can you be scared after all I did for you? After the way I loved you and helped make life easy for you in prison?" His voice choked. "I gave up everything for you. My wife. My job. My home." Tears coursed down his cheeks.

Angie nodded vigorously at Connie, trying to get her to answer him.

"Tell me I was wrong about you," Lexington pleaded. "Tell me you still love me."

Angie gave Connie a kick, but she was too scared to reply.

"Damn you! Talk to me!" He fired the gun. Connie and Angie screamed and cringed. "This time I won't miss!"

"Don't! Please," Connie whimpered.

"Veronica?" he whispered, then stepped closer. "Veronica, is that you?"

"Yes," Connie murmured.

"Oh, God!" he cried, joyous now. "I thought you were dead. I thought I'd killed you. But then I saw you near the jail, and I realized how much I still love you. We'll go away like we planned. I never cared about the money. I just want you."

As Lexington spoke, Earl and Vinnie quietly eased a package of firecrackers out of one crate, Roman candles and bottle rockets out of another.

"Come on, Veronica. If you love me, you'll come to me."

Suddenly, a man's voice shouted from the kitchen, "Hello? Is Angie Amalfi around? My God! There's a man hurt here!"

Angie and Connie exchanged glances. "I'm here!" Angie yelled. "I'm downstairs! Call the—"

Lexington spun around as footsteps hurried down the stairs and a little man wearing green clothes and a sour expression limped into the storeroom. He stormed past Lexington as if the pudgy bald fellow didn't exist. "Where are you, lady? Is this another one of your stupid charades?" He walked right up to the crate Angie hid behind. "I see you! You can't hide from me!" He threw the car keys on the crate. "I tried to give it to him, I really did. I want my money!"

Angie gaped at him. She'd forgotten all about the new car she'd ordered for Paavo.

"Shut the hell up!" Lexington roared.

Angie covered her head with her arms.

The leprechaun whirled around. "Who do you think you're—" His gaze dropped from Lexington's face to the gun in his hand. "Ohmygod! You mean that guy upstairs was really . . ."

"Get over there!" Lexington ordered, waving his gun. The human pickle turned chalky white.

Suddenly a barrage of what sounded like machine-gun fire erupted. Lexington dived to the ground, firing as he hit.

The leprechaun bolted into a corner. At the same time, Vinnie lit a Roman candle and Earl a bottle rocket.

Connie reached into a crate and came up with a handful of cherry bombs. She grabbed a couple of Vinnie's matches, lit the bombs one by one, and tossed them at Lexington.

He crawled from one side of the storeroom to the other to avoid the firepower.

Pinwheels skittered across the floor, whistling and shooting off multicolored sparkles. Aerial spinners whirled overhead, missles and rockets launched, starbursts lit the ceiling, while more packets of firecrackers blasted.

The leprechaun sobbed.

"You tricked me!" Lexington shrieked. "You don't love me. This is a game." He stood, pointing the gun. "Another of your games."

While Earl and Vinnie tried to figure out how to

light a smoke bomb, Angie pulled a can of hairspray out of Connie's purse, then grabbed one of Vinnie's matches.

Earl, Vinnie, and Connie saw what Angie was up to, and all began to shout, "No! Don't!" as she aimed a plume of hairspray at a box of firecrackers and then threw a match at it.

The spray ignited and she lobbed the hairspray canister onto the crate.

Angie and her friends hit the ground, arms over their heads, as Lexington raised his gun at Connie.

The crate exploded, knocking Lexington across the room. He hit a wall and dropped.

Fire from the first crate caused the others to go off,\ and the room became a smoke-filled mass of firecrackers, sparklers, whistles, and lights. A Fourth-of-July vision of hell.

When the smoke and ringing in her ears lessened, Angie heard Paavo's voice. "Angie, are you in here? Can you hear me?"

"Hide!" she cried. "It's the parole officer! He's a killer."

"I know. I've got him handcuffed."

At his words and calm tone, Angie popped her head up over what remained of the fireworks crates. Her hair was singed, her face, clothes and hands black with soot. "Thank God!" she said, and ran into his arms. "What are you doing here?"

Paavo held her, then brushed some soot from her nose and cheeks. "I came to tell you to stop sending people in crazy costumes to see me. Also, to warn you to watch for Lexington, especially after learning the Fresno police suspected he killed a pawnshop owner." He faced Lexington. "Was it to hide your trail, or to make Veronica seem more dangerous, or both?"

Lexington, who was sitting handcuffed on the floor, stunned and looking crazier than ever, didn't answer.

As Paavo spoke, Connie, Earl, and Vinnie also stood and dusted soot and gunpowder off themselves. He scrutinized them. "What the hell happened in here?"

"Lexington confessed," Angie blurted, with a quick glance at her friends. "That's all."

As Paavo's eyes narrowed and his lips tightened, the sound of police entering the restaurant reached them. Paavo pushed Lexington ahead of him up the stairs. The others followed.

In the kitchen, Butch had stopped the flow of blood from Pagozzi's shoulder, and Dennis was conscious. Angie called for an ambulance as the place filled with cops responding to Angie's and Butch's earlier nine-one-one calls, plus several neighbors' complaints about an all-out war having broken out in the small restaurant.

Paavo Mirandized Lexington and turned him over to the uniforms for the trip to City Jail.

"You used me," Lexington yelled at Connie as he was being led out the door. "You deserved to die! I loved you, you bitch! And I killed you! Maybe I'm not as dumb as you thought, *Veronica*!"

Finally, the paramedics took Dennis to the hospital, Butch with him, and Angie, Paavo, Connie, Vinnie, and Earl were left alone in the restaurant, shaken and saddened by all that had occurred.

Paavo went back down to the storeroom and looked at the now burned and smoldering crates with Chinese lettering, the firecracker paper, rocket and sparkler remnants lying all over the floor. "What is all this stuff? It looks like fireworks, but they're illegal in this city."

"It's confetti," Angie said immediately.

"That's right," Vinnie agreed. "Chinese confetti."

"We had some popcorn down here, too," Connie added. "When Lexington wasn't looking, Angie put it in a box of confetti and lit the box."

"Yes!" Angie cried, giving Connie a thumbs-up. "It began to pop, and this is the result."

Paavo frowned. "If that's the case, where's the popcorn now?"

"I was hungry," Earl said. "Sorry, boss, but I t'ink I ate da evidence."

Paavo looked from one to the other, then said simply, "Let's get this mess cleaned up."

A charred and still smoking green hat popped up from behind a cabinet in one corner and a quaking voice called out, "May I please go home now?"

Chapter 33

 Exhausted, Connie entered her apartment, kicked off her shoes, and flopped onto the sofa. The insurance claim on her shop had been approved, and for the past week she'd been picking out paint colors and wallpaper, and had gone on a buying spree for figurines and knickknacks, plus a line of more upscale home decorations—brass and pewter and pottery pieces, unique tea, coffee, and chocolate sets, rustic crockery—things Angie had convinced her to buy, the kind of merchandise shoppers couldn't find at Macy's home store. It was fun and filled her with new enthusiasm for her business.

She flipped through her mail and stopped at a letter from Zakarian Jewelers. Inside was a check for $10,000 in reward money. Her heart nearly stopped at the sum.

She and Angie had retrieved her porcelain-face doll from a pawnshop with the ticket found at Veronica's. At first, they were puzzled, but soon realized what the doll had been used for. Angie handed Connie the doll, saying it was hers to do with as she wished, and then left.

A half million dollars' worth of diamonds lay hidden in the doll's stuffing. Connie could have tried to smuggle them out of the country, fenced them, or turned them in. Her choice.

Her life.

Angie was giving her the chance to do with it as she wanted, but she'd seen firsthand what wrong choices could do to a man, or a woman. She'd turned them in, and then offered to split the reward, if any, with Angie.

Angie refused any part of it, only saying she was glad for the choice Connie had made.

Check in hand, Connie brewed a cup of tea, glancing again and again at the tidy sum.

After all the trouble she'd had, it was only right to do something special with at least a small part of the money. But what?

This whole mess had started with a blind date, a date who'd stiffed her. Maybe she could create a dream date for herself. One so hot it sizzled.

Carmel was one of her favorite places. What about a date there? Romantic images filled her head of a helicopter ride down the Pacific coast to Carmel, dining at the very best restaurant, dancing at the most fun nightspots, a helicopter ride back to the city, and then breakfast at dawn at the top of the Fairmont. Yes! She could really get into this.

Her dream bubble burst. Who would she take?

Girlfriends were out for something like that, fun though it would be to go with Angie, or even Helen Melinger, whose latest motorcycle-riding companion bore a striking resemblance to one of the inspectors Paavo worked with. What was with that?

Anyway, Helen wasn't much fun, and Angie was too busy trying to convince Paavo to take the Corvette she wanted to give him. So far, he was stubbornly refusing.

For something this cool, Connie needed a male friend.

If she took Stan, she'd have to shoot herself.

Max was a possibility. The other day, she'd run into him on the street near Wings. The money Veronica had embezzled had been recovered and used to settle claims from his investors and insurance company, with some left over for his own losses. He seemed to be well on the way to regaining some of the old fire that had made him one of the top financial advisors. He acted as if he wanted to talk to her, but she was going to meet Dennis for dinner and couldn't take the time.

Which brought her to Dennis. His career was on the rocks, and he was going to have to find out what he was all about after a lifetime of having had it—in many ways—too easy. He needed to learn about right, wrong, and consequences, and how lucky he was that Max hadn't pressed charges against him for conspiring with Veronica, and that there was no proof he'd profited from Wallace Jones's counterfeit autographs.

He was thinking about opening a video-game shop, something that would appeal to major gamers and technophiles like himself, as well as first-time Nintendo buyers. It was work he'd enjoy, and, she was sure, could make a go of.

And of course there was Kevin. After learning all she'd been through, he'd begun calling her regularly. He hadn't been lying when he'd said he'd been clean for over a year, which was a record for him. The last time he'd called, they'd talked for over an hour without getting angry or uttering a single swear word. A record for them.

What to do?

She decided to sleep on it, and when she awoke the next morning, she had her answer. When she thought of the way all this had started, it wasn't about a blind date. The date had come later.

She got into her car, glad she'd have another week before her shop would reopen. After a drive across town, she pulled into a parking lot and went into a city building. The doors had just opened to the public.

She filled out the necessary forms, waited in line, and when it was her turn, went up to a clerk, her heart pounding at what she was about to do.

"I'd like to adopt a dog," she said. "I live alone, with a goldfish." She forged ahead, her words a torrent. "I'd like a female. She doesn't need any fancy pedigree, just a mutt is fine. I don't want one that's big, and not too little, and not a puppy. A dog with a few years on her, some maturity, a little experience in the ways of the world, so to speak. One that doesn't want or need much exercise. A walk a few blocks each day, and one who doesn't mind hanging around a shop with a small backyard while her owner works. Just a nice companion."

The woman studied Connie's face. "Maybe a dog who's known love, but has had some disappointments—I mean, misfortune—and now hopes to settle down in a quiet but warm and loving home."

Connie brightened. "Exactly."

"Come this way."

Nervously, Connie followed her to a small room. About ten minutes later, the woman led in a medium-sized dog that resembled a cream-colored dustmop. Its stumpy tail wagged, and, peering at her through silky hair, its enormous dark brown eyes melted Connie's heart.

"Her owner was an elderly woman who died recently. She's been here a month already, but few people seem to want an older dog, especially a mixed breed. She's five years old, well trained, well behaved, quiet, and loving."

Connie knelt down to play with her a bit, then lifted her onto her lap. "She seems perfect. What's her name?"

"Oddly, she was named after a woman of ill repute in the Old West called 'Diamond Lil'—she's called 'Lily.'"

Diamond? Connie laughed. Definitely perfect. She looked the dog in the eye. "Lily, my girl, it's you and me, now."

Lily gazed up adoringly, and happiness filled Connie head to toe.

How great was that?

From the Kitchen of
Angelina Amalfi

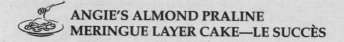

ANGIE'S ALMOND PRALINE MERINGUE LAYER CAKE—LE SUCCÈS

ALMOND PRALINE

½ cup blanched almonds
½ cup sugar
3 tablespoons water

To make the praline, spread almonds on baking sheet and roast at 350 degrees for 10–15 minutes, until brown. Stir several times. Combine sugar and water and set over medium-high heat. Stir occasionally as liquid boils and turns thick. When sugar is caramel brown, remove from heat, add almonds, mix, and turn onto lightly oiled tray. When cold and hard (about 20 minutes), break up and grind in electric blender.

MERINGUE

1–2 tablespoons soft butter
¼ cup flour
6 oz. ground blanched almonds
1 cup sugar
1½ tablespoons cornstarch
6 egg whites
⅛ teaspoon salt
¼ teaspoon cream of tartar

3 tablespoons sugar
1½ teaspoons vanilla extract
⅛ teaspoon almond extract

Preheat oven to 250 degrees. Rub butter over two large baking sheets, then dust with flour. Using an 8-inch cake pan or pot lid, make three 8-inch rings on sheets by placing the pan on the sheet and marking around edges with tip of rubber spatula. Set aside.

Mix together almonds, sugar, and cornstarch. Set aside.

Beat egg whites until foamy. Add salt and cream of tartar and beat to soft peaks. Add sugar, vanilla, and almond extract and continue to beat until egg whites form stiff peaks.

Using about ¼ of the almond-sugar mixture at a time, rapidly fold into egg whites, deflating eggs as little as possible.

Use pastry bag or spatula to place egg mixture into areas marked on baking sheets. Bake about 30–40 minutes at 250 degrees. They will not rise, but will lightly brown and are done when they can be easily pushed loose from baking surface.

BUTTER CREAM AND CHOCOLATE FROSTING

1 cup sugar
6 egg yolks
½ cup hot milk
12 oz. (3 cubes) unsalted butter
1 teaspoon vanilla extract
3 tablespoons kirsch (or dark rum or strong coffee)
2 oz. unsweetened baking chocolate, melted
½ cup almond praline (from recipe above)

In heavy saucepan, beat sugar and egg yolks until they are a thick, pale yellow. Gradually stir in hot milk and set over medium heat. Stir 4–5 minutes until thick enough to coat spoon but do not allow to a simmer. Remove from heat. Quickly add butter a little at a time, stirring to melt and absorb. Last, mix in vanilla and kirsch.

Remove a quarter of the mixture. Add chocolate to it and set aside.

Add almond praline to the remaining (¾) butter cream.

Putting it all together:

Build cake by placing one meringue on a cake rack. Cover with ⅓ of butter cream. Add second meringue and spread ½ of remaining butter cream on it. Cover with final meringue. Spread remaining butter cream over sides of cake. Spread chocolate frosting over top of cake.

Optional: Press ground almonds all around sides of cake.

PAAVO'S KARELIAN HOT POT

1 lb. boneless beef chuck, cubed
1 lb. boneless pork, cubed
1 lb. boneless lamb, cubed
2–3 large white onions, sliced
1½ teaspoons salt
White pepper to taste
2 tablespoons allspice
Butter

Lightly brown the meat, a little at a time, in butter. Sauté the onions.

Using a casserole, layer the meat, onion, salt, pepper, and allspice.

Add enough water to almost cover the meat. Place a tight cover on top. Bake in a 325-degree oven for 2½– 3 hours or until meat is tender. (If too much water remains in the pot—it should be almost dry—cook for 10 minutes or so at the end with the lid off.)

Serve spooned over hot mashed potatoes or cooked wild rice.

ANGIE'S TUSCAN BREAD SOUP

Tuscan bread soup, or *"ribollita"* (reboiled), is made with leftover minestrone.

DAY 1, MAKE A THICK MINESTRONE

4 oz. pancetta (or bacon), diced
⅓ cup olive oil
1 white onion, diced
3 garlic cloves, minced
4 red potatoes, diced
3 carrots, diced
2 celery ribs, diced
2 zucchini, diced
3 cups fresh or canned tomatoes, diced
20 sprigs parsley, leaves only, chopped
¼–½ teaspoon crushed red pepper (to taste)
¼ teaspoon dried oregano
2 bay leaves, broken in half
3 cups canned white kidney beans, drained
8 large cabbage leaves (or Swiss chard), finely shredded
Salt
Ground black pepper

Place olive oil in heavy 8-quart pot with lid over medium-low heat. When hot add the pancetta or bacon and cook, stirring occasionally, until lightly browned. Next, add the onion, garlic, potatoes, carrots, celery, zucchini, tomatoes, parsley, red pepper, oregano, and bay leaves. Stir to combine, then cover the pot and cook for 10 minutes.

Add just enough water to cover the vegetables, and stir. Raise heat to high until liquid just begins to boil. Immediately reduce the heat and simmer, uncovered, until potatoes are tender (15–20 minutes). Add beans and cabbage, stir to combine, and simmer until cabbage is tender (another 15 minutes or so). Season with salt and black pepper to taste. Remove and discard bay leaves.

DAY 2 (OR LATER) WITH THE LEFTOVER SOUP

Cut up one loaf Italian (or French) bread. Place it on the bottom of a casserole, pour soup on the top. If you have enough soup, make another bread and soup layer. Bake the casserole at 350 degrees until the soup is hot. It will be thick. Serve garnished, to taste, with thinly sliced red onion, a little Parmesan cheese, and a drizzle of olive oil.

Enter the Delicious World of Joanne Pence's Angie Amalfi Series

From the kitchen to the deck of a cruise ship, Joanne Pence's mysteries are always a delight. Starring career-challenged Angie Amalfi and her handsome homicide-detective boyfriend Paavo Smith, Joanne Pence serves up a mystery feast complete with humor, a dead body or two, and delicious recipes.

Enjoy the pages that follow, which give a glimpse into Angie's and Paavo's world.

*For sassy and single food writer Angie Amalfi, life's a
banquet—until the man who's been contributing unusual recipes for her food column is found dead. But
in* SOMETHING'S COOKING, *Angie is hardly one to
simper in fear—so instead she simmers over the de-
lectable homicide detective assigned to the case.*

A while passed before she looked up
again. When she did, she saw a dark-
haired man standing in the doorway to her
apartment, surveying the scene. Tall and broad shouldered, his stance was aloof and forceful as he made a
cold assessment of all that he saw.

If you're going to gawk, she thought, come in with
the rest of the busybodies.

He looked directly at her, and her grip tightened on
the chair. His expression was hard, his pale blue eyes
icy. He was a stranger, of that she was certain. His
wasn't the type of face or demeanor she'd easily forget. And someone, it seemed, had just sent her a bomb.
Who? Why? What if this stranger. . .

As he approached with bold strides, her nerves tightened. Since she was without her high heels, the top of
her head barely reached his chin.

The man appeared to be in his mid-thirties. His face
was fairly thin, with high cheekbones and a pro-
nounced, aquiline nose with a jog in the middle that
made it look as if it had been broken at least once.

Thick, dark brown hair spanned his high forehead, and his penetrating, deep-set eyes and dark eyebrows gave him a cold, no-nonsense appearance. His gaze didn't leave hers, and yet he seemed aware of everything around them.

"Your apartment?" he asked.

"The tour's that way." She did her best to give a nonchalant wave of her thumb toward the kitchen.

She froze as he reached into his breast pocket. "Police." He pulled out a billfold and dropped open one flap to reveal his identification: Inspector Paavo Smith, Homicide.

In TOO MANY COOKS, *Angie's talked her way into a job on a pompous, third-rate chef's radio call-in-show. But when a successful and much envied restaurateur is poisoned, Angie finds the case far more interesting than trying to make her pretentious boss sound good.*

Angie glanced up from the monitor. She'd been debating whether or not to try to take the next call, if and when one came in, when her attention was caught by the caller's strange voice. It was oddly muffled. Angie couldn't tell if the caller was a man or a woman.

"I didn't catch your name," Henry said.

"Pat."

Angie's eyebrows rose. A neuter-sounding Pat? What was this, a *Saturday Night Live* routine?

"Well, Pat, what can I do for you?"

"I was concerned about the restaurant killer in your city."

Henry's eye caught Angie's. "Thank you. I'm sure the police will capture the person responsible in no time."

"I'm glad you think so, because—you're next."

Henry jumped up and slapped the disconnect button. "And now," he said, his voice quivering, "a word from our sponsor."

312

Angie Amalfi's latest job, developing the menu for a new inn, sounds enticing—especially since it means spending a week in scenic northern California with her homicide detective boyfriend. But once she arrives at the soon-to-be-opened Hill Haven Inn, she's not so sure anymore. In COOKING UP TROUBLE, the added ingredients of an ominous threat, a missing person, and a woman making eyes at her man, leave Angie convinced that the only recipe in this inn's kitchen is one for disaster.

She placed her hand over his large strong one, scarcely able to believe that they were here, in this strange yet lovely room, alone. "But I am real, Paavo."

"Are you?" He bent to kiss her lightly, his eyes intent, his hand moving from her chin to the back of her head to intertwine with the curls of her hair. The mystical aura of the room, the patter of the rain, the solitude of the setting stole over him and made him think of things he didn't want to ponder—things like being together with Angie forever, like never being alone again. He tried to mentally break the spell. He needed time—cold, logical time. "There's no way a woman like you should be in my life," he said finally. "Sometimes I think you can't be any more real than the Sempler ghosts. That I'll close my eyes and you'll disappear. Or that I'm just imagining you."

313

"Inspector," she said, returning his kiss with one that seared, "there's no way you could imagine me."

Cold logic melted in the midst of her fire, and all his careful resolve went with it. His heart filled, and the solemnity of his expression broke. "I know," he said softly, "and that's the best part."

As his lips met hers a bolt of lightning lit their room for just a moment. Then a scream filled the darkness.

Food columnist Angie Amalfi has it all. But in COOKING MOST DEADLY, *while she's wondering if it's time to cut the wedding cake with her boyfriend Paavo, he becomes obsessed with a grisly homicide that has claimed two female victims.*

"You've got to keep City Hall out of this case. As far as the press knows, she was a typist. Nothing more. Mumble when you say where she worked." Lieutenant Hollins got up from behind his desk, walked around to the front of it, and leaned against the edge. Paavo and Yosh sat facing him. They'd just completed briefing him on the Tiffany Rogers investigation. Hollins made it a point not to get involved in his men's investigations unless political heat was turned on. In this case, the heat was on high.

"Her friends and coworkers are at City Hall, and there's a good chance the guy she's been seeing is there as well," Paavo said.

"It's our only lead, Chief," Yosh added. "So far, the CSI unit can't even find a suspicious fingerprint to lift. The crime scene is clean as a whistle. She always met her boyfriend away from her apartment. We aren't sure where yet. We've got a few leads we're still checking."

"So you've got nothing except for a dead woman lying in her own blood on the floor of her own living room!" Hollins added.

"We have to follow wherever the leads take us," Paavo said.

"I'm not saying not to, all I'm saying is keep the press away." Hollins paced back and forth in front of his desk. "The mayor and the Board of Supervisors want this murderer caught right now. This isn't the kind of publicity they want for themselves or the city. I mean, if someone who works for them isn't safe, who is?"

"Aw heck, Paavo." Yosh turned to his partner. "The supervisors said they want us to catch this murderer fast. Here I'd planned to take my sweet time with this case."

Paavo couldn't help but grin.

"Cut the comedy, Yoshiwara." Hollins stuck an unlit cigar in his mouth and chewed. "This case is number one for you both, got it?"

In COOK'S NIGHT OUT, *Angie has decided to make her culinary name by creating the perfect chocolate confection:* angelinas. *Donating her delicious rejects to a local mission, Angie soon finds that the mission harbors more than the needy, and to save not only her life, but Paavo's as well, she's going to have to discover the truth faster than you can beat egg whites to a peak.*

Angelina Amalfi flung open the window over the kitchen sink. After two days of cooking with chocolate, the mouthwatering, luscious, inviting smell of it made her sick.

That was the price one must pay, she supposed, to become a famous chocolatier.

She found an old fan in the closet, put it on the kitchen table, and turned the dial to high. The comforting aroma of home cooking wafting out from a kitchen was one thing, but the smell of Willy Wonka's chocolate factory was quite another.

She'd been trying out intricate, elegant recipes for chocolate candies, searching for the perfect confection on which to build a business to call her own. Her kitchen was filled with truffles, nut bouchées, exotic fudges, and butter creams.

So far, she'd divulged her business plans only to Paavo, the man for whom she had plans of a very different nature. She was going to have to let someone

317

else know soon, though, or she wouldn't have any
room left in the kitchen to cook. She didn't want to
start eating the calorie-oozing, waistline-expanding
chocolates out of sheer enjoyment—her taste tests
were another thing altogether and totally justifiable,
she reasoned—and throwing the chocolates away had
to be sinful.

Angie Amalfi's long-awaited vacation with her detective boyfriend has all the ingredients of a romantic getaway—a sail to Acapulco aboard a freighter, no crowds, no homicide-department worries, and a red bikini. But in COOKS OVERBOARD, *it isn't long before Angie's* Love Boat *fantasies are headed for stormy seas—the cook tries to jump off the ship, Paavo is acting mighty strange, and someone's added murder to the menu . . .*

Paavo became aware, in a semi-asleep state, that the storm was much worse than anyone had expected it would be. The best thing to do was to try to sleep through it, to ignore the roar of the sea, the banging of rain against the windows, the almost human cry of the wind through the ship.

He reached out to Angie. She wasn't there. She must have gotten up to use the bathroom. Maybe her getting up was what had awakened him. He rolled over to go back to sleep.

When he awoke again, the sun was peeking over the horizon. He turned over to check on Angie, but she still wasn't beside him. Was she up already? That wasn't like her. He remembered a terrible storm last night. He sat up, suddenly wide awake. Where was Angie?

He got out of bed and hurried to the sitting area. Empty. The bathroom door was open. Empty.

The wall bed was down. What was that supposed to mean? Had she tried sleeping on it? Had she grown so out of sorts with him that she didn't want to sleep with him anymore? Things had seemed okay between them last night. He remembered her talking . . . she was talking about writing a cookbook again . . . and he remembered getting more and more sleepy . . . he must have . . . oh, hell.

Angie Amalfi has a way with food and people, but her newest business idea is turning out to be shakier than a fruit-filled gelatin mold. In A COOK IN TIME, *Her first—and only—clients for "Fantasy Dinners" are none other than a group of UFO chasers and government conspiracy fanatics. But when it seems that the group has a hidden agenda greater than anything on the* X-Files, *Angie's determined to find out the truth before it takes her out of this world—for good.*

 The nude body was that of a male Caucasian, early forties or so, about 5'10", 160 pounds. The skin was an opaque white. Lips, nose, and ears had been removed, and the entire area from approximately the pubis to the sigmoid colon had been cored out, leaving a clean, bloodless cavity. No postmortem lividity appeared on the part of the body pressed against the ground. The whole thing had a tidy, almost surreal appearance. No blood spattered the area. No blood was anywhere; apparently, not even in the victim. A gutted, empty shell.

The man's hair was neatly razor-cut; his hands were free of calluses or stains, the skin soft, the nails manicured; his toenails were short and square-cut, and his feet without bunions or other effects of ill-fitting shoes. In short, all signs of a comfortable life. Until now.

*Between her latest "sure-fire" foray into the food in-
dustry—video restaurant reviews—and her concern
over Paavo's depressed state, Angie's plate is full to
overflowing. Paavo has never come to terms with the
fact that his mother abandoned him when he was
four, leaving behind only a mysterious present. But
when the token disappears in* TO CATCH A COOK,
*Angie discovers a lethal goulash of intrigue, betrayal,
and mayhem that may spell disaster for her and
Paavo.*

 The bedroom had also been torn apart and
the mattress slashed. This was far, far more
frightening than what had happened to her
own apartment. There was anger here, perhaps hatred.

"What is going on?" she cried. "Why would anyone
destroy your things?"

"It looks like a search, followed by frustration."

As she wandered through the little house, she realized he was right. It wasn't random destruction as she
had first thought, but where the search to her apartment
had appeared slow and meticulous, here it was hurried
and frenzied.

"Hercules!" he called. "Herc? Come on, boy, are
you all right?"

Angie's breath caught. His cat . . . He loved that cat.

"Do you see him?" she asked, standing in the bedroom doorway.

"No. They better not have hurt my cat," he muttered, his jaw clenched. They looked under the bed, in the closets, and throughout the backyard.

She was afraid—and for Hercules, more afraid that they'd find the cat than that they wouldn't. If he had run and was hiding, scared, he should return home eventually, but if he was nearby, and unable to come when called . . .

They couldn't find him.

Finally, back in the living room, Paavo bleakly took in the damage, the ugliness before him. "Who's doing this, Angie, and why?

For once Angie's newest culinary venture, "Comical Cakes," seems to be a roaring success! But in BELL, COOK, AND CANDLE, *there's nothing funny about her boyfriend Paavo's latest case—a series of baffling murders that may be rooted in satanic ritual. And it gets harder to focus on pastry alone when strange "accidents" and desecrations to her baked creations begin occurring with frightening regularity—leaving Angie to wonder whether she may end up as devil's food of a different kind.*

 Angie was beside herself. She'd been called to go to a house to discuss baking cakes for a party of twenty, and yet no one was there when she arrived. This was the second time that had happened to her. Was someone playing tricks, or were people really so careless as to make appointments and then not keep them?

She really didn't have time for this. But at least she was getting smart. She'd brought a cake with her that had to be delivered to a horse's birthday party not far from her appointment. She never thought she'd be baking cakes for a horse, but Heidi was being boarded some forty miles outside the city, and the owner visited her on weekends only. That was why the owner wanted a Comical Cake of the mare.

Angie couldn't imagine eating something that

looked like a beloved pet or animal. She was meeting real ding-a-lings in this line of work.

Still muttering to herself about the thoughtlessness of the public, she got into her new car. A vaguely familiar yet disquieting smell hit her. A stain smeared the bottom of the cake box. She peered closer. The smell was stronger, and the bottom of the box was wet.

She opened the driver's side door, ready to jump out of the car as her hand slowly reached for the box top. Thoughts of flies and toads pounded her. What now?

She flipped back the lid and shrank away from it.

Nothing moved. Nothing jumped out.

Poor Heidi was now a bright-red color, but it wasn't frosting. The familiar smell was blood, and it had been poured on her cake. Shifting the box, she saw that it had seeped through onto the leather seat and was dripping to the floor mat.

Tasty mysteries by
JOANNE PENCE

Featuring culinary queen Angie Amalfi

IF COOKS COULD KILL
0-06-054821-5/$6.99 US/$9.99 Can

BELL, COOK, AND CANDLE
0-06-103084-8/$6.99 US/$9.99 Can

TO CATCH A COOK
0-06-103085-6/$5.99 US/$7.99 Can

A COOK IN TIME
0-06-104454-7/$5.99 US/$7.99 Can

COOKS OVERBOARD
0-06-104453-9/$5.99 US/$7.99 Can

COOK'S NIGHT OUT
0-06-104396-6/$5.99 US/$7.99 Can

COOKING MOST DEADLY
0-06-104395-8/$6.50 US/$8.99 Can

COOKING UP TROUBLE
0-06-108200-7/$5.99 US/$7.99 Can

SOMETHING'S COOKING
0-06-108096-9/$6.50 US/$8.99 Can

TOO MANY COOKS
0-06-108199-X/$6.50 US/$8.99 Can

Murder Is on the Menu
at the Hillside Manor Inn
Bed-and-Breakfast Mysteries by
MARY DAHEIM
featuring Judith McMonigle Flynn

CREEPS SUZETTE	0-380-80079-9/ $6.50 US/ $8.99 Can
BANTAM OF THE OPERA	
	0-380-76934-4/ $6.50 US/ $8.99 Can
JUST DESSERTS	0-380-76295-1/ $6.99 US/ $9.99 Can
FOWL PREY	0-380-76296-X/ $6.99 US/ $9.99 Can
HOLY TERRORS	0-380-76297-8/ $6.99 US/ $9.99 Can
DUNE TO DEATH	0-380-76933-6/ $6.50 US/ $8.50 Can
A FIT OF TEMPERA	0-380-77490-9/ $6.99 US/ $9.99 Can
MAJOR VICES	0-380-77491-7/ $6.50 US/ $8.99 Can
MURDER, MY SUITE	0-380-77877-7/ $6.50 US/ $8.99 Can
AUNTIE MAYHEM	0-380-77878-5/ $6.50 US/ $8.50 Can
NUTTY AS A FRUITCAKE	
	0-380-77879-3/ $6.50 US/ $8.99 Can
SEPTEMBER MOURN	0-380-78518-8/ $6.50 US/ $8.99 Can
WED AND BURIED	0-380-78520-X/ $6.50 US/ $8.99 Can
SNOW PLACE TO DIE	0-380-78521-8/ $6.99 US/ $9.99 Can
LEGS BENEDICT	0-380-80078-0/ $6.50 US/ $8.50 Can
A STREETCAR NAMED EXPIRE	
	0-380-80080-2/ $6.99 US/ $9.99 Can
SUTURE SELF	
	0-380-81561-3/$6.99 US/ $9.99 Can

And in Hardcover

SILVER SCREAM
0-380-97867-9/ $23.95 US/ $36.50 Can

....